We Were the Bullfighters

We Were the Bullfighters

a novel

MARIANNE K. MILLER

DUNDURN PRESS

Publisher: Kwame Scott Fraser | Acquiring editor: Meghan Macdonald | Editor: Robyn So
Cover designer: Laura Boyle
Cover image: Ernest Hemingway (c. 1923) Ernest Hemingway Collection Photographs / John F. Kennedy Presidential Library and Museum; Kingston Penitentiary (c. 1901): Image from page 11 of "Souvenir views of the city of Kingston Ontario, Canada, and the Thousand Islands, River St. Lawrence" (1901), Internet Archive Book Images

Library and Archives Canada Cataloguing in Publication

Title: We were the bullfighters : a novel / Marianne K. Miller.
Names: Miller, Marianne K., author.
Identifiers: Canadiana (print) 20230569021 | Canadiana (ebook) 20230569064 | ISBN 9781459753600 (softcover) | ISBN 9781459753624 (EPUB) | ISBN 9781459753617 (PDF)
Classification: LCC PS8626.I45225 W42 2024 | DDC C813/.6—dc23

We acknowledge the support of the Canada Council for the Arts and the Ontario Arts Council for our publishing program. We also acknowledge the financial support of the Government of Ontario, through the Ontario Book Publishing Tax Credit and Ontario Creates, and the Government of Canada.

Printed and bound in Canada.

Dundurn Press
1382 Queen Street East
Toronto, Ontario, Canada M4L 1C9
dundurn.com, @dundurnpress

For Bill, Sarah, Jasper, and Violet

&

My sister, Trish

This is a work of fiction, except for the parts that are true.

The world's a jail and we're going to break it together.

— Hadley Richardson to Ernest Hemingway, 1921

⊹⊹

Prologue

For the past week, Ernest Miller Hemingway, late of Oak Park, Kansas City, Northern Michigan, Chicago, and most recently, Paris, has not been sleeping well. He dreads the fate that awaits him on this day.

There is a scream inside of him that he wants to send out across the universe: He is too young to be a father. Hadley knew there wasn't supposed to be a child.

The unborn child has brought him here to this country and this long day of servitude at the *Toronto Daily Star*. Brought him here to this late-night train.

Hemingway pulls the covers over his eyes and moans as the train crawls through another Ontario town. In the darkness he counts the things that are making him unhappy: not happy about running around Toronto hunting for news, not happy about being sent out of town, not happy about being a father, and most of all, not happy about leaving Paris.

Yet unhappy or not, here he is exhausted but wide awake, travelling through the middle of the black Canadian night. All because his wife got pregnant and five convicts at Kingston Pen chose this day to go over the wall.

1

THE CONVICTS, NORMAN "RED" RYAN, ED MCMULLEN, TOMMY Bryans, Arthur Sullivan, and Gordon Simpson, are also having a long day. A day that is not following Red's carefully laid plan.

Set fire to the prison stable; use the smoke as a screen from the guards in the tower; scale the twenty-foot wall; steal a wealthy neighbour's high-powered car. Outrun the police. That is how it was supposed to go.

But on the other side, the powerful car is nowhere to be found. There's only a lowly Chevy owned by a man painting the house. It will have to do. Off they go: Ed McMullen driving; Thomson, the painter, screaming, as they peel out onto the street.

Two guards are close behind, first on foot, then when they commandeer a vehicle, by car. Policemen arrive on motorcycles. Nearby residents volunteer their cars as more and more guards respond to the prison alarm's incessant wail. Wah-oo, wah-oo, wah-oo. Work gangs outside the walls are hustled back inside.

Red looks in the rear-view mirror and sees the guards getting closer. Closer. They all crunch down when the rear window shatters and bullets whistle through, barely missing Tommy Bryans's head.

"Good thing you're a little guy," Red Ryan says. "If you were any taller, you'd be dead."

Ed McMullen cries out when a bullet hits the steering wheel, splits it in two, and rips through his index finger. The wounded hand and the damaged wheel make it hard to steer.

They race through the streets of Kingston, heading north. The Chevy is not up to the role it's been drafted to play. The engine whines. Fire and smoke spew from the exhaust.

When Red looks back, they are the first car in a fast-moving parade. They cross the railway tracks and, at last, city starts to give way to country. As they go over the crest of a hill, Red studies the road ahead.

To the right and the left, he sees long stretches of dense woods. The lead chase car is about two hundred yards away. Guards lean out the windows firing as they come. In the distance he can see a curve to the right. They will be hidden from the guards for a moment or two. He tells McMullen, "After the curve, swerve hard, hit the left shoulder."

When Ed does, they jump out, run across the road, and head for the bush on the other side. Ed, his face white, his body shaking, his prison greys covered in blood, tries to keep up.

-+-+-

That evening guards with rifles station themselves on the four roads that surround McAdoo's Woods. Five guards on horseback patrol the path that cuts through seven hundred acres of trees. Red Ryan, Sullivan, Simpson, and Bryans have left Ed McMullen behind.

2

HEMINGWAY GETS OFF THE TRAIN AND LOOKS AROUND IN the early morning dark. The grey stone station is out in the sticks. "Land speculation," the station master tells him. "Somebody got wind the railway was looking and land got too expensive in the city. But there's a shuttle," he says. "We hook the sleeping car up to it. We'll get you downtown."

In the waiting room, everyone is talking about the prison break. This isn't the first attempt on Warden John C. Ponsford's watch. The prison is a terrible place, they say, where terrible things happen. No wonder people want to get out.

There is a copy of yesterday's *Daily British Whig*, the Kingston paper, abandoned on a train station bench. Hemingway picks it up. "Where's McAdoo's Woods?" he asks the station master, pointing at the headline: "Five Prisoners Escape from the Penitentiary."

"Northwest of here. Not too far." The station master motions for Hemingway to come closer. "Red Ryan met this guy, McMullen, on a train," he whispers. "Both bank robbers on the way to the Pen. Buddy of mine's a conductor. He says the two of them got pretty darn chummy during the trip."

"Who let them get away with that?" Hemingway asks, rummaging in his pocket for his notebook.

The station master rolls his eyes. "The last time Red Ryan was in the Pen, they let him out to fight in the war. Gave him a full pardon."

"That's probably where he learned about smokescreens," Hemingway says. He begins making notes, drafting the story in his mind. Use short sentences. Use short first paragraphs. Use vigorous English. The rules he learned before the war as a teenage reporter on the *Kansas City Star.*

The station master walks toward the door. Hemingway follows him, scouring the landscape in the semidarkness. From what he can see, everything north of the station looks like dense, wooded terrain. It shouldn't be too hard to lay low.

The sound of the shuttle coupling with the Pullman car makes the station master turn around. "You better get going, young fella. They'll be leaving without you."

Hemingway swings on board and climbs back up to his berth. As they roll toward the city, he thinks of the men loose in the bush. If it was him, he'd know how to survive on the run. His father taught him how to hunt at their summer place in northern Michigan. Hell, he's even hunted pigeons in the parks of Paris to stay alive, wringing their necks before they had a chance to squawk.

The shuttle train follows a gentle slope down to the banks of a river. He can see hard-edged buildings here and there. Almost as if someone had shaken them like dice and then let them fly across the landscape. Every now and then, as they rattle along, there is a house with a golden glow spilling out from a window. Nothing like Paris, crowded and glittering all night long.

Yesterday he was up at six to report for work at seven. The sky still dark. The hard light of the city room blinding him, stabbing at his eyes.

His new colleagues clutched mugs of coffee as they studied the assignment sheet. When he approached, they moved aside. He was to pass the day picking up photographs, stalking the corridors of city hall, hanging around the King Edward Hotel. Just in case something happened or someone important showed up.

His fellow labourers in the field of spot news studied him, exchanging glances over the warm mugs in their ink-stained hands. These, he knew, were not the writers, the literary aspirants of the *Toronto Weekly Star* whose gentrified offices were but a flight of stairs away. These were the foot soldiers in the news wars, the staff reporters. At the *Toronto Weekly Star*, it's about the writing; at the *Toronto Daily Star*, it's about selling papers.

They didn't try to hide their smiles. Behold the *Star*'s great foreign correspondent. He's not cruising around the capitals of Europe anymore on the company's ticket. He won't be hanging out in cafés. He'll be out on the streets of Toronto the Good, gathering the news, just like them. Write it up, get it in, then forget it, and start all over again.

The shuttle clatters over the mangle of rail lines that cross the bottom of the city. There is a grain elevator and huge cargo ships in the harbour. The fall sun is still below the horizon but the mist that's hanging over the water is starting to glow red.

Last night in the club car, Hemingway heard more rumours than a freshman in a locker room. The convicts are in the city; the convicts are out in the country, hiding in a barn; the convicts stole a rum-runner's boat and headed across the river to the U.S. of A. Everybody has a theory, but nobody knows.

The brakes squeak as they bump to a stop at the inner station. It's only five thirty in the morning. He asks about hotels and gets sent to a grey stone building down the street.

"Good morning, sir," the hotel clerk says to him as he puts his valise down on the front desk. "Welcome to the Prince George Hotel."

"Hemingway, *Toronto Star.* I need a room and a photographer."

"You're just in time for breakfast," the clerk says, swivelling the hotel register around for Hemingway to sign. The smell of bacon frying fills the air.

3

RED RYAN IS NOT HAPPY TO SEE THE SUN COME UP. DARKNESS is your friend. During the day you have to keep moving. Night should be like the Christmas Day ceasefire during the war. Everything should stop. Everyone needs a little peace. In the dark you can tell when someone is approaching you with a torch. At night you can rest. Or at least three can rest while one of you stands watch. But now, with the darkness turning into day, the hunt for them will be back on. He can already feel the tightness creeping up his body. The sun is making the morning sky glow blood red.

All day yesterday he felt good. If he'd looked down, he might have seen his heart beating in his chest. When they broke through the line of guards into the north end of McAdoo's Woods and headed farther into the swamp, he felt like he used to when he won a race at school, when he won the first-place ribbon. Their prison greys, their prison shoes, and their prisoners' caps all stink of stagnant water but he doesn't care. It's better than being covered with the stench of the prison and the hard dust of the yard. It's better than looking up at the high walls that surround you, guards in the towers with their loaded rifles pointed down, aimed right at your heart or your head.

Freedom is like a drug circulating through his veins. Yesterday he wanted to keep running. He thought he could run all day and all night. He thought he could run forever.

But today he notices the swamp has a smell that is soft and dank like an old familiar mattress. The bulrushes are spongy and the reeds are beginning to turn brown.

He looks over to where Sully, Tommy Bryans, and Gord Simpson are still sleeping with nothing for pillows on a small circle of dry ground. Look like wee little angels, a mother might say. That's true of some of the toughest guys he's ever run across. You can always see the boy the man used to be when he's asleep.

Bryans is a murderer, Gord and Sully are petty thieves. Red's the only bank robber, sentenced to twenty-five years for robbing two banks on consecutive days. Bank robbers get the lads' respect in the Pen. Ed McMullen was a bank robber too.

"Small-time crooks," Ed used to say, looking at the men circling the prison yard. "They don't have the big picture. Why bother with petty shit? If you're going to go, you might as well go for something big."

Sully rolls over, opens his eyes, and looks around. Red can tell that for a moment Sully is wondering where he is as he pushes up onto one elbow and scans the swamp and the forest around him until he gets to Red sitting on the rock. "What time is it?"

"What's the matter, Sully? You waiting to hear the warden's bell? You wondering if you can go down to the dining hall for breakfast?"

Some men who are in prison too long get used to the routine: the identical rhythm of every day; the rules; the being told what to do; the living their lives to the clanging of that damn bell. There's no requirement to think. They've forgotten they are men, not sheep. The smallest decision about the smallest thing becomes a burden, a trial. When nobody is telling them what to do it doesn't feel right anymore. They're paralyzed.

A flock of geese goes by and Red gazes up at the sky. It's losing its summer glow even though it's only early September. Yesterday they were lucky. The weather was good. But this morning there's a coolness in the air. Something is coming. Over to the east, there's a kind of white light behind the blue sky as if winter is waiting to make its move somewhere just over the horizon.

Far to the north of them, the land pulls away and begins to rise. Maybe he'll send Tommy Bryans up a tree like a cabin boy to the crow's nest of a sailing ship. The rest of them will stay back a safe distance in case there's trouble.

He turns toward Sully and mouths, "Get up." Then he walks over to Gord and Tommy and gives them both a kick on the shoulder with his prison-made boot. "Get up," he growls in a whisper. The two of them open their eyes. He can tell both of them are ready for a fight until they remember who he is and where they are. Gord stands up first with Tommy right behind.

"We need to get moving," Red says.

"Jesus, Red," Gord says. "Give me two minutes to take a piss."

"Yeah," says Tommy, taking a step toward Red. "Give us a minute. I need to take a piss too."

They go behind a tree and start to relieve themselves. Sully gets up and joins the other two.

Red watches the three grey backs standing in a row.

⁂

The forest is so dense that as the sun comes up, everything on the ground is bathed in green light. Red can see steam coming off the earth where the three streams of hot urine hit. The three of them together can't replace Ed. If he had a gun, he could take the three of them out right now. They wouldn't know what hit them. He could go it alone. One man, not four. Much easier going in the bush.

He had been so sure, so very damn sure, that they would outrun the police. He didn't think they would need to know anything about the land north of Kingston except where the roads were. Instead, here they are with no car, lost in a stinking never-ending swamp.

Last night Tommy said they had to be careful or they'll go around in circles. He's from Northern Ontario. He says he knows a lot about the bush. "We have to mark where we've been," he said. "Rip the leaves off the underbrush in a certain pattern."

Maybe not a bad idea but the way the kid said it, it was like he was the sergeant and they were the privates. Or he's one of the goddamn guards. It started a fight.

"No way," Sully said, "It'll be like those marks they put on silver. The guards will get wise."

"What the hell are you talking about?" Tommy said.

"That's how I got caught."

Tommy looked over at Red. "What?"

"I think Sully stole some silver from some rich dame's house in the west end," Red said.

"We were melting it down back at our boarding house when the old lady who ran the place caught us and called the cops. And that's why I'm telling you, leaving a trail in the bush is like getting caught with some dame's monogrammed silver."

"Not really, Sully," Tommy laughed. "That was dumb. This is smart."

"Who you calling dumb? You were sitting in the same prison he was," Gord said.

"Yeah, for murder, not shoplifting," Tommy said.

"We stole safes," Gord says.

"From magazine stores. How much money you get, a dollar and a quarter?"

Sully and Gord both got up. Red stood up and grabbed their arms.

"Calm down, the pair of you. And you watch your mouth, Bryans. I don't need no fighting. We got enough to worry about."

They have no idea what's around them, other than the farmhouses to the south they saw on the way in. They can't go anywhere near the road, too easy to be spotted. They need to steal another car or hop a train and get the hell out of here, fast.

"Let's go," Red says. The three grey backs startle and the trio turn to face him. Each one with his dick still in his hands.

"Hey!" Gord says, giving Tommy a shove. "Watch what you're doing kid, you're pissin' all over me."

4

When Hemingway gets out of the photographer's car, the sun is clearing the tops of the trees in McAdoo's Woods. He crosses a field wet with dew and approaches a small group of men gathered at the edge of the forest. In the centre is a short man with slicked-down hair wearing a rumpled grey flannel suit. He has the ramrod bearing of a military officer.

"P-o-n-s-f-o-r-d, John C.," the man says.

Ah, thinks Hemingway, *it's the keeper of the keys himself.* He joins the other reporters whose pencils scribble as the man talks.

"We have the woods surrounded. It is an ever-tightening cordon." The warden of Kingston Pen twists his hands like he, too, has strangled a pigeon or three in his day. "We'll squeeze them out of their hiding place."

Hemingway casts his gaze over the thick underbrush that marks the beginning of the woods. The edge of the road is lined with cars and there are guards strolling, guards sitting, guards smoking, guards reclining on the grass. It doesn't look like a manhunt to him. Give these guys some parasols and they could be enjoying an afternoon on La Grande Jatte.

He approaches a small cluster of men. "Good morning," Hemingway says. His new boss, Harry Comfort Hindmarsh, gave him a letter that identifies him as a reporter for the *Toronto Daily Star*. As he pulls the envelope out of his pocket, one of the guards stomps his cigarette out and walks toward him.

"*Toronto Star*," Hemingway says, holding the letter up so the small group of guards can see the letterhead. "Can I talk to you about the prison break?"

All the guards look in the direction of Warden Ponsford. He's still holding the attention of the other reporters, gesturing toward the woods like a referee calling a penalty at a football match.

"What do you wanna know?"

"How many men are out on the hunt?" Hemingway asks. The other guards get up off the grass and form a tight khaki circle around him.

"Where'd you say you were from?" one of them asks.

"*Toronto Daily Star*."

"Big city paper, huh?" says a red-headed man with a droopy moustache. The hairs that droop down over his lips become stained brown as he spits tobacco juice in the direction of Hemingway's feet.

"We all got ordered out here, including the off-duty guys and the guys on vacation," says a man with a scarred face. "Ain't hardly anybody left back at the prison. It's on lockdown."

"Them convicts did us a favour, if you ask me." The voice belongs to a tall, slim boy, so young that Hemingway wonders if he has ever drawn a razor across his face.

The red-headed guard puts his arm around the kid's shoulder. "If you think they'll pay us overtime, you're dreaming, probie. You better tell that new wife of yours to get out her old flannel night-gown because you won't be home for a while."

Hemingway turns to see what the photographer is doing. He'd like to remember these guards with their rough skin and hollow eyes. Not for the paper but for himself. He tries, with a wave of his hand, to catch the photographer's eye, but he's sitting in the car, head back, eyes closed. This is what happens when you drag a portrait photographer out on a newshound's mission.

"Who you waving at?" A stain of brown tobacco juice lands on the toe of Hemingway's shoe.

"I was hoping to get a few pictures."

The guards close around him in a circle. The man with the moustache takes a step closer. "No photographs," he says. "We don't want no trouble."

Hemingway's been a reporter long enough to know that when you meet resistance from the people in authority it's better not to confront them. Withdraw, regroup, and make another plan of attack.

While the reporters continue to buzz around the warden, he walks back to the car. "I'll distract him," he says to the photographer, pointing in Ponsford's direction. "While I'm talking to him, you take some pictures."

He moves back to where Ponsford is still holding court.

"I am certain the four men are within a few hundred yards of the abandoned car." Same old stuff. Ponsford is as well-rehearsed as a defence witness at a trial.

Hemingway pulls out his notebook and writes it down.

"My men have the area covered," Ponsford says with his arm raised in the air as if he is Marc Antony addressing the Romans. "There's no need for the army or the mounted or the provincial police."

Where the hell is the photographer? Hemingway looks back at the car. The photographer is struggling to get the huge camera out of the back seat.

"My men are the best men for this job." Warden Ponsford's voice rises above the questions yelled at him by the crowd of reporters.

"Why is that?" Hemingway hears himself say. He has pushed his way to the front and stands facing Ponsford across the wet grass.

The warden of Kingston Pen stops and turns. He slicks a long hank of hair back down across the top of his head. "It's obvious. Only the guards will recognize the convicts on sight."

As Hemingway scribbles this down, he hears a loud whirring noise. Oh Christ, it's the goddamn camera. A hand comes from behind him and clamps around his wrist. His pencil falls into the dirt.

"I told you no pictures, Toronto," says the guard with the tobacco-stained moustache.

The camera whirs again and the guard tightens his grip. Hemingway can feel the skin on his arm starting to burn. His wrist starts to ache. He may not be a concert pianist or a surgeon but he sure as hell relies on his hands to make a living.

"Tell him to knock it off or that idiot is going to get you both in a wagonload of trouble."

"Get your hands off me," Hemingway says, trying to pull his arm free, but the guard doesn't let go. Instead, he wrenches Hemingway's arm back and up behind him. He can feel the pressure on his bones. The son of a bitch is trying to get him down on his knees.

The other reporters have turned away from Ponsford and are beginning to stare. The camera whirrs again. Hemingway jabs his free elbow back with as much power as he can muster. Tobacco-soaked breath hits the side of his face when the burst of air leaves the guard's lungs. But it doesn't work. The guard gets him in a chokehold, then lets him fall to the ground.

"Tell him to put that camera away, Toronto, or I'll tell my men to open fire."

Hemingway gets up, his fists tight, his jaw clenched, and turns to face the guard, who takes a step back, his gaze focused on a point somewhere past Hemingway's right shoulder.

When Hemingway turns, he sees the young guard with the new wife drop his cigarette in the dirt. He flips his rifle up against his shoulder and stares down the barrel as he walks toward them. The sharp crack of the kid's rifle makes the assembled press corps dive for the dirt.

⁂

On the way back to Kingston, the photographer can't stop talking about what happened. He clutches the steering wheel so hard his knuckles turn white. He says over and over, "I thought we were going to die."

"They wouldn't have killed us," Hemingway says. "Too many witnesses."

"The Penitentiary Department will pay fifty dollars for information leading to the arrest of each escaped convict," the photographer says. "Farmers up here are searching their sheds and their barns."

"Maybe you should go and get a few pictures," Hemingway says with a smirk.

The photographer doesn't get the joke. He furrows his brow, thinking it over, entertaining it as an idea.

Hemingway tucks his notebook back into his pocket and turns in the passenger seat. Just beyond the photographer's face, through the driver's side-window, he can see the harvested yellow fields and the red autumn woods and the cold grey rock of the pre-Cambrian landscape going by.

⁂

Back in Kingston Hemingway begins his trek up to the hotel's third floor. The stairs creak the way they did in Oak Park when he tried to sneak in late at night. He's only been here a few hours but Kingston seems a lot like Oak Park: a place where even young men who have been injured in a war are not free to express their opinions at Sunday dinner.

His suitcase and his portable typewriter relax on his bed. He pulls his notebook out of his pocket and sets it down beside the faithful Corona. On the drive back, he bought a copy of the *Daily British Whig*. He sits down beside the window and reads. "Wounded Prisoner Found Exhausted," the headline says about Ed McMullen's capture.

His eyes travel up and down the columns as he turns the pages. The Tokyo earthquake has killed hundreds of thousands in Japan. The Prince of Wales will arrive in Quebec on Wednesday. On Friday Luis Ángel Firpo will fight Jack Dempsey in New York.

He reads the report about the convicts again, underlines things that might be of interest to the readers of the *Toronto Daily Star*.

He's learned one thing writing for the *Star* in Europe. You don't have to be present at an event to cover it well; you just have to write like you were.

He opens up the Corona and begins. "Escaped Kingston Convicts Still at Large."

⁂

Pleased with what he wrote, Hemingway sits in the hotel dining room going over the copy he telegraphed to the *Star*. He can sense the waiter reading it over his shoulder.

"I hear," the waiter says from behind him, "there've been a lot of resignations in the last few years."

"At the newspaper?"

"No, at the penitentiary. If you ask me, it's not natural to be your brother's keeper."

The waiter retreats through the swinging doors to the kitchen. Hemingway takes the napkin off his lap and pushes back his chair. A woman at the next table turns and faces him. She says, "I hear the salaries are low and the hours long at the prison."

She is young and pretty with long brown hair. Her skin is translucent white. Her eyes are blue and a small blue vein runs beneath the cameo at her throat. He finds himself looking at her left hand, to see if there's a wedding ring. Ezra always said there is a direct connection between the crotch and the creative brain.

The woman twists a strand of her hair. Her head is raised, her eyes focused upwards, as if she is studying the pressed tin ceiling.

When she turns her head and lowers her eyes, he knows she has caught him staring. He picks up the carbon of his story again and pretends to study it while he thinks about this.

She's beautiful but he is, after all, married to Hadley. He is not Ezra Pound. Ezra's wife, Dorothy, accepts his itinerant behaviour.

The waiter comes back with a pot of coffee and Hemingway raises his hand. The woman says, "May I please have some too?" The waiter changes course and scurries to her side. Hemingway's eyes follow the dark brown liquid as it descends like a muddy waterfall into her empty cup. He can see her breasts rise and fall with every breath beneath the white fabric of her dress.

When the waiter leaves, the woman turns to him again and smiles. The spirit of Ezra clutches at his elbow. *Ernest, Ernest, do something. Art, Beauty, Truth, Sex, they all go together. A man needs a regular bath in bodily fluids to get the creative juices going.*

Every time the woman moves, her perfume floats across the dining room and caresses Hemingway's cheek. When she lays her napkin down, the waiter reappears and slides her bill across the table.

There is something about the movement of the waiter's long fingers across the flat white linen that Hemingway does not like. It's too slow. It's making him angry. It's like another man leaving his hand a moment too long in the small of your wife's back.

"Charge it to my room," the woman says. "Two-oh-four."

The waiter pats his chest like a gorilla in heat until he finds a silver fountain pen.

The woman signs and starts to walk away. Her waist is small, her legs are long, her shoes a soft grey. When she reaches the arched dining room door, she turns and smiles. Hemingway sits a little straighter. His face begins to flush.

Opposite him, slumped in his chair, the shade of Ezra shakes his head.

The first time Hemingway met Ezra Pound, he thought Ezra was a joke. His hair was wild, he dressed in a velvet jacket like some kind of nineteenth-century poet. All those literary manifestos, pretentious nonsense he thought at first. But after his time in Paris, there are different things that he would hold up to ridicule, his parents' rigid beliefs for one. Some things matter less to him now than they used to. Some things matter more. He's beginning to believe artists do think differently. Artists, like convicts, lead different kinds of lives.

He rubs his ear to keep Ezra's voice out of his head, but it doesn't work.

It's easy, Hemingway. No true artist would ever love just one woman.

5

Everywhere Red looks all he sees is swamp. There's a mist hanging in the air and a bird that sounds like it's laughing at them. He can't sleep. Gord volunteered to stand watch tonight so the rest of them can sleep but nobody trusts him. He spooks too easily. He always thinks he hears things in the woods: men calling or men cocking their rifles or branches moving or dogs howling or dogs sniffing their way through the underbrush.

Tommy sits beside Red on a fallen log. Red studies the kid he never wanted to bring along in the first place. At least he knew all the other guys. Somewhere along the way, Tommy's lost the identification number off his sleeve.

Tommy picks up a blade of grass and rolls it between his palms. His hands are small, the fingers short and stubby. Red knows there are crescents of dirt under those nails, blacker than the night that descends on them.

While he watches Tommy, strands of clouds come together and then separate around the moon. The crickets keep singing. The bird laughs at them again. The wind blows through the trees. Far off in the distance Red can hear geese honking, getting ready to head south. Gord stands up and looks around.

"It's geese for Christ's sake, Gord," Tommy says. "Calm down."

Red knows tomorrow he'll have to do something or he will go crazy. He doesn't want to hear the slosh of their legs wading through the swamp again. Their movements separate the bright green scum on the top of the water, leaving a trail. All that wet around their ankles travels up their pant legs. It feels like a day when the prison won't give you a change of clothes even though you've been out working in the rain.

Gord's afraid of every damn noise in the bush. Tommy is terrified of leeches. Next time Red Ryan'll chose his travelling companions more carefully. Next time he escapes from anything, he does it with a gun. It might come in handy should he need to cull the herd.

Tommy drops the blade of grass. "That was a little too close last night. I almost caught a bullet."

Gord says, "I almost shit my pants."

Tommy twists a branch until it comes free. "You ever had the lash?" he says to Red, flicking the branch like a whip. Flick-snap, flick-snap, flick-snap, against his leg. Like he's jockey and horse or warden and prisoner all in one.

"Stop it," Red says.

Sully looks up from his place on a moss-covered rock. "What's going on?"

"Nothing. Lie back down and get some sleep," Red says, giving Tommy a look. He doesn't want to think about what will happen if they're caught. All he wants to think about is how to get out of this goddamn swamp. He doesn't like travelling blind in the bush. He's a city boy. He wants to get back to Toronto.

"It's awful quiet out here at night," Sully says. "It gives me the creeps."

"Quiet?" Gord says. "Are you crazy?"

Red lights up the last of his cigarettes, takes a draw, and holds it out to Gord. Maybe a smoke will calm his nerves.

Sully, not Gord, comes over and takes the cigarette from Red. Sully's hand shakes but he manages to get it to hold steady. He sucks the tobacco smoke in and a look of satisfaction spreads across his face. He keeps it there, in his lungs; time stops while Red waits for Sully to exhale.

"Jesus, that's good." Sully's nostrils flare as he blows the smoke back out.

"What was that? Did you hear that?"

Even though Red knows that Gord sees bogeymen behind every tree, images of bloodhounds and German shepherds and guards with rifles are beginning to invade his thoughts too.

"Don't get spooked," Tommy says. "It was only an owl. They like to hunt at night."

"Hunt what?" Sully says. "It didn't sound like there was anything out there."

"Oh, there are things out there. There are always things out there."

Sully signals with his hand and Red leans in closer. "We have to do something, Red. Tomorrow morning it will be forty-eight hours without water or food." He nods his head in Gord's direction. "I think it's beginning to show."

"I guess we'll find out who's made of what, Sully," Red whispers.

They hear a scuffle in the bush, the sound of leaves beaten by wings and the half-cry of a startled animal. Gord stands up, looking like he's ready to run off or turn himself in. "What was that?"

"Sit down," Tommy says. "It's just that old owl. He got something I guess."

⁂

It's the harsh, cold air that wakes Red up. They have made it through another night but the morning sky is full of dark clouds. His stomach rumbles, his mouth feels like it is full of cotton balls.

There is an ache in his head. He wonders if they should travel by night and rest during the day. But it's hard to navigate a swamp in the dark. His prison greys feel like they will never get dry. Gord and Sully are asleep, each on his bed of rock or branches. Behind him, the leaves rustle. Tommy Bryans is walking out from behind a clump of bushes.

"My piss is down to a trickle," Tommy says. "We need to get some water."

What's the plan here? It's driving Red crazy that he doesn't know the answer. He'd like to find a place to think. "Tommy, you stay here. I'll see if I can find some water."

When he stands up his head feels light. His temples pound. With each throb, the trees go in and out of focus. He slept but he's exhausted. He reaches out and grabs for the lower branch of a dead tree. It comes off in his hand.

As Red struggles to keep his balance, Tommy laughs and starts to unbutton his shirt. "It's something my old man taught me," Tommy says. "If you need water, tie your shirt around your ankles and walk around in the dew. When your shirt gets wet, you suck the water out of your shirt."

For a moment Red wonders if the kid is pulling his leg. Their shirts are the last article of dry clothing they've got.

"Trust me," Tommy says. "It works. It saved my life once. The dew is nice clean water, not like the stinking swamp."

Tommy bends over and wraps his shirt around one calf. He takes the sleeves and ties them together. "We came through that little open patch of dry land last night just before sundown. It can't be too far away. Before the sun is truly up, there'll be dew there for sure."

Red looks over at where Sully and Gord are sleeping, unbuttons his shirt, too, and pulls it off. The cold morning air turns his skin to goose flesh.

"Come on," Tommy says.

Red leans down to tie his shirt around his calf the way Tommy did, but his head starts to spin again.

"Sit down," Tommy says. "Give me your shirt. I'll tie it on."

Tommy is down on his knees. Red studies the top of his head; Tommy's ears stick out at an angle from his skull, partly hidden by his too-long prison hair. The kid winds the grey cotton around Red's leg like puttees in the war and secures it with the same two-sleeve knot. The cuffs hang down like the lock on a set of leg irons.

They head out through the underbrush. Why didn't they wait to take their shirts off?

When they reach the open patch, Tommy shuffles along, dragging his feet through the dew-covered grass. Red does it too. They scuffle in circles until their shirts are soaking wet.

Tommy leans down and unties his shirt and sucks on the sleeve.

Red thinks, *I have done some crazy things in my time but sucking on the sleeve of my prison shirt like a baby at a tit has to be about the craziest.* But it works. The water fills his mouth, a hint of grass in the taste. The coolness of it traces its way down, down his throat, through his chest, to his stomach. He runs his hand over his shirt looking for the next wettest spot and then he suckles there too.

After a few minutes, his temples don't throb and the trees have gone back into place. No more lightness in his head. They might make it after all.

⁂

Red leads the way back to the place where they spent the night. When they get close, he can see Gord Simpson pacing back and forth. "Where the hell have you two been?" Gord says. "Sullivan is sick."

Red walks over to where Sully lies on the ground, shivering. Sully stares up at him with eyes that have sunk into his skull. He looks like a tired old man.

"Call the guards, Red."

"What?"

"I need to go to the infirmary." Sully's head rolls from side to side. His tongue hangs out of his mouth. "Bang on the bars, Red."

"Sully," Red says, "look at me. You're not in your cell."

Sully turns his head and stares up at him.

"Are we out in the yard?" he says. "I shouldn't lie down in the yard. I'll get in trouble."

"I think we're already in trouble," Tommy says.

Sully's breath comes in blasts, in and out, in and out.

"Lie still, you aren't in the goddamn yard," Red says. "And shut up. Do you want to get us captured?"

Red puts his hand on Sully's throat. "His heart is beating like crazy," he says. "Give him your shirt, Tommy. He needs water bad."

Tommy holds out his shirt. Red grabs it and holds it close to Sully's mouth. "Here, suck on this." Sully tries to lift his head, but it sinks back down again. Red wrings some water out of the shirt and lets it drip onto Sully's parched lips.

"We need to get out of here and find some food," Gord says.

"Sully," Red says, "do you think you can get up?"

Gord and Tommy grab Sully by the arms and try to lift him to his feet. His legs spread and dip. His body flops like he has no bones. When they try to put his arms around their shoulders, he can't hang on.

"I don't think Sullivan can walk, even with our help," Gord says.

6

HEMINGWAY REACHES OUT HIS HAND, BUT THERE IS NO Hadley next to him on this rainy Kingston morning. He pulls the covers over his head. Two years ago he and Hadley were on their honeymoon.

On his way into the dining room, he picks up today's *Daily British Whig* from the front desk. There is still no trace of the escaped prisoners. Rumours spread faster and faster. The *Whig* reports every one of them. The convicts boarded a train. The convicts are in a nearby town.

"There's a telegram for you," the waiter says when Hemingway sits down. He eyes the beige-coloured cable. "Mr. Hemmingway," it begins.

A few short months ago, the *Toronto Daily Star* had praised his dispatches from Italy and Turkey and Switzerland. Now his new boss, Managing Editor Harry Comfort Hindmarsh, can't even spell his name right.

He sticks the telegram under the sugar bowl, unfolds his copy of the *Whig*, and starts to read again. The postmaster at Collins Bay is in possession of a convict-tracking bloodhound. Mrs. Victor Long of Glenburnie says she's sure she saw one of the convicts right in her own backyard.

The waiter arrives and puts Hemingway's breakfast down, chasing away the images for his report collecting in his head. He should have brought his notebook.

He takes his fork and breaks open the yolks of his two fried eggs. Hindmarsh's telegram stares up at him from underneath the sugar bowl. "Bastard," he says out loud as the yellow yolk streams across his plate toward him. "There is only one goddamn *m* in Hemingway."

The dining room window looks past Ontario Street onto the train yard and the ships in Kingston harbour, the harbour on the river that flows toward the sea, past the towns and the islands, past the cliffs of old Quebec, where he landed with Hadley barely a week ago. It is the river that sails past the farms and the hills, past the Gaspésie, out into the Atlantic Ocean, the highway back to Paris where his friends are. Where his friends published his little book in August, *Three Stories and Ten Poems*.

He handed a few copies out at the *Star*. Somebody told him that was a mistake. Well, Hindmarsh better get ready because there's more coming at the end of the year. Eighteen sketches this time. Some of them will be in the "spring" edition of the *Little Review*, too, if it ever comes out. It's a different kind of writing, things boiled down to their essence, like poetry, only it's prose. What's not there is more important sometimes than what is. To evoke emotion, not report it. What's going on underneath the words, not seen, makes the reader work, participate in the story.

Hemingway finishes his breakfast and gets up after he signs his bill. His hand moves toward the sugar bowl but he pulls it back. The telegram can stay right where it is. He walks out onto the hotel's steps, breathing the fresh air and studying the harbour and the grain elevators. The rail yards in Kingston separate the city from the water. Lines of track run across its foot and curve west past city hall and his hotel.

Past the rail lines, past the shoreline, he sees something he hadn't noticed before, a short, grey stone tower out in the water. It is the same tower that sits in Sandy Cove, Kingstown Bay, Dublin, in real life and in the opening pages of *Ulysses*. It is Stephen Dedalus's Martello tower reincarnated here in another King's town, thousands of miles across the sea.

Stephen Dedalus, who walked around Dublin trying to decide — journalist or writer? To be or not to be.

⁂

In his room Hemingway sits down at the desk, takes two sheets of paper, puts a carbon in the middle, and snaps them on the writing desk to get all the edges straight. He rolls the paper down into his typewriter, the faithful portable Corona #3 Hadley gave him for his birthday the summer of 1921.

The sound of the paper rolling through the carriage is so familiar that it makes his chest ache. He still remembers the first thing he wrote on it. He was turning twenty-two. He was so in love with Hadley. It was right before their wedding.

He wrote about desire.

That is what he and the Corona were made for.

Not this.

The keys on the Corona make their familiar tap, tap, tap. He gets up, he pours a glass of water, he walks around. He sits back down and picks up the *Whig* and reads again. Parts of this convict story are pretty funny.

The convicts as dinner for the postmaster's underfed bloodhound. The convicts assigned the making of ladders at the prison. The multiplicity of convict sightings.

There must be almost as many convicts on the loose by now, Hemingway writes, as there are citizens in the good city of

Kingston. It's simple mathematics: the number of convicts multiplied by the number of sightings. He laughs. The Corona jumps across the desk, he bangs on it so hard.

They say the guards have set up dummy cars without spark plugs to try and entice Red Ryan and his gang out of the woods. One guard says maybe it's dummy banks they should set up.

Hemingway gets up from the desk and watches the dark clouds form over the river. The buildings and the rooftops of Kingston are still wet from an early morning rain. He wonders if the convicts found shelter from the storm. At night a swamp and the woods can be a frightening. Sometimes the silence can be as terrifying as the sounds in the forest. That's what it was like in the war. It was the silence that terrified you.

He thinks about Hadley alone at the Selby waiting for him. The heaviness of her breasts, the huge curve of her belly: round and swollen like the hulls of the old wooden ships in Kingston harbour.

The baby happened in January, when they were in Chamby. But that didn't stop them. They travelled to Rapallo to visit Ezra, then to Milan and Cortina. Fresh air and skiing and hiking. Ten days off in April to work for the *Star* on the French-German troubles at the Ruhr, then back to Cortina, then back to Paris, then to Spain without Hadley. The ratio was right in those days, life to work. In May he saw his first bullfight. Then in July he brought Hadley to Spain because Gertrude Stein had told him — you have to see the running of the bulls in Pamplona.

The problems of life come at you like a bull sometimes, huge and terrifying, skidding and snorting behind you while you run on cobblestones, slick, shiny, soaked with rain.

Every man wants to escape the danger and run. A bullfighter has fear but he stays and fights. The bull is bigger but the bullfighter makes the bull dance to his tune.

⁂

Outside the window over the river, the clouds have cleared away. The sun is setting, glowing red and low in the September sky. The grey, curved stone of Joyce's Martello tower sits alone in the harbour.

It is one hell of a book Joyce wrote. It takes courage to break all the rules.

Perhaps it is time to find his own courage. There is a bottle of absinthe in his satchel. A silver spoon rolled up in his extra pair of underwear, a little stemmed glass stolen from a restaurant in the Marais.

Time to find himself in *la Fée Verte*.

In Paris, after a few glasses of absinthe, he would sit down and write: drunk but not whisky- or wine-drunk. An omniscient drunk. Clear-headed. About everything. Today he feels clear-headed about nothing, not Hadley, not the baby, not writing, not the *Toronto Daily Star*.

He stands by the dormer window, looks out at the Martello tower, and pours three fingers of absinthe into the heavy Maraisian glass. He places the filigreed spoon across the rim. It is stolen but he cannot remember from where. From his pocket he pulls out the square of sugar from the dining room, the compacted essence of childhood winter memories. He places it carefully on the spoon.

He gets another glass of ice-cold water from the bathroom and drips it ever so slowly onto the cube, watching the sugar dissolve. The water does not mix with the oils in the absinthe, and it clouds into pale opalescent green before his eyes. The smell of flowers fills his nostrils, and images of Paris and the Jardin du Luxembourg fill his head. He stops because he wants the ratio, absinthe to water, to be high.

Once the sugar has dissolved, he gives the glass a stir and stands up. He raises it in the air. He feels like a sorcerer or maybe a god.

Somewhere below him in the streets of Kingston there are ordinary people who've never been to Paris. Somewhere north of Kingston there are convicts on the run. Somewhere in Toronto there is a baby waiting to be born.

Despite the baby he will have to win the fight. Tonight he will have to find the fortitude. He will be brave or act brave or believe he is brave enough.

He, Ernest Miller Hemingway, needs the world to know his name.

⁂

"Mr. Hemingway." Someone is knocking ever so softly. "Mr. Hemingway," the voice whispers. "Are you awake?"

Hemingway looks at his watch. It's nine fifteen. The tapping comes again.

"Mr. Hemingway, there's something going on, out at the prison. It's me, Bernard, from the dining room; I thought you'd like to know."

When Hemingway opens the door, the man who serves him dinner is standing there, still wearing his waiter's attire under a brown coat. On his head is a black peaked cap.

"I was having a drink with a friend of mine after I set the tables for breakfast tomorrow. He told me the convicts are singing."

"Who told him that? One of the guards?"

"He didn't need a guard to tell him. He lives a couple of blocks away from the prison. He said you can hear them singing at the top of their voices. So clear you can make out the words. I guess they don't like being confined to their cells."

"I don't blame them."

"Started after lights out. I thought you'd like to know."

⁂

Hemingway pulls on his jacket and shoves his notebook and pencil in his pocket. He walks up to King Street to get the street railway. When the car arrives, it's full. The good citizens of Kingston have heard there is some entertainment to be had out at the penitentiary.

He pushes his way through to stand near the back door and looks out the windows as the car heads west.

The houses on King Street give way to an open view of the lake. To the south the water stretches out to the horizon. On the shore there is another short, grey stone Martello tower reminding him of his dilemma. The car moves on, and he moves to the back to keep it in his sight as long as he can. He hasn't read all of *Ulysses*, parts of the first half and the soliloquy at the end. But what he has read amazed him.

Closer to the penitentiary they pass the corner where Ed McMullen got shot. His head's a little foggy from the absinthe, but he starts to hear the low hum of male voices.

Standing across from the grey columns of Kingston Pen's front gate, he can make out the words.

> It's hard to be locked up in prison
> From all the joys and the comforts of life.

He stands and listens as the convicts sing louder and louder. It is hard to be locked in a prison. Particularly one of your own making.

7

Red gets up on one elbow and looks around. The glow of dawn is crawling above the tree-covered horizon. Carrying Sully yesterday he felt like he'd been on a work detail at the prison for too many hours. If only he was on his own. He could move through the woods like a fox. Sure-footed and quiet.

Gord gathered some branches and made himself a lean-to off the side of a rock. He said tomorrow they could weave some more branches into a sort of duck blind, a camouflage, and if they find some water and berries, they could stay here for a while and rest, with the rock to protect them.

But Red doesn't want to stay by the rock. Today he wants to get to the top of the hill to see what's around them. They should have let Tommy drive the car, somebody expendable. He and Ed planned this together. The two bank robbers. Now, without Ed, he's left to make all the important decisions on his own.

"I'm going to scout around today," he says, "by myself."

Nobody disagrees with him. One benefit of them being tired and hungry. He could use some time on his own to think. But as he's about to head off into the bush Tommy says, "I'm coming with you."

"No, you're not."

Tommy crosses his arms like a defiant child who had been told to go to bed. "How do we know you won't take off and decide not to come back?"

⊹⊹

Tommy breaks branches behind them as they go along. Good thing Sully isn't here, and Red's not sure he cares anymore. He's decided: This is their last day in the bush.

The weather is colder. The sky is blue with only one cloud off to the left. Tommy says it looks like a naked woman bending over, washing her hair. Off in the distance, Red hears a train whistle. He could hear them at night in the prison, the loneliest sound in the world.

They walk toward the echoing, plaintive sound, through the underbrush; saplings slap their faces as they go by.

Then Red can see it, he can tell by the light. It's the place where the undergrowth and the trees come to an abrupt halt. But when they get to the clearing, it isn't railway tracks, it's a road: a silver, gravelled, straight-as-an-arrow road heading north, judging by the sun, up over the top of a rise.

Tommy runs out into the middle and dances up and down.

"Get back here." Far down the road, a cloud of dust heads their way.

But Tommy keeps scuffling through the gravel in the middle of the road. The cloud of dust is getting closer.

Red looks both ways again and steps out from behind the tree onto the road. He grabs the collar of Tommy's shirt and pulls him back toward the bush. "We stay inside the woods until I say we don't."

Tommy breaks free and throws a punch in Red's direction. Red grabs Tommy's wrist and twists his arm behind his back.

"Look kid, you better tow the line, or I'll leave your sorry ass right where you stand," Red says, pushing Tommy back toward the bush.

Tommy turns, lifts his head, and looks Red dead in the eye. "If you leave me and the cops find me, I might sing to the guards about how your brother Frank helped you escape."

Red throws Tommy down in the dirt and before he can struggle to his feet, Red stomps his foot down on a sapling and twists until it rips free. He thrashes it across the back of Tommy's legs. Down, again and again, the branch whips through the air, landing on the kid's legs and arms, neck and shoulders. Screaming, Tommy flails his hands to protect himself.

"Stand up, you little jerk," Red says, throwing the sapling aside. "You'll stay right beside me in the woods, or you'll get a whupping like your mama never gave you."

⁂

As they move up the incline, Red can feel spongy forest floor give way to firmer ground. Every few yards he looks to his left to make sure the road is still there. And it is. It doesn't desert him.

At the top of the hill, they see a sign that says, "The Village of Glenburnie Welcomes You." The woods have started to thin. Off in the distance, there are a couple of houses and a general store with a car and a horse and wagon parked out front. Behind the houses, there are barns and sheds sprinkled over the fields. Off to their right, down the crossroads, they can see the spire of a limestone church.

"We should rob a bank," Tommy says.

"Even if there was a bank in this one-horse town, I wouldn't rob it with you, kid," Red says. "Shut up and follow me."

Crouching down and keeping inside the protection of the trees, Red moves closer to the crossroads. Judging by the rising sun, he was right about the direction; they are moving north and the other road runs east and west.

If they keep heading north, they have to go out into the open and cross the road. If they go west, they have to cross a road. To the east of the crossroads, there are three or four small houses, all on the north side of the road. Then, the trees close in again. Past the trees, Red sees the church, straight and utilitarian. "Methodists," he says. "I'd bet money."

There's a barn behind the last house and over to the right, just before a stand of pines. The barn is grey and weathered, its big sliding front door long since gone. Daylight shines, like a prison lantern, through the gaps between the boards.

⁂

Sully gazes up at Red when they get back. He sits on the rock eating berries from Gord's cap, his skin porcelain white, his lips and his chin stained blackish red. Like someone punched him in the mouth.

"Did you find the train tracks?" Gord says, holding out his cap.

"Found the end of the swamp, a road, and a town," Red says.

Sully looks up and smiles with red-stained teeth.

"We aren't safe yet, Sul. Who knows where the guards are. They could be fifty feet away."

"This is what I think we should do," Tommy says, walking over to Gord and Sully.

Red straightens to his full height. "I decide what we do and when we do it. You and Gord look after Sully. I'm not carrying anybody."

He will lead them, like Moses, out of the swamp, farther and farther from the stone walls and the chains and the guards at Kingston Pen. They will find good, dry shelter in that barn and get some rest. They need real food. They need a car. Then they will go to Toronto, where he knows the streets and the back alleys as well as he knew every square inch of his cell at the Pen.

8

THIS MORNING, IN THE HOTEL DINING ROOM, HEMINGWAY hears people talk of other things: the earthquake in Tokyo, the arrival of the Prince of Wales. The convicts share the front page of the *Whig* with the news of a revolution in Spain. Spain is uncharted territory. No English writer has claimed it yet.

It's too early to start working so he turns to the sporting section. On Friday, at the Polo Grounds in New York, Jack Dempsey will fight Luis Firpo. The Argentinean outweighs Dempsey by about thirty pounds, the paper says.

Hemingway's right hand gives a little jab across the table. His chin lowers into his chest. He could go a couple of rounds right now if there was a worthy opponent on the premises.

He reads the *Whig*'s latest report on the prison break. The best part of the story: a rumour about a trick perpetrated on the guards. If the rumour is true, these convicts have friends on the outside.

"Excuse me, sir," the waiter says. He holds out a piece of paper. "One of the guards from the prison brought this."

The paper says: "12:30 today, my office, Kingston Penitentiary. Warden J.C. Ponsford."

Hemingway stashes the *Whig* under his arm and gets up from the table. He should probably go upstairs, but instead he walks out of the hotel and heads down Clarence Street to the place where the river flows into the lake. There is a strong breeze blowing and the wind skims across the water like it is trying to strum a guitar.

⁜

At noon, sitting on the street railway on his way to the prison, Hemingway holds yesterday's edition of the *Toronto Daily Star* like a curtain in front of his face. He doesn't want to smile, talk, or look at anyone else.

What he wouldn't give to be heading for a drink with Ezra. Ezra, the first, the only man he has ever confided in. Is it wrong for a man to long for the sight of another man the way he longs for the sight of Ezra?

Ezra understands what he is trying to do. And who he wants to be.

The street railway shakes and clangs its way along King Street. As they pass the other Martello tower, the *Star* catches the breeze blowing off the lake. It rattles and flutters trying to get his attention.

His last report — still no byline — is on page four: "Provincial Police Are Taking Up the Chase." Hindmarsh is losing interest but it's a big mistake. Those damn convicts are giving everyone the slip.

The car comes to a stop across the street from the high walls and columns and the guards' towers of Kingston Pen.

⁜

When he goes through the large oak doors with the heavy, round metal handles, he sees not cells, but grass. The prison is like a city within a city. A wide expanse between the offices. Over to the right, the workshop; over to the left, the cellblock with its giant dome. The charred stables. He tries to picture the scramble that must have happened in the yard on Monday morning while he roamed the streets of Toronto collecting bits and pieces of nothing about nobodies. He can see it all: the smoke, the fire, the neighing horses, the makeshift ladder.

Warden Ponsford and another man stand as two guards escort him into the warden's office. Ponsford introduces Gilbert Smith, the Inspector of Penitentiaries, there to conduct an investigation into the escape.

"I heard a rumour that some of the guards were on the take. That Red Ryan's brother had something to do with it," Hemingway says after they sit down.

Warden Ponsford doesn't answer. He turns in his chair and points to a map on the wall behind his desk. There are red dots spattered across it like drops of blood. "Six teams of guards are out on the road searching the woods," Ponsford says. "Combing the countryside in twelve-hour shifts."

Hemingway does not honour this repetition of everything he already knows by writing it in his notebook. He sits and says nothing. Sometimes silence encourages those who do not wish to speak to open up.

Ponsford stands and walks over to a picture hanging on the wall where he poses with the prime minister of Canada, William Lyon Mackenzie King. "The search is very methodical and well-organized. We have a trolley truck that brings out food for the guards."

Hemingway's closed notebook remains in one hand, his pencil in the other.

"Isn't that what you did in the war, Mr. Hemingway?" Ponsford says, running his finger along the bottom of the picture frame.

"Brought coffee and chocolate to the soldiers? You weren't a soldier. You worked for the Red Cross."

Hemingway looks up. He could roll up his pant leg and show Warden Ponsford his scars. Two hundred pieces of shrapnel from an Austrian mortar shell. July 8, 1918, on the Piave river in Italy.

There is a cruel streak in a man who wants to put another man down, find a weakness he can use. No wonder Red Ryan and his pals wanted out of here. Did Warden J.C. Ponsford go out of his way to try and find out what he did or did not do in the war?

"A farmer reported that his shotgun was stolen from behind the kitchen door," Hemingway says. "Have you looked into that?"

"We'll find them."

"I read that you were warned Red Ryan would try and escape."

"Quite the contrary, Mr. Hemingway." Ponsford takes a sideways glace at the two guards by the door. "I warned my staff to keep a close eye on him."

Inspector Smith stands up and says, "I will be covering any and all leads in my investigation."

The two guards who escorted him in stand at attention. His time is up. He didn't get much.

"When will you return to Toronto," Gilbert Smith asks.

"Not for a day or two."

"Then I suggest you contact me at the end of the week. Perhaps we can talk again."

Outside on King Street, he walks past the prison and turns back to look at the southeast corner where the convicts made their escape. Those bastards had big brass balls. That wall is high.

⁂

When the street railway stops at market square, the place where the farmers sell their vegetables and hawk their homemade wares,

Hemingway calls out, "Anyone live out by McAdoo's Woods?" The clock on Kingston City Hall sounds the three-quarter hour.

"Who wants to know?" an old man in dirty overalls answers. He smells like horse manure.

"I'm looking for a ride." Hemingway pulls a five-dollar bill out of his pocket.

"Convict hunting?" says the old man, hitching up his overalls.

"Maybe."

⁂

As Hemingway climbs into the cab of the farmer's rusty truck, he thinks about the swamp and the rock and the dense bush and the map he saw on Ponsford's office wall.

"How far's the railway from McAdoo's Woods?"

"Just southwest of Glenburnie," the farmer says. "I'll let you off up top the hill just before the village."

"Appreciate it."

"How you getting back?"

"I'll walk. I'm used to hiking."

"You got a flashlight? Gets dark early these days."

"Damn. No, I don't."

"You city folk beat all," the farmer says. "There's a flashlight under the seat. You can have it for another fiver."

Hemingway pulls out another bill, stuffs it in the old guy's pocket, and then reaches under the seat. The flashlight is old and rusty but when he tries it, it still works.

They drive along in silence past the outskirts of the city, past the same rocks and trees he went by on his first morning covering the escape.

"Take it nice and slow once we get past the place where they dumped the car."

As they slow down, he can see the prison guards are now almost outnumbered by the Ontario Provincial Police. They're going to broaden the search, he'd read in the *Whig*. Now there are two camps. Each group surrounding a tin drum spitting flames. The smoke spirals up into the sky. Some of the men stand with their hands over the fire. One of them looks up as the truck drives past.

"There's a road up here," Hemingway says, "that cuts across the property."

"Just before the rise. Bush is pretty dense."

"Slow down," Hemingway says when they are out of sight of the guards and the police.

"This is the best time of day for tracking," the farmer says. "The sun is casting long shadows."

"I know. I've spent a lot of time in the bush."

"Not this bush, with four convicts on the loose. You should have a gun."

"I know."

The farmer pulls over to the side of the road. "Look, son, I don't mind giving you a ride but I gotta be getting home. The cows will be waiting at the gate."

⁂

The truck leaves a trail of dust as it drives away. Hemingway walks along in the grass at the edge of the bush. The air smells fresh and clean, with a touch of woodsmoke. If you don't know where you're going, a road is a good thing to follow, like a river or a railway track. Surely, the convicts know that too.

Off to the south, there is another cloud of dust, this one coming in his direction. He ducks down behind the thick trunk of a fallen tree. When the car passes, he can see there are two men in the front seat. The man on the passenger side has the business end of a rifle sticking out the window.

The tree trunk is covered with moss and the sinking sun is laying a line of brightness on it like a spotlight. His hand sweeps across it. It's warm and soft but untouched, like a clean towel at a fine hotel. Whatever the old farmer thinks about him, he does know a thing or two about tracking. Granted, it's tracking animals not people but it couldn't be that different. He tries to remember everything his father taught him about being out in the woods. Keep looking down. Look for rocks that have been kicked or branches broken or paw prints on the ground.

The bush lines the road about three feet in. He enters the green cool of the forest and the underbrush drags on his pant legs. They'd have to come out of the forest and cross this road at some point to get to the railway tracks. The bush is so dense and the undergrowth so thick that four men would leave a trail. He keeps his head down looking for signs that something, anything, has been disturbed.

After about half a mile, he makes his way back out to the road. From the map he saw in Ponsford's office, there should be a crossroads and a village up ahead. His legs are tired and his hands and face scratched from fighting his way through the bush.

A couple of yards ahead, he sees a sapling lying on the ground. Out on the road, the gravel is kicked around. When he looks deeper into the woods, he sees what he's been looking for all along. The grass is trampled down. There is an opening in the undergrowth about two feet wide. Somebody came through here.

He walks back out to the middle of the road and scours the bush on the other side. Nothing, but his heart is beating, boom, boom, boom, boom against his chest. The convicts had been smart enough to throw the car left, then run to their right into McAdoo's Woods. Maybe they used a branch to smooth the gravel and hide their footprints. He walks about fifty feet back but there is no sign of anything being disturbed in the gravel or in the woods. No footprints on the west side of the road. He travels back, crouching, studying the dirt, to where he found the switch and then searches again another fifty feet in the other direction. Nothing on the road or the grass or the forest on the west side of the road.

The switch hasn't been cut, it's been ripped. The yarn-thin end with the newest growth is cracked and broken. Somebody got a whippin' like his dad used to give him in the woodshed.

The sun is low in the sky. A bird cries out. In the shadows every noise seems unfamiliar and magnified. He walks into the bush, his eyes scanning left and right over the multiple shades of green. Judging by how the undergrowth is beaten down, looks like they went back in where they came out. He moves north and east inside the cover of the trees. What is he looking for exactly? The old guy was probably right. He should have a gun. What if they find him? He's outnumbered and they're desperate. He could die right here. But if he survives, his reports would be back on page one tomorrow morning.

9

Red takes them back along the trail Tommy left until he sees the unfiltered light off in the distance. The road is still there, right where he left it. Daring him to step on board.

There are fewer cars now. Red moves closer to the road but he makes the rest of them stay well back in the trees. As the sky gets darker, a strange fatigue sets in. It's like whenever he pulled a job, he'd be high for a while but then, an hour later, he'd want to lie down and go to sleep. They should have waited until the morning.

A dog barks in the distance. Red squints his eyes and tries to see through the shadows to the place where the sound came from. Standing dead still, not breathing. There is a flashlight dancing like a firefly in the twilight way off to the south. The dog barks again. A flock of birds takes flight. "Get down," he says. "Somebody's coming." The beam of the flashlight moves back and forth and then focuses in their direction.

"Halt!" a voice cries. A shot rings out. Red's heart stops. Jesus, is this it? Is it over? Is this all they get?

The dog stops barking and Red can hear the sound of leaves brushing against clothing as men crash their way through the woods. When Red looks up, it looks like there is a whole posse, maybe four or five, about twenty yards away.

"Move and you're a dead man," the voice shouts. Red stops breathing. The shadows and the beam of light get closer. Now it's about ten yards away. "You, hands in the air."

"Don't shoot."

Red cannot believe his eyes when a man steps out from behind the trunk of a large pine tree, hands reaching for the sky. The beam of the flashlight moves up to find the man's face. He is young, tall, dark-haired, with a moustache.

"Jesus Christ, Toronto!" Red recognizes that voice. It's one of the guards. "What the hell are you doing way out here? Trying to get yourself killed?"

Then another voice he recognizes. "Knew you were trouble the first time I laid eyes on you and your little black notebook."

The first guard signals to the other men and they grab the young guy by the arm and pull him off to the west toward the road. "Warden Ponsford's been telling us what you wrote in your big city paper, Mister whatever-your-name-is. Said it reads like you were out there with us that first night, riding right along beside us, searching the bush, looking for those guys. Tryin' to make out like you're a brave bastard but you're not even man enough to put your name on what you wrote."

"His name's Hemingway," one of the guards says, walking up close to the man and shining his flashlight onto his face. "He's from the *Toronto Star*. The boss told me he hauled him in this afternoon."

"You find anything, Hemingway?" one of the guards says.

Red holds his breath but the young man with the moustache shakes his head.

The guard with the flashlight sends a beam of light up into the treetops and Red sees two headlights advancing along the road from the south. The flashlight goes out. The men tighten up on the dog's leash, grab the young man with the moustache by the arm, and get into the car.

"Hemmyway," Red says under his breath.

"That was close." Gord says. "He might have found us. He wasn't far away."

"He's just a newspaperman," Tommy says, "trying to make a name for himself. Big deal. Probably doesn't know a damn thing about tracking something in the woods."

"What makes you such an expert?"

"Spent more time in the bush than you ever did, city boy."

"Stop it," Red says. "No fighting. That's a sure way to get caught. We gotta stick together."

Tommy moves toward the road. "Let's get out of here. They're gone. We don't have to worry anymore."

"You little asshole," Red says. "If it wasn't for that Hemmyway fellow out here snooping around, the guards might have found us."

"We owe you one, mister," Sully says.

Red gives the signal and they pick their way through the undergrowth, staying under the protection of the tall black trees. "We rest tonight and then keep moving."

They find the road and follow it north from a safe distance inside the bush until they reach the crossroads and then head east. "There it is. There's the barn."

"Doesn't seem to be anything happening," Gord says. "No cows getting milked or cattle being fed."

"No reporters," Tommy says with a laugh.

Before Red lets them leave the safety of the woods, he takes one last look down the road past the little group of pine trees and the church that stand to the north. He gives the signal and they start to move. The grey cavity that is the entrance to the barn looks like a monster's mouth waiting to swallow them whole.

10

HEMINGWAY SITS IN THE BACK OF THE GUARDS' CAR AND listens to them talk about him as if he isn't there. How lucky he was that they didn't put one right through his heart.

"What were you planning to do out there anyway, Toronto, if you found them?"

He's been asking himself that question ever since he heard he was going to cover the story. What would he do if he found them? Turn them in, end their story? That doesn't feel right.

"Big feather in your cap if you did, right?"

But he's not in this for glory. All he wants is a goddamn byline. In some ways he believes Red deserves his freedom. No person is meant to be a prisoner. And no person, in his opinion, is meant to imprison other people.

The real question is not what would he do but what would Red do? If the rumour about the stolen gun is true, Red probably would shoot first and ask questions later. So really, Hemingway, it's a moot point.

"Out you get, Toronto," the driver says when they pull up to his hotel. "Stay out of trouble. You just keep writing your newspaper stories. You could be trampling on evidence out there. Leave the convict hunting to us."

Hemingway nods but he's already decided, moot points aside, he's going back out there tomorrow and see what he can see. Somebody scuffled on that road. Looks like there's dissent in the convicts' ranks.

In his hotel room, he draws a sketch of the area he went through, the hill, the road, what's up ahead.

At dinner he asks Bernard about the territory. "Little town up there, Mr. Hemingway. Not much to it. General store, church, a couple houses. Doesn't take long before you're back in farm country."

"Close to the railway track?"

"Yeah, it's just to the southwest of the crossroads. Why you asking?"

"I wonder if Red Ryan knows that?"

He's about to sign for his meal when the desk clerk walks into the dining room. "Mr. Hemingway, I'm glad I caught you." He holds out a telegram. His Royal Hindmarsh has decreed in boxy telegraph type: "Return Toronto tonight. New assignment."

He walks up the stairs to his room and stares at the darkness descending over the river. The portholes on the ships in the harbour shine golden, moving up and down, like a string of lights swaying in a summer breeze. People pass by on the street below. He's looking down on something he has lost but he doesn't know what it is. No more Red Ryan for him. Hindmarsh has lost interest. Tomorrow, the klieg light glare of the *Toronto Star*'s city room will be burning into his eyes.

The first time he was in Toronto, in 1920, he stayed with Ralph and Harriet Connable. Ralph is the head of Woolworth's in Canada. Woolworth's is a big advertiser with the *Toronto Daily Star.* Ralph lives in a mansion, but he talks like a woodsman. In

Michigan he worked for his dad's company in the bush. He's full of stories.

"Who would have thought," Ralph told Hadley at dinner the first night they arrived in Toronto, "that when we hired young Ernie to keep an eye on Ralph Jr. while we were away, he'd end up writing for the paper and turn into the *Star*'s big-time foreign correspondent."

Well, that was Paris and this is Toronto.

⁂

The worn shuttle train arrives, and on his way to the outer station Hemingway watches as the buildings go from the solid limestone structures of downtown, the city hall, the barracks, the armoury to the one-storey shacks of railway workers that run along the river. Other people on the train rattle and read their newspapers or chat to their seatmates. He watches the trees and the water and the sky, remembering how they look on a mid-September day.

At the outer station, the Toronto train releases a hiss of steam and begins to follow the long curve of track that starts them facing west. Hemingway stares out the window and records the scene as it goes by, the dark green pine, the birch, the reeds and bulrushes around a lake. In his head he is a convict, running, scared but bold, out in that bush. His lungs on fire. In his head he is an erstwhile writer wondering if he should have jumped on one of those ships in the harbour or said yes to that woman in the dining room when he had the chance.

II

Red swings down off the hayloft and heads toward the barn door. Even a dog knows you don't piss where you sleep. He sticks his head out and looks toward the house. All is darkness.

As his eyes adjust to the gloom, he can see a privy. Leading up to it there is a gravel path. He can see the outline of an old tree stump next to the outhouse door. There is a hatchet driven into it and a small pile of kindling on the ground.

When he reaches the outhouse, a flock of geese honk their way overhead. The door creaks as he pulls it open.

The rough wooden hole smells of piss and shit. Even so, what a luxury. Solitude at last. Time to think. No Tommy Bryans buzzing around him like a wasp. He can sit and look at the stars through the quarter-moon cut-out in the door.

The sound of crunching gravel interrupts his thoughts. He struggles to pull his pants back up from around his ankles, getting ready to face whoever or whatever is out there. There is nothing to use as a weapon, only the spike and twine that holds a catalogue on the wall. He tries to pull the spike out but it's driven in too far. Red squints through the quarter moon. There is a dark shape walking toward the stump in the path.

His heart is beating, banging against his chest like a battering ram, as he presses himself back against the privy wall. Stay calm, stay calm. He takes another look. No more noise. No more crunch on the gravel. When he counts to one hundred, he will open the door.

When he undoes the latch, there is just the sound of the wind blowing through the pine trees on the other side of the barn. But the hatchet is no longer stuck in the stump. It is resting on the pile of kindling. On top of the stump there is a burlap sack. He picks it up and holds the rough brown cloth close to his eyes. Food, he can smell it. Ham.

The name on the burlap is stencilled in red, "Wagner's Oats." The same oats they use to feed the horses in the prison. He wiggles his finger into the little rose of fabric that the bailing twine drawstring has created and pulls the two sides apart.

⁜

Red sets the contents of the sack out on the floor of the barn like a farmer's wife laying out lunch for hands in the fields. There is ham. There is cheese and some milk in a jar. There is a knife, a utensil, a tool, and a weapon.

He finds a loaf of bread wrapped in a linen towel. It's real bread like his mother used to make in the woodstove in their kitchen: crusty on the outside, soft and sweet on the inside. At the bottom he discovers a crock of butter wrapped in layers of newspaper, still cold from the icebox.

Below the butter he finds more newspapers, the smell of the printer's ink still on them. Underneath it all he finds a crudely drawn map and two one-dollar bills.

The money goes under his cap as he studies the map. He recognizes the church, the pines, the house, the barn, the crossroads, and the general store. Over to the west of the crossroads, there is a curving ladder of a line that he knows stands for the railway tracks. Somebody has straightened them out.

Outside the barn all is quiet. He stands clutching the food sack to his chest. All he can hear is the soft sound of snoring coming from the loft.

When he gets to the top of the ladder, he bends down and gives Sully's shoulder a shake. "Wake up," he says. "I know where the train tracks are now. And I've got food."

"Food?" Sully looks at him as if he is speaking a language no one could understand. Sully yawns and a blast of bad air strikes Red's face.

"Get up, Sul. We don't have any time to waste. Wake up Gord and the kid. If we leave now, we can get down to the tracks before the sun is up."

⁂

Even before dawn Red is still afraid of walking out in the open. They take a circular route, going south back into the woods, crossing the gravel road, then heading north again. Until at last they see the clearing where the trains run through.

There is a low stand of bushes along the track, leaves crimson and orange like a low-burning fire. Red can see how the line curves to the west. "Trains slow here," it says with an arrow on the crudely drawn map.

He signals to the others to stay back while he pushes his way through the scrub brush. No sign of anything. He moves out and puts his hand on the rail, then his ear. Nothing, no vibration. He crawls back to where the others are waiting.

"Well?" says Tommy.

"One of us needs to watch for the train," Red says.

There is a red glow in the sky as the sun tries to clear the tops of the trees. Tommy is reading the newspapers from the food pack.

"Too bad we don't have the Toronto paper; we could see what that Hemmyway wrote about us."

He holds the papers up for Red to see, the September 10, 11, and 12 editions of the *Daily British Whig*, the headlines all screaming of their escape.

"Hah, look at this," Tommy says. "They think we're far away. Not like that reporter out in the bush."

"Anything about Ed?" Red asks.

Tommy riffles through the crumpled pages and reads, "Wounded prisoner found exhausted."

"That's too bad," Sully says.

Tommy points at Ed's picture. "I hope he doesn't start singing."

"Quiet," Gord yells. "Do you hear something?"

Sully pulls on Red's arm. "I've never hopped a freight before."

"I'll help you, Sully. It's not dangerous if you wait for the right moment."

"You never hopped a freight?" Gord laughs. "Well, get ready. Even though it's going slow, be prepared. You're going to get yanked when you grab on."

"Not if you get your speed up at the same time the train is slowing down to go around a bend," Tommy says. "That way it's not so much of a jolt."

"A kid I went to school with lost a leg trying to jump a train," Sully says.

"It's easy. I did it all the time up north," Tommy says. "You have to go for it at exactly the right moment. You grab hold with one hand and then the other hand. You don't let your feet leave the ground until then."

"You have to watch for the right car," Gord says. "Oil tanks, no good. Fruit cars, too many flies. Coal cars, too dirty. Cattle cars, they stink. Make you want to puke. The cattle are spooked; they're all crapping themselves."

"Yeah," Tommy says. "Cows know they're heading to their death from the minute the farmer rounds them up and puts them on the train."

Sully says, "Maybe we should forget about the train."

"Empty boxcars, that's what we're looking for," Red says. "Gord, go put your ear down on the rail."

Gord slowly moves away from the underbrush and heads toward the track. He gets down on all fours and puts his ear on the metal rail and then his hands down on the track.

Red gives Sully what's left of the sack of food and says, "Here, you hold this." He goes out, looks up and back, and then joins Gord down on his knees.

"I think I feel something," Red says. "There's a train coming but it's far away."

They crane their necks until, at last, they can see the black plume of smoke and the light of the headlamp coming toward them from the east. Red motions to them all to get back behind the bushes.

"Once the engine goes by, we need to start running."

"You gotta board her before she's going too fast for you," Tommy says.

Please God, let there be an open car, Red says to himself. He leads them to the place where the track makes a left turn and heads toward Toronto. He can hear the train now, chugging and rattling, the couplings creaking. The ground begins to rumble. He can smell it too, the smell of steel grinding on steel.

"Ready," Red says as the engine chugs past them. "You stay close to me, Sully. There's an open car."

"Watch the wheels," Gord says. "That's how you know she's speedin' up."

"Now, now, now," Tommy yells. "She's starting to move."

12

BACK IN TORONTO, HEMINGWAY STANDS OUTSIDE THE SELBY Hotel and waits for the Sherbourne streetcar. There is no swamp, no forest, no woods into which he can escape, just this journey through the cold, red-brick canyon of Sherbourne Street in the early morning dark. He stares at the People of the Blank Faces, the People of the Empty Eyes. He is one of them now.

The streetcar turns onto King. The businessmen fold their newspapers under their arms and talk about sports. Dempsey fights Firpo in New York tonight.

When the car stops at Yonge, people stand and, with them, Hemingway moves toward the door. As he walks west on King Street, he can hear the hymns floating up from the basement of the *Toronto Daily Star*, the typesetters singing while they work.

Is this his fate? To be imprisoned in a den of Methodists? Shades of Oak Park, where there were so many damn churches people called the place "Saints' Rest."

Ezra would fall off his chair laughing if he knew.

⁂

When Harry C. Hindmarsh arrives at his desk, the men in the city room scatter.

"Good morning, Mr. Hem-ming-way."

Hindmarsh says Hemingway like he writes it, with two *m*'s, enunciating the syllables hem-ming. Like lem-ming. On the desk between them, Hindmarsh puts down three folders, papers spilling out, each one about a foot thick.

The other reporters develop a new-found fascination with their typewriters or their fountain pens. The pendulum of the regulator clock sways back and forth behind Hindmarsh's head. The time is 7:05 a.m. Hemingway's eye catches two words, coal and Sudbury, on the folder closest to him. Sudbury? Where the hell is that?

"I have assembled everything written in the *Star* and the *Globe* about this British Colonial Coal Mines business in Sudbury, and all the background material we have amassed over the years. I suspect they may be misleading their investors."

Hindmarsh riffles through the papers like a banker counting other people's money until he locates a thick report with a blue cover. "Someone let this file languish. I think it bears further investigation."

According to the faded library date stamp, the *Star* received the report quite a while ago. In Hindmarsh's brain this, not Red Ryan, is what bears further investigation?

"British Colonial Coal's offices are just around the corner in the Temple Building," Hindmarsh says, pointing in the direction of Bay Street. "I want your piece on my desk first thing Monday."

After Hindmarsh leaves Hemingway walks over to the window and looks north and west across the top of the new addition to Simpson's department store. If the British Colonial Coal Mines

Limited is in the Temple Building at Bay and Richmond, they aren't sparing any money on rent. Its round turrets stand out against the sky. The Temple Building is the best business address in Toronto.

He walks down the three flights of iron stairs to the lobby. Outside, the air is fresh, free from the smell of printer's ink. The typesetters are still singing.

> A thousand ages, in thy sight,
> Are like an evening gone,
> Short as the watch that ends the night,
> Before the rising sun.

A group of men rush by him on the sidewalk, running to catch a streetcar. His eyes move from face to face to face, searching under caps for a flash of red hair, a scar, that grey pallor that prisoners have.

The convicts have fallen off the face of the earth.

He pulls the *Star*'s front door open and goes back inside. The fancy criminals in the Temple Building can wait.

The librarian smiles at him when he walks into her basement domain. He had given her a copy of his *Three Stories and Ten Poems*. She said she liked it, particularly the stories, although the one with the girl and the boy on the dock made her blush. She said he showed promise.

"What can I do you for, young Mr. H? I hear you are getting that phoney coal mine scandal dumped on your plate."

Hemingway shrugs. "You know this guy Ryan who broke out of Kingston Pen?" he asks, sitting on the corner of her desk.

"Yes, well done. Good reporting. Very vivid."

"We got anything on him besides what I wrote?"

"Are you joking? He's been at it for years. His family wants to disown him. One of his brothers changed his name. One of his sisters got fired after he robbed the place where she worked."

And Grace and Ed think he's a problem.

"Sit tight. I'll go get the whole kit and caboodle. They say he used to play baseball in Willowvale Park."

The librarian comes back and puts a large file down in front of him.

Hemingway starts reading, making a note of all the places that the Ryan family lived, all the neighbourhoods where he might have friends: Esther, now Augusta, Street, Markham Street. He scribbles it all down as fast as he can. There was a girlfriend over a bank at Bathurst and Bloor, maybe even a child. Red's dad was a tinsmith, worked at Bathurst and Olive.

"He's been in the paper since 1912. I think they lived on Wyndham Street then, near my cousin Agnes. Cried like a baby when he got sent to Kingston Pen the first time. His Ma and Pa are dead now, I think. Just the brothers and the sisters left, three of them are pretty young. It's all in there. Put it back on my desk when you're done."

Jesus, Hemingway says to himself, looking at the clippings. Red Ryan shot a goddamn horse.

"Can you keep this out for me? I'm supposed to be over at the Temple Building."

"So you did end up with that coal mining thing?"

"Yeah."

"Is everybody crooked?" she says.

"Allegedly."

"Everybody except you and me."

He watches her move the file of clippings over to one side of her desk. So Red Ryan has deep Toronto roots. He'll be back in the city as fast as he can do it.

⁂

When Hemingway reaches Bay and Richmond, he leans his head back and looks up into the fall sky. The Temple Building claims the entire block for its own. Eleven stories high, a solid structure trying to convince you the business inside is just as solid.

He waits for a couple of cars to pass and then he heads across the street. The building's doors are copper, carved like a Florentine cathedral, the lobby polished marble.

"Floor, please," the elevator operator says as Hemingway steps inside.

"Eleven."

The elevator moves through the dark brick shaft. There is a flash of light every time another floor goes by. He counts them out in his head like someone laying out a straight: four, five, six, seven. Stencilled yellow numbers, once bright, now shadowy and grey.

At the end of the hall on the eleventh floor there is a set of double doors that bear the words "National Finance, Suite 1103" in gold letters. National Finance is the company issuing British Colonial coal-mining stock.

His pencil and notebook shoved deep into his suit coat pocket. Watch, listen, wait. He learned that from the Native kids in Michigan.

Inside suite 1103 there is a young woman sitting at a small desk. "Ernest Hemingway, *Toronto Daily Star*."

"One moment," the receptionist says and disappears through a frosted glass door.

Hemingway sits down in a black leather chair and picks up the morning edition of the *Star*. His last prison escape story, how somebody tricked the guards. Told them the convicts were found two miles away and when the guards rushed there, Red and Company made their escape from the woods.

HCH may have lost interest, but Hemingway hasn't. Red's crafty but he's the real thing. No pretty secretaries, oak-panelled offices, fancy addresses, or sham stock offerings for Red Ryan. There's no behind-the-scenes, under-the-table, double-dealing shim-sham. Red and his pals get their hands dirty. They rob you the old-fashioned way, face to face.

The longer they are free, the longer their freedom is dangled in front of him like a worm on a hook, the more something in him cheers for them. Because if they can go over a wall and get free against all odds, maybe so can he.

⁜

After the interview he leaves the Temple Building and crosses Queen Street to city hall to make some notes. The marble foyer is almost empty. Two sheriff deputies grip the arms of a man whose eyes are hollow and whose legs are shackled. The chains clack against the floor as they push him, shuffling like a slave, toward the elevator that goes down to the cells. That's a humiliation anybody would do anything to avoid.

When Hemingway arrives back at the paper, there is a group of young reporters standing around the doorway of the radio room. The *Star* is broadcasting the Dempsey-Firpo fight tonight. Luis Ángel Firpo, the Argentinian *toro de las pampas*, and Jack Dempsey, the heavyweight champion of the world, who for three years has kept his title. Not hard to do since all he'd fight were exhibition bouts. Refused to fight any challengers.

Hemingway used to box in Paris. He used to take Hadley to the fights in Paris too. There was a Negro he liked, a Canadian named Larry Gains.

He pushes his way to the front and sticks his head in. It's not very big, the radio room, but somebody has sure cleaned away all its experience for the occasion. It smells of furniture polish, like his mother's parlour in Oak Park. He can hear the wires crackling and hissing all the way from New York, the rumble of the crowd at the Polo Grounds growing louder and louder.

Jimmy Cowan's there. So is Greg Clark. The more senior staff members sit on chairs and desks and tables staring at the receiver. Not one of them is Harry C. Hindmarsh. Has he gone home and left the inmates in charge of the institution for once?

Hemingway listens as the announcer describes the scene: the red, white, and blue bunting, the brass marching band, the rows of videographers perched on crow's nests high above the crowd.

Greg and Jimmy are betting on Dempsey but Hemingway always goes for the underdog. "A buck on Firpo," he says. Someone has tacked up a picture of Dempsey, fists up in a fighting pose, and one of Firpo sitting with his manager and his trainer in an arena. The trainer has his hand on Firpo's shoulder.

Hemingway tries to imagine those two finely tuned bodies in New York. Not frozen still as they have been captured by the camera, but alive and breathing, bobbing and weaving, keeping themselves moving in their dressing rooms, waiting to enter the ring.

Left to the chin, a right cross to the jaw, that's Dempsey's favourite combination and one of his too. He's gone more than a few rounds in his time. "You have to begin a fight with a plan," he says to no one in particular.

They pay no attention because Dempsey has entered the arena in New York. He has climbed through the ropes and the crowd is roaring. They have all come to their feet, the announcer says. Men are standing on chairs leaning over the balconies to get a better look at Jack Dempsey in his white trunks. The first cheers have not died down when the chorus of voices rises again and the announcer describes Firpo as he comes into the hall. Somebody in the radio room says eighty-six thousand people can sure make a lot of noise.

Hemingway bobs and weaves and throws a few punches in the doorway. Jimmy Cowan takes a step back into the hall to avoid being hit.

You have to make it your fight, his father always said. Never forget that. If you don't, the other guy will make it his. You have to seize control.

Dempsey doesn't waste any time. Firpo is barely out of his corner, the announcer says, when Dempsey comes two-thirds of the way across the canvas to meet him.

Hemingway watches the people in the room listening to the bodiless voice from New York. The announcer is making them experience the fight, the tight muscles and the sweat and the energy of the crowd, the sensation of being there, blow by blow. It's what he wants to do with his stories. Make you feel the emotions when you read it, not what you are told to feel. Make you believe you are there.

Dempsey is ducking to avoid Firpo's blows. Then he hits Firpo with a left upper cut and Firpo goes down on his knees. He gets up. He goes down again. Dempsey is standing right over him.

"What's the matter, Gallagher," somebody in the radio room yells at the referee. "Did somebody forget to teach you the rules?"

As if he's heard the voice from Toronto, the referee warns Dempsey to get back. Firpo starts to rise. Suddenly, he rushes Dempsey and knocks him out of the ring. The crowd at the Polo Grounds goes crazy and the crowd in the radio room at the *Star* goes crazy too.

Then Dempsey is back in the ring, and the announcer says that the reporters in the front row may have pushed him back up onto the canvas.

The people in the radio room all look at one another. There's no ruling about what just happened and round one goes into round two.

Now Firpo is taking a beating. Two left hooks, two right uppercuts, and a left to the body when Firpo tries to go into a clinch. Dempsey shakes him off and drives in a series of blows. Firpo is down. At the count of five, he is back up. But Dempsey gets in close. A left to Firpo's midsection, then a right to the jaw. Firpo goes down. Dempsey moves back to his corner. Firpo isn't moving when the count reaches ten.

The announcer says this may go down as one of the greatest bouts in boxing history. Three minutes and fifty-seven seconds and it's all over.

Money is changing hands again in the radio room. "Son of a bitch," Greg Clark says, "that's not right." Hemingway can hear the librarian's voice — "Is everyone crooked?"

The reporters and secretaries and typesetters drift out into the hall, still talking about the fight. Hemingway moves with them. He waves goodnight to Greg and Jimmy.

It's dark out now and the lights from King and Yonge shine in the windows of the *Star* building with a hazy glow. When he gets back upstairs, a figure steps out from the darkness and turns on the lights. "How was the boxing match, Mr. Hem-mingway?" Harry Hindmarsh is standing there, his shadow stretches halfway across the floor.

"I need your notes from today first thing in the morning, and I have another file for you."

Hemingway senses that he is supposed to respond with enthusiasm to this information but he keeps silent. His overloaded satchel is already in danger of falling apart.

Hindmarsh walks toward the stairs and then stops and turns around.

"Who won?"

"Dempsey"

"I knew that he would."

⁂

Hemingway walks down the stairs to the lobby to get some air. How angry will they be in Argentina when they hear about Firpo's defeat?

Greg and some of the other reporters stand and smoke on the stoop, settling up their bets.

"Hey, Hem," Greg says. "While you were out investigating coal mines, word came in that the guy from Kingston Pen who got captured may be singing like a birdy."

He feels his breast pocket for the notes he took down in the library. No honour among boxers or thieves.

The snooty higher-up from Ottawa he met in the warden's office is conducting an investigation, according to Greg. It's been five days now since they went over the wall.

"I'll bet McMullen's just trying to lighten his punishment for trying to escape," Greg says.

"Maybe their buddy's trying to throw the cops off the trail."

"Mark my words, they're lying low. Waiting," Greg says.

"For what?"

"The word. Boy are you naive."

Greg is seven years older than he is. Greg was working for the paper when he was writing stuff for his highschool newspaper. And sometimes Greg likes to rub that in. Treat him like he's a kid.

"I lost my naïveté working on the crime beat at the *Kansas City Star* and you know it."

"Then you know somebody will get the word to them, the arrangements will be made, then they'll move. Somebody will help them just like those reporters in the front row helped Dempsey tonight. And by the way, Hem, you owe me a buck."

⁂

Hemingway walks along King jingling what's left of the change in his pocket. He salutes the doorman at the King Eddy as he passes by. He is holding the door of a taxi as an elderly gentleman in an ill-fitting tuxedo gets in.

"Firpo lost," Hemingway says as the doorman folds his tip and puts it in his pocket. "Not a fair fight."

"The best laid schemes o' mice and men," the doorman says.

"You don't have to tell me that."

Will he go down for the count at the *Toronto Daily Star*? The tales of the fallen are whispered in corners and washrooms all around the paper. But even if it kills him, he will not be one of them. Maybe, someday, if it's a fair fight, it will be Harry C. Hindmarsh who will go down. Maybe Hemingway'll be the victor. However, he, unlike Hindmarsh, is not married to the daughter of the owner of the *Toronto Daily Star*. Life isn't always a fair fight.

It sure wasn't tonight in New York. Firpo was robbed. It's a violation of the Marquess of Queensberry rules for anyone to push a fighter back into the ring.

He looks back at the King Eddy as the doorman holds the arm of another well-dressed guest as he stumbles up the broad stone steps.

"If either man fall through weakness or otherwise, he must get up unassisted," Hemingway says out loud. "That's the rule. That's what it says."

⁂

Back at the Selby, he opens their hotel room door by inches trying not to wake up Hadley. His satchel has pulled the shoulder of his jacket off to one side. He puts it on the desk and sighs but it falls over, and papers from his new assignment slide out across the scratched and stained mahogany and fall onto the floor.

His hand goes to his eyes and then his forehead, as if he is trying to wash something away. The old desk chair creaks when he sits down. A pencil-thin column of light from the street lamp falls across Hadley's face.

When he got back from Kingston, she wanted to write to Grace and Ed about the baby. But he doesn't want them messing in, helping out. Ezra can help them, Gertrude and Alice can help them, his old friends from his first time in Toronto can help them, but not his parents. Just the thought of his parents and he is back on his knees in the front parlour feeling guilty about some childhood peccadillo while his mother banged out "Onward Christian Soldiers" on the piano.

Hadley stirs and then opens her eyes and stares at the papers all over the floor. She slides the covers down past her belly and swings her feet onto the faded rug. Her hair has fallen across her face. "Tiny," she says, coming over and touching his shoulder. "You're very late."

His body jumps at her touch. "I listened to the fight. Firpo lost, then Hindmarsh nabbed me. That guy never leaves the building." The chair complains as he sits up and swivels around to face her. "I walked home."

His arms encircle the place that once was her waist. His hands slide down her hips and move across her thighs. He rests his head on her belly and reaches up to touch her breast.

"Tiny," she says, taking a step away from him. "I need to ask the doctor."

"But I miss you," he says, standing up to face her and taking her hand, "I love you."

13

THEY ARE ON A SIDING, SAFE, AT LEAST FOR THE NIGHT. Tommy is propped up in a corner of the car snoring away. Gord has made himself a bed out of a bale of hay. Only Sully is awake. "I've decided to do a little exploring on my own," Red says. "A reconnoitering mission, like I used to do in England during the war."

He slides the door of the freight car open and jumps down onto the ground. The night is cold. Mist comes off a pond at the bottom of a small hill.

He skulks down and moves from scrub brush to scrub brush until he reaches a round patch of gravel that he figures is the dead end of the road. There is a house about a half a mile away. He can see a light on over the barn door but otherwise the place is in darkness. He can make out a pickup truck in the yard and a clothesline weighed down with overalls. He sneaks over to the line, pulls the overalls off, and rolls them into a tight, round parcel that he tucks underneath his arm.

A dog barks and an upstairs light comes on. Goddamn dogs. He retreats behind a large maple. He hears a woman's voice but he can't make out what she's saying. When he gets up the courage to look again, the light has gone out. He starts back down the road again. The distance between the houses is getting shorter.

There are no streetlights, but even in the dark he can tell that somebody cares a great deal about the next house. The shrubs and bushes are wrapped in burlap for winter. The flower beds are covered with hay. The front porch smells of a new coat of paint.

He climbs the four wooden steps and tries the handle on the front door. The latch clicks and he's inside. Down the front hall, he can see a kitchen and over to the right, a parlour.

In the parlour a picture on the piano stops him dead. The girl in the picture is almost as beautiful as the preacher's daughter they used to see every Sunday at the penitentiary. She played the organ and led the hymns for her father. The first Sunday of every month, whether you were protestant or not, you had to go and listen about God's forgiveness and the evil of your ways.

Once a con saw the preacher's daughter, he didn't mind. Her pastel skirts echoed her shape as she sat on the organ bench. On a platform, raised up in case they hadn't realized, she was far above them all. Every Sunday night she was the subject of much speculation. What would she look like without her pale blue dress, that long dark hair spread out on a pillow?

The thought that this beautiful girl in the photograph might be sleeping in a room right above his head excites him. What if he went upstairs? Her room would smell clean and sweet, like violets.

He drops his bundle of clothes and his hand slips down to the baggy crotch of his prison greys. She is so close. Safe and snug in her bed, believing as her life is today so it will be tomorrow, and the next day, and the day after that. He could change it all in an instant. Right now, he is a god or a puppet master pulling strings.

A dog barks, again. He cannot stay here; he has to go back. The clock on the mantlepiece says one o'clock. They need to find a car; they need to get off the train. He needs to get to Toronto.

The front door creaks as he passes into the night, heading for the train with the stolen clothing under his arm. She will never know, that beautiful girl in the photograph, he has spared her. He has chosen to let her live her uneventful little life.

14

RED AND SULLY RUN FROM TREE TO TREE UNTIL THEY REACH the churchyard. It's a small square church in another small Ontario town. They've left the freight train behind. Tommy and Gord are waiting for them in the bush.

They can hear the hymns from inside, "Blessed be the ties that bind," the women's and the men's voices. That was one of Red's favourite things about services at the prison, the soft, high voices of the women. That, and watching the backside of the reverend's daughter.

There are about twenty cars, road dust–covered, parked in the fall sun outside the church's double oak doors. Red's eyes wander among the Model Ts looking for the right car, one with some power. His eye catches something shiny and red with a hood ornament gleaming in the sun. This is the kind of car that a man like him should drive. A brand new 1923 Buick touring car. He saw an advertisement for it in a magazine in the prison library. It's not dust-covered and it's parked right where it should be, out of the sun, next to a flower bed, surrounded by russet and yellow chrysanthemums.

Red ducks down and runs between the Model Ts until he is standing next to the shiny red thing. He leans in over the polished wooden steering wheel. The keys are there. He slides his hand around the pale blond circle of wood, then lets it fall down to caress the black leather driver's seat. His fingers find the keys. He takes them out of the ignition and then he puts them back in.

The organ stops inside, the sermon begins. The minister's voice is low and slow, like one of the old lifers at the Pen speechifying about their adventures when they were young.

"Red!" Sully's head peeks up from behind a rumble seat. "That's not a good car. It's red. We'll be a sitting target in something like that."

"I'm changing the plates." Red holds up the knife from the food package. He kneels in the dirt behind the Buick, pushes the tip into the centre of the screw's head and gives it a firm turn to the left.

Sully is shaking his head and pointing at a Ford. "They'll be watching for us. We don't want to stand out."

But Red wants to stand out. Stand out against his brothers, his father, the other guys in the Pen, the chumps too afraid to break out with them. The Model Ts are black and boring.

He moves the knife away from the plate and, with his hand, makes a few more turns of the screw in the plate's upper right corner.

"Probably made these plates in the prison," he says.

Sully doesn't laugh. "If we take a Model T, there's so many it'll take them a while to figure out one of them is missing."

Red reaches out to give the shiny red metal one last caress. It's hot from the autumn sun. His fingers slide down until his whole palm is flat against the car, feeling the warmth, disappointed that they will not share this great adventure together.

"What about this one?" Sully stands beside the dustiest car in the lot, parked closest to the road. "The keys are inside," he says. "Come on, get in. Gord and Tommy are waiting for us."

The low and slow voice inside the church has stopped. The organ starts to play a hymn, the go-out-in-the-world-and-do-good-works-for-Jesus hymn. Or, if you are a convict in a penitentiary, the get-back-in-your-cell-and-think-about-your-sins hymn.

Sully holds the door of the Model T open. "You drive. I'll crank her up."

Red takes one last look at the shiny red car. "Too bad we can't take her." He's walked away from more than one broad with less sorrow in his heart.

⁂

The breeze is fresh and cool as Red drives along. Gord and Tommy sit in the back, Sully beside him. Wearing the overalls he stole in the village, they look like a crew of farmhands off to help with a harvest.

They pass through another town and the road turns toward the lake. Halfway up a hill, the Model T coughs.

Red noticed a feed store with a gas pump a few miles back. He looks to the left and the right and then turns the car around and heads back. "Going to gas her up."

He parks across the street. There is a dusty blue truck sitting next to the pump. A tall man in a dark blue suit tucks his tie into his shirt front, walks over, flips the lever, takes the nozzle down off the gas pump, and shoves it in. Truck and store both carry a gold-and-black banner: "Phillip's Farm 'n' Feed." There is a sign in the window that says, "Sorry We're Closed." In the truck is a woman wearing a dark blue hat. They like to dress alike, these two. But the man's face is drawn and tight. He's angry. Red can hear her voice, high and loud, but he can't make out what she's saying. The man pulls out a pocket watch, holds it up to her, and then turns back to the pump. Ah, she's saying they're late. Good.

People who are in a rush make mistakes. They forget to do things, like lock up the pumps.

The man finishes filling the tank and shakes the nozzle dry into the warm September air. The sun is getting high in the sky. Red hears the woman's voice again. The man takes out a handkerchief, wipes off his hands, and then opens the truck's door. As he and the missus pull out into the street, Red puts the car in gear.

The Model T creeps onto the lot until she's parked beside the pump. "I'll stand guard," Sully says. He stations himself at the sidewalk, looking right and left, up and down the street.

Red puts his hand on the pump and pulls on the nozzle, out it comes. Good, not locked. Gas begins to gurgle into the tank. He can tell by the sound of liquid on metal that they were pretty close to empty.

"Red!" Sully has left his post. He's waving his arms and moving faster than Red has seen him move in a long while. "The feed store guy. He's still three blocks away but he's coming back."

Damn. Mr. Farm 'n' Feed remembered he didn't lock up. The tank isn't full. The gas still sounds like a rock falling into a well.

Come on, come on. He opens the nozzle wide as it will go. Fill 'er up. Fill 'er up. He doesn't want to stop again. They should have checked for a car with a full tank back in the churchyard. Goddamn Methodists!

He hears the truck backfire. Mr. Farm 'n' Feed must have stepped on the gas. Aoogha, aoogha! They can see Red helping himself to their gas.

He pulls out the nozzle, dropping it on the dusty ground.

Aoogha, aoogha!

"Get in, Sully!" Red screams as he jumps into the car and starts to drive out of the lot. "Keep looking behind us, Sul. If they follow us, we may have a great big problem on our hands."

The road out of town is level and dry. They can see the truck never leaves the feed store's yard.

"Next stop, Toronto," Sully says.

"I bet his old lady is going to be mad." Red laughs.

The most the damn car can do is thirty miles an hour and sometimes the road is so bad they barely make it above walking speed. Still better than standing in a swamp up to your ass in leeches or getting shot for borrowing a little gas.

⁂

When they get to Toronto, Red ticks the streets off as they drive along Danforth Avenue: Woodbine, Coxwell, Pape, Broadview. The wide expanse of the new bridge stretches out before them. The lights of the city sparkle like the stars you wish on.

On the other side of the Don River Valley, Red pulls over and throws the keys to Gord. "Dump her in the Don somewhere where she won't be found."

"Where are you going to be?" Gord asks.

"I told you, we'll see you at Carlton Street." Red gives the Model T's rear fender a kick. "You've got the address. Just make sure this hunk of tin sinks."

The lawns and the fall flower gardens on Bloor Street are better kept than Red remembers, almost as well kept as the convict-tended garden at Warden Ponsford's house across the road from the Pen.

"Let's head down Sherbourne," Red says, running across the pavement.

15

HEMINGWAY LOOKS UP TO SEE THE LIBRARIAN TAPPING THE eraser end of a No. 2 pencil on the palm of her hand. "It's time to close up," she says. "I only let you stay this late because I was working on something for Mr. Atkinson. I'm off home and I want you to tidy up."

Hemingway studies the files he has spread out on the library table, half hidden underneath the day's papers. He is only halfway through.

"What are you hoping to find, young Mr. Hemingway?"

Hadley asked him the same question the other night when he was sitting on the floor of their hotel room with the *Toronto Daily Star*, the *Globe*, and the *Telegram* spread around him.

"Greg says sometimes crooks communicate by using the personals," he'd told her. "I'm looking for something suspicious."

"Don't you think they'd make it look ordinary?" Hadley said. "I think it would be something like a sale or a party on this date. I bet they have code words."

For someone who has lived a very sheltered life before she met him, Hadley has a lot of worldly ideas. He hates that. Greg is a newspaperman and fought in the war. Greg's been around. So has he. He is the worldly one, not her.

"What is it with you and these convicts anyway?" Hadley said, picking up Héloïse and Abelard. "Are you mad because Hindmarsh wouldn't keep you on the story and you want to prove him wrong?"

He has had to admit to himself that sending that funny piece in to Hindmarsh from Kingston probably wasn't such a good idea for his second day on the job. Probably it had something to do with getting pulled off the story. His attempts at satire have gotten him in trouble before. Sometimes he's not as clever as he thinks he is, and although she doesn't know anything about the tongue-in-cheek, extremely amusing story he submitted, goddamn it, Hadley knows that to be true. She's told him so. Sometimes he thinks she knows him better than he knows himself. It's irritating.

"Besides," Hadley said, "why would they send messages to anybody in Toronto?"

"Maybe he has a girl. Maybe he's lonely. He has a brother here."

"I don't want you skulking around after convicts. You could get killed."

"Leave me to it."

"Is there a reward?"

"Yes, there's a reward. You know that. You read the paper."

"Is that why? To get money for Paris?"

"That's not why."

"Promise me that you won't go chasing after these guys. They're bad apples. I don't like it."

He'd turned and walked into the bathroom. "Don't worry, Hash," he called out to her, "they're probably in Hawaii living the high life by now." He couldn't look her in the eye. He didn't believe it for a minute.

⁂

He gathers up his notes and waits while the librarian does a check around the cavernous room. Every day he's trying to think like a guy on the run. Hell, in some ways, he is a guy on the run. He's going to be late getting back to the hotel again and this time it's not even Hindmarsh's fault. Well, not directly. He forgot about the time until he heard the pencil tapping. He forgot to call the hotel. To be honest he hates leaving messages with the desk clerk. But in his defence, not that Hadley will like it, there was lots about Red and Gord Simpson and Arthur Sullivan in the files. Not much on that Bryans kid but he isn't from Toronto.

When he gets near the Selby, he can see Hadley standing in front of the hotel, the desk clerk right at her elbow. That damn clerk acts like he's more worried about her having the baby than he is. It's almost one a.m. Sherbourne Street is very quiet. The streetcars stopped running long ago.

Far above Hadley's head, the pineapple drawn in stained glass on the transom is backlit, bright yellow glass, green leaves on the top, outlined in grey lead: the universal sign of welcome. But Hadley is not in a welcoming mood. Hemingway can tell by the set of her body she is angry.

At the corner just south of the hotel, he sees two women. They have bobbed hair and bags slung over their shoulders. A long, low car purrs past the Selby and stops. One of the women walks over and leans in on the passenger side.

The clerk tries to block Hadley's view of what is happening, moving in front of her and straightening to his full height. Then, his hand is on her elbow, trying to guide her back into the hotel.

The two women disappear into the car. The lights from the Selby's lobby shine through the front door and fall across the clerk's face.

"Please, come inside," Hemingway hears him say.

Hadley puts her foot on the first step and then turns to look back down the street. "There he is," she cries out. "Ernest!"

Hadley's voice is like a slap on his face. She has climbed to the top step. She pulls his old grey sweater tighter around her, arms resting on her belly, waiting. "Come inside."

In the lobby he can see her cheeks are streaked with tears.

"Where were you?" Anger has replaced concern many hours ago.

The hotel clerk stands beside her like an elderly chaperone. "Mrs. Hemingway has been a little upset."

Her old dress wrinkled, her hair pushed back from her face, she walks toward the stairs up to their room.

"Where were you?" she says again, looking back. "It's past one o'clock."

"At work."

"But why are you so late?"

"I had to finish."

"Finish what? Why didn't you call the hotel?"

He walks ahead of her across the lobby. "Let's go upstairs. I'm not talking about this in front of a stranger."

"No!" Her voice is high and cracking. "Stop! I want to know where you were."

"Mrs. Hemingway was very worried that something had happened to you," the clerk says, back at his station behind the polished oak desk.

Hemingway straightens to his full height and walks toward the desk, his hands forming into fists. "You, sir, have no right to comment on my ... on our ... personal business."

"I've seen more of this gentleman than I have of you in the last two weeks," Hadley cries.

Hemingway sizes the clerk up like he does any opponent. The guy has probably never raised his fists in his life. He could take that skinny bastard in two minutes. He could send the clerk flying through the brocade window curtain with one punch, throw him out onto Sherbourne Street in a heap.

"Ernest," Hadley cries as if she's read his mind, tears streaming down her face. "You touch him, and I'll never speak to you again." The dark look in her narrowed eyes makes him stop.

She catches up to him but all the way up the stairs, Hadley says nothing. She is so big with child, she moves very slowly now.

When they reach their room, she starts to undress for bed. She lets her nightgown float over her head and begins to twist her way out of her clothes. She doesn't like to undress in front of him anymore. He can tell she is trying to hold back the tears. Her shoulders shudder. He begins to unbutton his shirt.

"Ernest," she says again when her undressing is complete. "Where were you?" Her round belly, her heavy breasts, her nipples swollen and dark show under the thin white cotton of her nightgown. She begins to cry again.

An exhaustion so profound settles over him that he thinks for a moment he will lose consciousness and fall onto the shopworn rug.

"I'm sorry, Hash."

Hadley wipes her tears and slips in front of him, putting her arms through his.

But he disentangles himself from her and picks up the *Toronto Daily Star* that is lying on the desk and throws it on the floor. One day, on her own, she moved the desk next to the window so he could write, so he would have better light. So far, he has written nothing.

"Don't be mad at me, Hash," he says. "I was down in the library."

"This late? That's crazy. For work?"

"I was reading the files they have on Red Ryan."

"Oh, Tiny," she says. "Why are you doing this?"

"Greg says I'm doing it because I'm afraid to write."

"Is that true?"

"I'm afraid to start because I know as long as I'm working here, I will never finish anything and then I will lose it."

"Maybe if you didn't spend so much time on those men, you could write ... something."

Hadley wraps her arms around him. He can feel her warmth through the thin cotton nightgown. Through the window he sees two men in overalls on the other side of the street, one of them dancing, zigging and zagging, between the light and shadow.

16

RED STANDS ON THE PORCH OF THE HOUSE ON CARLTON Street and waits. It won't take Gord and Tommy long to ditch the car. They'll all be happy here. Clean clothes, real food, a soft bed, women. They can close their eyes without seeing the drool-covered teeth of a police dog or the barrel of a guard's gun.

Once they arrive the front door opens and his old friend Lillie sticks her head out. Her hair is tied back in a bun but she reaches up and lets it loose. A jumble of blond curls comes falling down. "Come in. Come in. Your brother told me you might be paying a visit."

Inside, Lillie's girls hover at the top of the stairs.

"Don't be shy, girls," Lillie says. "Come down and meet our visitors." Tommy's eyes grow wider and wider as one, two, three, four girls come down the oak staircase. "Let's go into the parlour, Red," Lillie says. "I just had it painted, a kind of aquamarine blue. It reminds me of the manor houses you see in picture books."

Red likes the walls. They are soft and cool. The girls in their dresses stand out against them, like candy wrappers floating on a summer lake.

One of the girls walks past Red. She is short, maybe five feet tall. Her hair is brilliant red. Her eyes are green. A waist so tiny he could encircle it with his hands. "Hello, I'm Babe," she says.

It's almost two in the morning but no one is tired. Lillie puts out a supper for them. Slices of ham and a pan of scalloped potatoes. Food that looks like food. Not cooked to mush in the prison kitchen.

While Red fills his plate, Babe talks to Sully. But she keeps looking over in his direction. As she talks she keeps pushing a piece of unruly red hair out of her eyes.

Lillie claps her hands and says, "May I have your attention." Her voice is not smooth and soft like butter anymore.

"The first thing I want to say is any friend of Red and his brother is a friend of mine. We go way back. They've always been fair with me. I've always been fair with them."

"Always gave them their money's worth, eh Lillie?" Tommy smirks.

"Shut up, Tommy," Sully says. "Get your mind out of the gutter for once."

A girl who had been talking to Tommy pulls her pink sweater around her, walks over to the window, opens it, and sits down on the sill.

"Here's the problem," Lillie says. "I need to know what the plan is. My girls have some regular customers. You can't stay here for long. You'll need to move. Might be smart to spread out."

"Yeah!" Tommy hollers grinding his hips, "Let's spread ourselves around."

The girl on the windowsill rolls her eyes and lights a cigarette.

⁂

Babe's touch is like an electric charge. She knows what she is doing, this red-headed girl. Red wants to ask her how long she's been in her line of work, but he doesn't think he should.

"Lillie said you rob banks," Babe says, pulling the sheet up to her chin. Underneath the blankets her hand wanders across his chest. "How'd you get started doing that?"

"When I was twelve, I stole a bicycle. It was shiny red. It belonged to a doctor who lived up the street. I kept my eye on it for weeks and when I saw my chance, I grabbed it. It was a beauty. The cops took it away when they caught me."

"Sometimes," he says, tugging the sheet away from her chin, "I think I've been looking for that bicycle all my life."

There's a siren off in the distance. It's getting closer. But when Red gets up and goes to the window, Carlton Street is quiet. There is only a lowly streetcar, chugging and swaying along on its way to work, like a boat through choppy waters.

Babe gives the rumpled sheets a pat. "You don't have to worry about the cops. Lillie takes care of all that."

But he's not so sure. The siren is coming down Carlton Street now. Ignoring a stable of business girls is one thing, hiding escaped cons is something else. Lillie may not have enough money to make the cops turn a blind eye. From what he read in the *Whig*, all four of them have a fifty-dollar price tag on their heads.

While he watches, Babe lets her hand drift down the centre of her body, tracing circles with her long fingers as she goes. "Red, honey," she says, "come back to bed."

Every part of him wants to go back and join her but he has to pay attention or it could all be for nothing: the escape, the swamp, Ed's injured hand, Ed's capture.

He opens the curtains and presses his forehead against the glass. His breath makes a cloud that comes and goes on the windowpane. The sound of the siren is louder still.

Babe gets out of bed and stands beside him. "I don't mean to tell you your business or nothing, but take it from me, if the cops come to call, they won't be wailing the siren. They like surprise. It looks better in the papers." She takes his hand. "Look, they're going by."

When Red leans out, the police car is crossing Yonge Street heading west. The sound of the siren is gone, chasing someone else in the night. He jumps when the streetcar clangs its bell.

"You're tired. When I'm tired, I always get spooked."

"It's been a long week." Red lies down and he closes his eyes.

"I've been reading about you in the papers, the *Globe*, the *Telly*, but mostly the *Star*." Babe slides down beside him. "Don't be afraid." Her hand moves along his thigh. He can feel the tension starting to leave his body, floating off like the smell of gunpowder after you've pulled the trigger.

⁜

Four days later Red sits at Lillie's dining room table making a plan. Babe has fallen asleep on the sofa, a magazine lying open across her chest. It's going to be hard to leave her. But it's too dangerous staying in one place unless he wants to live indoors all the time like someone's pampered kitten. Might as well be in prison. It's time to go their separate ways, to get out of here. Babe says he can write to her at her mother's house and tell her where to write back.

Tommy comes down the stairs, walks over to Babe, and reaches for her magazine. She awakes with a start and grabs his wrist. "Just what are you doing, my lad?" Her fingers tighten and Tommy pulls his hand away.

"For God's sakes, Tommy," Red says. "I thought you were spending all your time with Vicky."

Babe gets up off the couch, walks over to Red, and gives him a kiss on the cheek. While her face is next to his, she whispers, "Victoria can't stand him."

When Sully and Gord come in from having a smoke in the back lane, Red holds up a piece of paper. There is a Bank of Nova Scotia at the corner of St. Clair and Oakwood that he knows as well as he is starting to know the hills and valleys of Babe's behind. Two years ago he worked there with his father, installing the tin lining of the vault.

He's sketched the layout from memory: the location of the manager's office, the placement of his desk, the vault, the distance from here to there, the telephones, the alley out behind.

"We'll do it just before a payday," he tells Gord and Tommy. "The bank'll be loaded with money. Just what we need, a small bank branch with a full safe. Then we can get out of town."

"I want to stay here," Tommy says. "What about Vicky?"

"She's a whore, Tommy," Gord says. "She doesn't care about you."

"The faster we get out of here, the better," Sully says. "Three of us from Toronto. Doesn't take a genius at police headquarters to figure we might come back."

The next morning, before dawn, Red and Sully run in darkness, like bootleggers, searching for a car lot. Not too far, not too close, not too small, not too big, but big enough that it'll take somebody a while to figure out a licence plate is missing.

When they find one, Red throws some pebbles up against the window of the office to see if there's a guard dog inside. Nothing. Moving across the lot, Sully right behind him, Red runs his hands across bumpers looking for the car that nobody wants, the one that has been here for a while. When his fingertip drops into a large dent, he's found the car. The bumper is covered with rust. Sully stands guard, moving his gaze back and forth along Davenport Road.

The licence plate is caked with mud. One tap and most of it falls off. Red spits on his fingers and rubs the numbers on the plate clean. 34-467. He jams the screwdriver in and twists until the screw surrenders. One, then the other, until the plate falls down onto the dusty lot. Now they just have to find the car.

⁂

The Overland was sitting outside of Toronto Western Hospital when they enlisted it in their cause. Not too hard to hot-wire. *A design mistake*, Red thinks. He steers it up Oakwood to St. Clair, Sully beside him, Tommy and Gord in the back seat. They've picked the right car for the getaway. He'll be sad to ditch it when the job is done.

⁂

The bank looks exactly as Red remembered it. They go past, turn right, and then turn right again onto the house-lined street that runs behind the bank. Gord will do a preliminary walk-through, ask to change a twenty, make sure Red's memory of the layout is correct. They all have revolvers; they're all armed and dangerous, courtesy of some bootlegger friend of Lillie's.

Trying to rob a bank on your own is foolish, an old con told Red once. You can't control a bank full of people by yourself. You need someone on the manager, someone on the tellers, someone guarding the door, someone driving the car. You need a sturdy canvas bag for the loot.

While he waits for Gord to come back, Red leans against the hood of the Overland and smokes his last cigarette. He can feel the engine hum and vibrate all through his body.

Gord appears from around the corner. "Let's go!"

Sully holds out his hand, it's shaking.

The clock on the drugstore across the street marks the time. It's exactly 1:15 p.m. Red pushes open the door of the little bank branch on the outskirts of the city.

Gord strides into the manager's office and shows him who's in charge.

Sully takes up his position in front of the main counter, revolver in hand, sweeping it back and forth across the room, shouting "Don't move." There are people in the bank, two women with a baby. When one of them cries out, Sully shouts "Keep quiet or I'll blow your brains out."

Red runs at the counter and vaults over. "Hands up!" One of the girls tries to hide underneath but he threatens her with his gun and tells her to stand with the others. He gets the keys to the teller's cage from the man guarding it. While he empties the drawers of paper money, loose change, and rolls of coins, he hears cries from the manager's office. Gord is really roughing the guy up.

"Open the goddamn vault," he can hear Gord screaming.

Red motions to the two girls and the man from the teller's cage to move toward the office. Another man comes into the bank and Sully threatens him too. The women are crying and one of them lets out a gasp when she sees the manager's bloody face. She wants to call a doctor. "This is a bank robbery, lady," Red says and rips the telephone wire out of the wall.

Gord tries to pull the manager toward the safe but the manager isn't co-operating. He goes limp like a rag doll and falls to the floor. "Get up, you coward," Gord screams, kicking him in the leg but the man doesn't move.

Red can hear the old con's voice. "Rob a bank by yourself and the whole thing can descend into chaos." Well, he's not by himself but that sure as hell is the way this is going. Chaos with a capital *C*.

There's a noise behind him and Red turns. A man in carpenter's overalls comes through the back door. Jesus! Red yells "Get in the office," but the guy turns and runs back out.

"That's it," Red says. "Pack the money into the leather sack. Time to go."

Around the corner they jump back in the car and peel away. Some kids from the high school across the street start screaming. The manager, brandishing a .38, fires a shot in the air and chases them down Oakwood Avenue. They drive east on Biggar and down Alberta, across Davenport, onto Ossington. The Overland is doing its job. Three grand and change. Not bad for twenty minutes' work.

"Red," Sully screams from the back seat. Red looks in the rear-view mirror but he sees nothing. "Not behind us," Sully yells, "ahead of us." There is a trio of police cars heading their way.

"Stop screaming and crouch down. Be ready to run if we have to."

A million scenarios go through Red's head. The unforgiving nature of the concrete walls of the underpass they are approaching terrifies him. The expression like shooting fish in a barrel enters his head. He tries to divine just how they would escape if the police suddenly block their path.

But the police keep right on going.

17

HINDMARSH DECIDED, AFTER HEMINGWAY HANDED IN HIS coal stock story, that he needed to travel to the scene of the crime: Sudbury, a town that looks like a moon crater.

Being a staff reporter is like being a student writing an examination. For the story he'd saturated his brain with geologists' reports and words like anthracite and anthraxolite, white quartz, iron pyrites, and then he'd vomited it back out for the pages of the *Toronto Daily Star* under the headline, "Search for Sudbury Coal a Gamble."

Hemingway sits in the library and looks at what he wrote. He did learn something doing that phoney coal mine story — what's real and what isn't.

Anthraxolite has a brilliant blue flame and a great heat. But all it leaves behind is a great mound of ash. Anthracite is the real thing, hard and pure. It lasts longer. When it burns, it burns clean.

Good writing is the real thing, too, clean, hard, pure, something that will last forever. Newspaper writing is like anthraxolite — it can be brilliant, too, but it's only meant to last a day.

For the first time, Hindmarsh gave him a byline for the coal story. When he saw it, all he could think was he didn't give a damn anymore. A byline for a story he could care less about. He deserved a byline from his first day of work. He deserved one for the convict pieces.

Two weeks ago Red Ryan and his gang were still in that prison at the mercy of Warden Ponsford with his manicured gardens and his rotunda bell that told them when to eat and sleep and walk and shit. The escape didn't go exactly as the gang hoped but they changed their plan and kept going.

This staff reporter job isn't going according to plan either. He can't sleep or eat. He works twenty hours a day. He finishes one story and is handed three more. He comes back from one trip and is sent on another. He has written nothing except reams of copy for the *Star.* So different from Paris where he wrote about whatever he wanted, when he wanted, unless he was on a special assignment. He hasn't even written any letters, his usual writing warm-up.

Hadley's handling everything. He worries about her too. About childbirth. Women have been known not to survive.

Hadley has rented an apartment. Harriet Connable helped her find it. It's in a place called Cedarvale Mansions, no less. Hadley says she will make sure he'll have a good place to write there. But she doesn't get it, he can't write. He's tried to explain. He's afraid to start because he knows he won't be able to finish.

He hasn't seen it but the new apartment sounds very different from 74 rue du Cardinal Lemoine in rent and accoutrements. They are to move in the first of the month. But he won't be here to help. He is being sent out of town again. Hadley says at the apartment there's a real kitchen, a bathroom, an actual bedroom, a fireplace, a sunroom, a washing machine in the basement for chrissake. She showed him the ad. North of St. Clair, Toronto's most exclusive neighbourhood, it said. One good thing. It's near the Connables.

Ralph and Harriet are ecstatic they will be so close. They are also thrilled about the baby.

Hadley is happy, Ralph and Harriet are happy, but he feels like he can't breathe. They made a mistake coming here. Hadley and the baby may be getting the best care but he is drowning.

Hadley told him that on the day they left Paris, Ezra pulled her aside and warned her about ever trying to change him. And although it is not her intent, a life he does not want is closing in around him like a prison cell. "No living creature likes to feel trapped," Ezra always said. "It's primal."

⁂

"Hem!" The voice comes from above him. "Hemingway." Greg Clark waves at him from the doorway. He's not sure how he feels about Greg anymore. He goes drinking but never gets drunk. Greg thinks Hemingway's lucky to be here. Greg is the son of a former editor. He gets to write the big stories for the *Daily* and the *Weekly*.

Greg's footsteps resound across the library floor like thunderclaps. He pulls out a chair with a screech that would break glass.

"Guess what."

"I'm busy."

"No, you're not. You're hiding down here."

"Okay, so I'm hiding. I'm entitled. I got sent to Sudbury for chrissake. I've been here since seven. What time did you get in?"

"Never mind that. Guess what's happened."

"Somebody cheat another bunch of shareholders with another phoney coal mine?"

"No. Somebody just robbed the Bank of Nova Scotia at Oakwood and St. Clair."

Hemingway looks at Greg Clark's five-foot-two frame perched on the library chair. His kind blue eyes are shining.

"Red Ryan?"

"That's what I think. The police are going crazy, chasing them all over town."

"So, they're in Toronto," Hemingway says, his pulse starting to race. "Hindmarsh should have left me on that story. I wonder where they were hiding out. I bet I could have found them."

"This'll sell a few papers."

Hemingway jumps to his feet and grabs his coat from the back of his chair. "Let's go."

"Where?"

"Where do you think? I'm getting back in on this. It's a great story. The guy's got balls, you have to admit that. He sent letters to Chief Dickson and to the Canadian Bankers Association saying he was going to rob a bank downtown. Then he robs a goddamn bank out in the sticks. Does he think the cops are that dumb?"

"I heard they stole a car and changed the plates," Greg says.

"You hear a lot of things for a guy who's upstairs half the time writing fancy pieces for the *Weekly*."

"Ear to the ground, my son, ear to the ground. Learned that during the Great War. It was some doctor's fancy car parked outside Toronto Western."

"Ha! Smart enough not to make the same mistake twice. In Kingston they stole a beat-up old Chevy."

"I know that, Hem." Greg says. "I read what you wrote in the paper."

"You coming with me?"

"Where?"

"I don't know. Got any ideas? You're the guy with his ear to the ground."

"If you find them, let me know," Greg says with a laugh. "Some of us have to get back to work."

Hemingway sits back down in his chair at the library table and tries to remember everything he knows about Red Ryan. He learned a few things about the underworld when he worked in Kansas City before the war. The city fathers were always trying to clean the damn place up. Booze, bank robbers, business girls plying their trade in so-called rooming houses, those who operated on the other side of the law had quite a network — the big three, gambling, liquor, and prostitution. You scratch my back, I'll scratch yours. You protect me, I'll protect you. Quid pro quo.

So Red and his gang are in Toronto. The cops won't like this. Right under their noses. Maybe right under his nose too.

Last weekend he'd worked past midnight on a misty Sunday night, trying to finish up that coal mining story for His Royal Hindmarsh. He decided to walk back to the Selby. At the corner a man lit up a cigarette. The smell of tobacco reminded him of Paris, where everyone smokes all the time. He can feel it even now here in the library, curling down into every cavity of his lungs.

That night he'd walked north on Yonge, past Queen, then Dundas. At Carlton he turned east. It was a warm night despite the rain that had fallen, unseasonably so for more than halfway through September.

Along the street he heard a woman laugh. It was past one in the morning. It was the kind of laugh his mother would have clucked over, sitting on the front porch in Oak Park.

"No lady laughs like that," she would have said. The laugh was loud and brassy.

He saw a group of people standing on a porch. As he got closer, a short woman with red hair pointed in his direction and they all moved inside like a flock of frightened birds. The light behind the drapes in the parlour window went out; where there'd been laughter, there was silence.

Squinting in the dark, he'd just made out the address, Number 52, the infamous Number 52 Carlton Street. For a known whorehouse, the clients and b-girls were being pretty brazen, laughing out on the front porch. Maybe that had been the convicts' safe house. Only blocks away from the Selby, damn it, and from him. Booze, bank robbers, business girls.

But that night, walking home, he wasn't thinking about Red Ryan. The joyful laughter made him think about Paris, the late-night dances at the Carré Contrascarpe, just up from their apartment at 74 rue du Cardinal Lemoine. The good times where he would dance with the prostitutes who plied their trade there. They would tell him about their lives. The memories made him sad. The misty night made him sad. Paris is beautiful after it rains.

Perhaps, while he was mooning about Paris, wondering who was sitting in Le Select, who was drinking, who was writing, who was making love, he may have missed Red Ryan and his friends, brazen and resourceful, sitting on a porch right in front of his eyes.

He startles to hear the rap of a pencil on the table next to him. The librarian is standing there holding a stack of papers.

"For me?"

"No, not for you. Mr. Hindmarsh just called down here asking if I'd seen you."

"Did you tell him?"

"No, but I can't keep lying for you. Get upstairs."

"Yes, ma'am."

⁂

Hindmarsh is standing looking out the window when he arrives. "Good news, Hemingway," he says as he turns around. "Please take a seat."

Oh my God, Hemingway thinks as he slides into a chair, *he's going to put me back on the story.*

"I want you to cover Lloyd George in New York City."

"Excuse me?" Hemingway says, leaning forward in his seat, the familiar tightness creeping back into his neck and his shoulders.

"You covered him for us before, at the Genoa Conference, when you were in Europe."

"Yes but ..." He is being damned by his own good work.

"But what, Mr. Hemingway?"

"I thought you might want to put me back on the Red Ryan business."

"I have someone else."

Hemingway stands up to face the man who is making his life so miserable. He's lucky there is a mahogany desk between them. "But this would be my third trip out of town in three weeks." His voice sounds high and desperate. He takes a deep breath.

"You were in the Great War. I thought you would be keen to cover the man who led Britain to victory," Hindmarsh says, sitting down.

"My wife is going to have a baby." Hemingway takes another deep breath. You should never let your opponent see you sweat.

"Not until the end of the month from what I hear."

Hemingway can feel his face starting to get hot, the anger is boiling up in him. From what he hears? Who's been talking to Hindmarsh?

Hindmarsh opens his desk drawer and pulls out an envelope. "Here are the train tickets and your letter of introduction and a hotel reservation in New York. Past that, Montreal, Ottawa, you'll have to make your own reservations."

Hemingway wants to pick up the envelope and throw it in Hindmarsh's face but instead tucks it under his arm and walks out of the office without saying another word. When he does open it, he sees Lloyd George is making some kind of goddamn grand tour. He won't be back in Toronto for days. Who knows what might have happened by then. He might officially be a father. Red Ryan might be captured or far, far away.

⁂

Harriet Connable is sitting in their hotel room when he gets back. "Hadley and I went shopping," Harriet says. There are parcels spread all over the room. With Harriet in it, the room smells of lavender.

"We bought linens for the bed, curtains for your new windows, too many things for the baby. I'm afraid I've worn your wife out, Ernie. Why don't you two come over for supper tonight?"

"We can't. Well, I can't. I'm going out of town again."

"What?" Hadley and Harriet say together.

"I was just heading home when Hindmarsh caught up to me and handed me this." He searches in his pocket and holds up the railway tickets and his letter introducing him to whomever it may concern as a reporter for the *Toronto Daily Star*. "I'm going to New York, to cover Lloyd George."

"You've just come back," Hadley says.

"Surely, once the baby's here, he'll keep Ernie closer to home," Harriet says. "Maybe I should get Ralph to say something."

"Say something to whom?" Hadley has sunk down onto the bed, wiping tears away with her sleeve.

"But children, this is ridiculous." Harriet walks across the room and sits beside Hadley. "Ralph is not without his connections. He introduced you to the *Star* in the first place."

"I don't. Want. That."

Harriet gets up and collects her red wool coat, one sleeve dragging on the floor. "All right, Ernie. I'll let you two talk." Her lips brush Hadley's cheek. "You'll be fine, darling. You're tired. We did too much today."

After Harriet leaves Hadley struggles to her feet and takes his hand. "I don't understand."

"I begged him not to send me. I don't like begging, Hash. It's humiliating."

"I don't like making a public display of myself in front of Harriet Connable either. Doesn't Mr. Hindmarsh know we're expecting a baby?"

"Oh, he knows. He knows I wouldn't be here except for the ..."

Hadley drops his hand and walks to the other side of the room and picks up a parcel wrapped in white tissue paper. She pulls on the blue ribbon that surrounds it. The tissue paper falls away, releasing a small yellow blanket. "I picked yellow because it's a happy colour," she says. "Are you blaming me and the baby for your problems at the paper? It was your choice to come here. We could have stayed in Paris. They have good doctors there. But you didn't want to. You said women having babies is a specialty here. You wanted a safe place. A safe place in North America. Well, you got what you wanted, here we are in your safe place."

18

The sky is dark. No moon in sight. The water looks black as ink. The lights of Detroit shine across the river. "What's the name of the boat?" Red says.

After the robbery they hitched a ride in a bootlegger's car from Toronto to Windsor. Lillie set it up. Red's paid off Tommy and Gord and they've gone their separate ways. Good riddance to both of them.

Export sheds line the Windsor shoreline. Dark soot-covered shacks. Some no bigger than an ice-fishing shelter. Coming toward them on the road Red can see convoys of trucks. A truck stops in front of a shed, men appear, unloading begins.

"Maybe we should talk to them about getting into this game."

"I don't know, Sul, I like to be my own boss. You need a whole network of guys if you're in the booze business."

"We can get a network, there's your brother, he'll help us. These guys are getting rich."

"My brother's helped us get out. That's enough. Here it is, the ABC Export Company."

The leaning shed looks like all the others, small, square, no windows, a small door. "We're supposed to slide around to the water side."

Red and Sully push their way along the small space between two greying clapboard walls. On the other side there is a sleek mahogany speed boat tied up to a long dock.

A short man dressed in overalls bends over the engine. He looks up as they come around the corner and wipes his hands off on an oily black rag.

"Frank sent me," Red says, and the man swings himself up onto the dock.

"Norm and Art, right?"

"Right."

"Call me Shorty. Glad you got here nice and early. Don't want any trouble, interferes with business."

There is a faded wooden bench pressed up against the shed and the man motions for them to sit.

"Where you headed, boys?" Shorty laughs. "Mexico? Cuba? Venezuela?"

"Detroit," Sully says.

"He knows that, Sully. He's joking."

"Soon as my cargo gets here, we'll take off. There's a little ledge built under the dock just above the water. I'm going to get you two to scoot down there when the truck comes."

The sun is still well below the horizon. Shorty turns and points across the river at Detroit. "That over there, my friends, is a parched city and behind it an even thirstier country."

The dock shakes and they hear the squeak of brakes and the rattle and sigh of an engine being turned off. "That'll be my load," Shorty says and points to a ladder at the end of the dock. "Just go a few steps down and you'll see the ledge." He disappears inside the shack and Red and Sully move slowly along the dock until they reach the end.

Red swings his leg over and starts down the ladder. "It's right here, Sully, right where he said it would be." Red crawls onto the square platform and moves over so Sully will have room. They sit cross-legged and hunched over, ears cocked. "Look at that thing," Red says. "It's one of the most beautiful boats I've ever seen."

They hear the rumblings of guarded voices, the short man's and one or two others. Then there are footsteps along the dock and the sound of crates being stacked on the boards above them.

"I never liked hiding and waiting," Red says. "It makes me nervous."

"You feel like a sitting duck."

"Exactly."

"Got any cigarettes?"

"We can't do that, Sully. They'll see the smoke, plus I don't think you are supposed to smoke around an engine, too much gasoline."

The footsteps on the dock above go back and forth, back and forth until, at last, they stop and Red breathes a sigh of relief. He recognizes Shorty's blue overalls as he comes down the ladder.

"Need some help?" Red says.

"No, you stay where you are 'till I get this stuff on board. Your faces are plastered all over the newspaper, don't you know that?"

"In Detroit?"

"Yeah, in Detroit. In Windsor. Toronto ain't that far away."

"Hey Red, we're famous."

"All that means, Sul, is we better keep moving once we get there."

"That would be my advice, Mr. Ryan," Shorty says. "Go somewhere where you can get lost in the crowd."

They watch the boat sink deeper into the water as Shorty loads crate after crate of liquor on board.

"I figure," Sully says, "between the two of us, we should have about sixteen hundred dollars after your Bank of Nova Scotia."

"Yep. We don't have to work for a while. Where do you think we should go? What about Cleveland or New York?"

"Let's just stay clear of anything that looks like a swamp."

"Or a cop," Red laughs.

After about ten minutes, Shorty swings into the driver's seat of the boat and says, "Okay boys, hop in."

"It's a joke," Red says. "You can make booze in Canada but you can't sell it."

"As long as the booze is headed anywhere but the U.S., it's all perfectly legal to export it. I'll be making five or six trips to Cuba today," Shorty says with a wink and a grin.

When the engine starts to roar, he holds up a piece of paper. "You see this. This is the golden ticket. The B-13 Canada Customs and Excise Form – Liquor in Transit."

"Golden ticket," Sully says.

The paper flaps in the breeze as they skim across the Detroit River.

⁂

"I'd get out of here if I were you, Red," Shorty says as he pulls up Detroit dockside. "Can't always control when the Feds want to make a show and bring the hammer down on us."

Red surveys the waterfront, with its wide wharf lined with brick warehouses. The dash across the wharf could leave them vulnerable if anyone is watching.

"Which way you boys wanna go? The booze is goin' all over the states. Somebody would let you hitch a ride." Shorty pulls out a long sheet of paper and starts counting off the crates of liquor by twos. When he reaches fifty, he stops and looks back at them.

"Well, my friends? We move fast in this business, make up your minds. Nobody's going to stand around waiting for you two clowns to decide to join them."

"Let me talk to my friend." Red and Sully move over and stand by two empty oil drums.

"I think we should go see my brother."

"One thing at a time, Sul. Let's tell Shorty we don't need a ride and get out of here without getting killed."

Red looks across the stretch of dock they have to cross. On the other side, someone has left a car running. Has the Almighty put the answer to their dilemma right in front of them?

Shorty grabs him by the arm. "Don't you dare."

"What?"

"I saw you looking at that car. You wanna end up dead faster than if the cops get a hold of you? You're going to have to find a way to get around somewhere else."

"Okay, okay."

"Don't say I didn't warn you if you get caught." Shorty reaches into a crate and pulls out two bottles of whisky. "Here, for the road. Good luck to the pair of you."

"Thanks," Red says then signals to Sully. They scurry across the slippery wooden dock. The morning mist has settled over everything on the Detroit waterfront.

"We could knock over a bank and then buy a car."

"Very funny."

"I'm serious."

"We gotta lay low like Shorty says."

"My brother could help us out."

The streets around the harbour are filled with trucks waiting to pick up the cargo coming across from Canada. But other than the people moving liquor from launches to trucks, there's not much happening.

"Red, look over here."

Behind one of the red brick warehouses is a long, low garage, last painted when the century began by the look of things. While Red stands watch, Sully wedges himself in between the garage and the building next door and looks in a window covered in grey dust. "There are three old jalopies, Red. Lined up in a row. Remember Shorty said that's what they use to pull the booze across the river in the winter. Doesn't matter if they fall through the ice."

"Well, she's not winter yet, is she, Sul?"

"No, she isn't."

"May take a while before anybody misses a jalopy or two."

"That's what I'm thinking."

⁂

Red slows down as they drive by the red brick building on Woodward Avenue. On top of the building, there are four tall smokestacks with the word "FORD" spelled out across them.

"I'm still not sure visiting your brother is a good idea, Sul. Straight-and-narrow guys don't want to help out guys like us."

"He's on easy street making those cars."

"If you like sitting in some factory all day long."

"Daniel says they can make a car a minute. And Ford pays good."

"They're making Model Ts. Big deal. You want a real car, like the REO. You stick with me. You'll be on easy street too."

Red pushes down on the gas and the old car coughs. "We'll both be driving classy cars, Sully. Not a tin can on wheels like this thing we borrowed."

"Slow down. That's his street. We can probably catch him before he goes to work."

Red sticks his arm out the window at a right angle to indicate his turn. "What's the number?"

Sully begins going through the pockets of his suit jacket, then his pants. "I know I have it. Maybe it's in my wallet."

The houses are large with sloping roofs flowing over long, solid verandas.

"Looks like your brother is doing all right for himself. Maybe he's selling booze on the side, like everybody else in Detroit. Has nothing to do with Mr. Ford and his factory."

The car shakes when a sudden gust of wind blows dust across a vacant lot and over the road. "Whoa, she's going to be a cold one," Red says.

"I like the way things look in the fall. The way the trees are so dark and the leaves are so beautiful."

"Never mind the poetry, Sully. Let's get this visit over with."

Red turns into the laneway. They can see the autumn sun starting to set behind the grey clouds. The lights shine yellow out of the front window. The lace curtains pull back and a child's face appears just barely above the windowsill.

"I'm not crazy about the idea of kids. They could go yacking to their friends at school about Uncle Arthur and his friend coming to visit. You didn't tell me he's got kids."

"Just stay in the car."

Sully makes his way along the front walk, up the veranda steps. He wipes his shoes on the front mat before he knocks on the door. It opens and Red can see a tall, thin woman with a child balanced on one hip and another clinging to her legs. She's not inviting Sully in as far as Red can tell.

Then, all of a sudden, the woman disappears and slams the door in Sully's face.

Red gets out of the car, stands next to it, and tries to wave at Sully to come back. But Sully is sitting on the veranda railing staring at the closed door. Red has an uneasy feeling in the pit of his stomach. Sully looks back at the window, a hand reaches up and pulls a roller blind down.

"Sully," Red cries out in the lowest voice he can. This time Sully looks up. Come on, Red gestures. When Sully reaches the bottom of the veranda steps, Red grabs his arm, opens the car door, and shoves him in.

"What'd she say?"

"The cops have been to the house, looking for me."

"That's just great," Red says, turning to look up and down the street. "We need to get the hell out of here and fast. Maybe we should head to New York. Nobody has any family there. It's too dangerous to stay around."

19

Hemingway lies back in the Pullman car and watches the Toronto skyline fade away. It will be a difficult job to cover Lloyd George all by himself, write it all up, and get it all in. He'll have to be up early, very early. Lucky for him he has a great memory and an even better imagination.

The other two reporters who were supposed to come with him were told to stay home at the last minute. Hindmarsh's decisions seem designed to confuse and anger him. Those two have nothing pressing like, say, the birth of their first child.

-+ +-

When he arrives in New York, there's a fog coming in. The ships blow their horns, low and craggy, on the Hudson River. Clouds of heavy mist float up the streets of lower Manhattan, the droplets like a soft kiss on his face.

As he works his way down to his hotel, the quadrangular bulk of Madison Square Garden comes at him through the fog. There's a fight tonight, White v. Moran. White is a hard hitter. Hemingway could use a little entertainment on company time, although he's tired from the long train journey.

The Garden is huge, with a rounded roof and boxes for those with money. His ticket gets him a place high in the rafters looking down on the smoke-filled arena. As the boxers enter, he takes his eyes off the boxing ring so far below and looks across the crowd to see who is there. It's a habit he picked up going to the pictures in Oak Park. See which local girls are there and with whom.

⁂

After a few lacklustre rounds, White gets serious in the eighth, almost knocking Moran out in the tenth, but in the twelfth Moran comes roaring back. White goes down. The crowd screaming when White, bleeding, goes down again in the thirteenth. The guy sitting next to him says, "The way White is fighting tonight he'll never get another crack at Benny Leonard."

Hemingway nods his head. Benny Leonard is the thinking man's boxer. He learns from his mistakes. He figures out your game and then he won't let you use it. He takes charge. That summer, 1920, Charley White fought Benny Leonard in Benton Harbour, Michigan. It was his first defeat.

Hemingway did some fighting that summer too: the returned soldier son versus the parents, discord that went more than a few rounds until he finally left home.

At the Garden, by round fourteen, White is done. The referee calls the fight.

People stand up, stretch, shake their heads, collect their belongings, and head toward the exits. Everyone is talking about Moran and how he won. The lights come on overhead, looking like stars on a summer night. Benny Leonard's biggest fan bids him a good evening and starts down the stairs.

Hemingway waits for a moment, holding his coat in his hand, watching the man's progress down the cement steps. That's twice White has been defeated. Across the rows and rows of emptying bleachers below him, two men catch his eye. They stand aside to let the other patrons reach the aisle but they do not leave. Hands on the seats of the row below, they are looking up at the Garden's star-filled dome. Although it is beautiful, the dome of Madison Square Garden reminds Hemingway of the dome he saw the day he went to interview Warden Ponsford. The dome in Kingston Pen where the ranges of cells converge. The dome with the bell that, he hears, all the prisoners hate.

They are not well dressed, these two urban stargazers. And suddenly, their eyes stop at him. One man pulls his ragged cap over his hair, yanks it down at an angle to hide his face, and turns away. The other man, shorter and thinner, seems to be trying to make himself invisible behind his tall friend.

Hemingway stands up, throws on his coat, and starts down the stairs. Could it possibly be? Would Red Ryan know who he is? There was speculation Red might head to New York. The smaller man pushes his friend toward the exit.

Hemingway picks up his pace, using the iron banister to vault two and three steps at a time. If he'd left with Benny Leonard's fan, he could have ended up standing next to them. Even now the two men are not that far ahead but the crowd is so thick it is hard to make any progress toward them. New Yorkers do not take kindly to someone pushing by them as if they are not there. He gets more than one hard shove as the patrons of pugilism react to his hurried assault. "Watch it, Mac! Where's the fire?"

When he reaches the floor seats, it's difficult to see over the crowd. He runs back up five or six stairs but there is no sign of the two men. Patrons stream toward the exits. Hemingway follows, out onto Twenty-Sixth Street, through the Garden's Moorish arches, bringing back a quick flash of memory — the Alhambra, the bull rings, the architecture of Spain. The mist still hangs over Madison Square Park, the trees and street lights, the buildings half-lost, appearing like ghostly giants. He jumps up on a park bench but still he does not see them. It's been about a week since the bank robbery. They would still have some money in their pockets. Why wouldn't they be here? But in Manhattan they could be anywhere, be staying anywhere. Or they could be staying right around here, like he is.

Streets spread out from the park. He starts down one but sees nothing. He comes back, then starts down another, then another and another. The doorways, the alleys, the speakeasies, the subway, it's impossible, too many places for the convicts to hide. He thinks of asking at the nearby hotels but of course they wouldn't use their real names. Damn, he had notes about Red's aliases when he was in Kingston but he's working in a new notebook now.

He walks back to his hotel, a drab six-storey affair in the shadow of the Flatiron Building. When he reaches his room, he hangs his jacket and pants across the arms of the tired and square wood chair that sits in the corner. The clothes have carried the misty dampness back with him. He slides into bed, the sheets, thank God, feel crisp and dry against his skin.

There is just something about Red Ryan's defiance, his confidence, his determination, his bravery in the face of very big odds. He's like Moran taking on that big puncher, White, and bringing him down. In his soul it is Red he is cheering for, not the warden or the priggish penitentiary officials or the cops. He's cheering for Red in spite of everything he's done.

-+ +-

Two men arguing on the street outside wake him up. He goes to the window and tries to hear what the trouble is but he's on the fifth floor. One has pushed the other to the ground. The argument makes him think about the fight. White losing to a thinker like Leonard, then losing to a scrapper like Moran. Losing, hell, humiliated. If it was best two out of three, White's done. Leaving the window, he turns on the bedside lamp and retrieves his watch from the nightstand. It's two thirty in the morning. The voices are just loud blasts in the night. He debates with himself about going down to see what the row is about but his pants and jacket are still damp. Instead, he goes back to bed and he pulls the covers up over his chin. At the moment he feels like he is zero for three and going down for the count. The baby, no writing, this pain-in-the-ass job. He has to be up in an hour to follow the New York muckety-mucks and their fancy limos down to the docks so he can report on Lloyd George's arrival in America. His pants and his jacket better be dry.

20

"That is one strange building," Sully says, pulling the faded curtain back and looking out at the lights of the Flatiron Building, "and this place is a dump."

"Somewhere respectable wasn't going to let us in dressed the way we are at eleven thirty at night."

"Damn, that fight lasted a long time," Sully says. "White was getting pummelled."

"And that reporter, the one from out in the woods, looking down at us. Maybe it was too early to go somewhere so public."

"What's the point of having money, Red, if you can't have any fun? Besides, do you really think he knew it was us?"

Red gets up off the bed, walks over to the window, and pulls the curtain shut. "Yes, Sul, I do think he knew it was us. You saw the way he vaulted down the stairs. He knew all right. What I'd like to know is what the hell is he doing here?"

Sully flops down on the bed. "You don't think he's after us, do you?"

The idea travels through Red's brain like a torpedo. What if that's true? What if the paper sent him here? What if it's this guy they have to worry about, not the cops? "I don't know, Sul. How the hell should I know?"

"Couldn't we have gotten a room with two beds? I don't want to sleep with you."

"I don't want to sleep with you either, Sul. But we aren't in a prison, a swamp, or a barn and we won't be staying here long. Use your head. If that Hemmyway fellow was at the fight, he may be staying in a hotel around the Garden too."

"You should dye your hair then."

"What?"

"That red hair of yours, it's a dead giveaway. You need to blend in with everybody else."

Red walks over, reaches under the bed, and pulls out the leather case where he keeps the money. The envelope is still bulging with twenties and tens. "Here, take a ten, find an all-night drugstore, and buy some dye, and, if you can, get us something to eat."

"Really?"

"Yeah, you had a good idea for once in your life. We'll dye my hair and then find a better place to stay."

"What colour?"

"Didn't you just say it? The same colour as everybody else. Check on the car while you're down there."

"Who would steal that old piece of junk?"

"We did. Just go." Red watches as Sully puts on his coat and hat and reaches for the hotel room's battered black door. "Don't be long," he calls out to Sully as it shuts with a click.

The click makes him think of the loud clang of a cell door being shut behind you. No matter. It is good being out in the real world. And once they get themselves organized it will be even better, just as long as they don't do anything stupid.

He pulls some stationery out of the battered desk in the corner and starts to write a letter to Babe. But after the first paragraph, after the first *I miss you*, he stops. There's no point writing to Babe because he is not sure where they're going to be so she can write back. He can't get the reporter out of his mind. Who would have thought they would run into him in New York? Why didn't he stay in Toronto where he belongs?

⸺

The sky is still dark when Sully returns with two brown paper bags. He walks over to the bed and dumps the contents out. "Car's okay. Got some pretzels," he says. "Three each and I picked out a fine jet-black colour for your hair."

"You ever done this before?"

"Sure, lots of times for my old lady only she's a blond. Go stand by the sink."

Red grabs a pretzel and takes a bite of its tough, salty skin as he pulls a chair over and sits down facing the wall.

"Close your eyes," Sully says unscrewing the bottle of dark black liquid.

"That stuff stinks. How long does this take?"

"Madame must be patient," Sully says. "You want a professional job, don't you?"

⸺

Red studies himself in the mirror above the sink. The room is a mess. Black dye on the floor, the hotel's threadbare towels destroyed. Some of the dye has attached itself to his forehead, the tops of his ears. He'll have to scrub like crazy to get this off. But he does look different, although his eyebrows are still a rusty colour. Sully wanted to dye them, too, but Red refused. He didn't want to go blind.

He collects a washcloth from the sink and dabs at his black forehead and grabs another pretzel. "I was thinking, now that I'm camouflaged, let's go find some decent clothes, then next time we'll stay in a fancier place."

⁂

They sneak down the back stairs of the hotel and out onto Twenty-Third Street until they reach Broadway. The city is quiet. The fog still hangs low. They see a small haberdashery shop and skulk down an alley until they find the back door. Sully holds up the tattered red blanket from the hotel when Red smashes the back window. Inside they find pants, sweaters, and jackets. Shoes with a shine. They grab everything they can, but as they go to leave a line of cars goes by the window.

"Hit the deck, Sul," Red cries and he and Sully crouch down behind a glass display case. "There are cops in those cars." At the end of the parade, there is a long black car.

"What's going on?" Sully says. "Must be somebody important."

As they poke their heads up above the display case, Red grabs Sully. "Look at that fancy car. It says City of New York. Who is that? The mayor?"

"You look," Sully says.

Red follows Sully's finger to see the reporter, with his baggy tweed suit and his moustache, walking in the same direction as the parade of cars.

"It's that Hemmyway guy."

"Why do we keep running into him? Let's get back to our room."

They wait and then retrace their steps out the back door, through the alley, and back to Twenty-Third Street and across Madison Square to the hotel.

-+-

"We've solved one problem," Red says as he tucks a bright white shirt into a pair of black slacks back in the hotel room. Then he slips on a jacket with beige silk lining. "But I think we need to keep moving."

21

It's five a.m. and the fog is still thick as Hemingway walks down to the docks. The City of New York has hired a Revenue Cutter to take journalists out to Lloyd George's ship. The *Mauretania* is in quarantine off Staten Island. The deputy mayor is coming out on his own steamer to collect the esteemed visitor and his family.

As the cutter pulls alongside, the vessel that looked so long and low and sleek to Hemingway from a distance appears in front of him like a tidal wave. Hem, he's often told himself, if it's time to go, a high dive off the deck of an ocean liner would not be a bad way to do it.

There is no time to contemplate that idea any further. Reporters and cameramen are scrambling aboard the *Mauretania* like pirates, combing the decks, looking for the man himself. How many of them, he wonders, are veterans of the Great War? It's not just the story of Lloyd George's visit they're after, they want to see the man whose name they heard every day in the trenches of the war to end all wars.

The first sighting is on an upper deck. Lloyd George stands high above them looking down, with his wife, Dame Margaret.

Megan, his twenty-one-year-old daughter, is in between. Megan looks frightened, although he has seen her play the shy ingenue before, at the Genoa conference in 1922. There are rumours that Lloyd George has a woman on the side but it's a happy family they are presenting to the world today.

Officially, the former prime minister is here to thank America and Canada for their help during the war but Hemingway wonders if he's here to relive past glories, the cheering crowds, the receptions. North Americans still honour and respect Lloyd George. Unlike the British, who unceremoniously threw him out of office.

Lloyd George comes down to the promenade deck. The last few years show on his face.

Reporters shout questions about the League of Nations and the Treaty of Versailles.

The deputy mayor's steamer, the *Macom*, pulls alongside and the city, as if waiting for its cue, appears out of the mist, tall, solid, and promising, reaching for the sky. Hands extend and Lloyd George, Dame Margaret, and Megan are all helped on board. They choose to sit out on the deck, holding onto the gunnel, breathing in the misty air. On shore there are hundreds of people waiting; the tip of Manhattan is a sea of black coats. Hemingway wonders if the convicts are there.

The steamer rises and falls as it cuts through the water. All around them immigrant ships are jamming up in the harbour, arriving full to bursting or getting ready to return with a sad cargo of hopefuls who arrived too late to make the admittance quota for their country.

Despite the thousands that are turned back, Manhattan seems overflowing with people from other lands; every language he has ever heard in Europe echoes in the streets.

Lloyd George's motorcade crawls up streets lined with people and policemen. The crowds are eight, ten, sometimes twenty, people deep. A reporter from the *Times* speculates the crowd is bigger than the one that welcomed home the troops after the war.

The tall buildings give way to the grass around city hall. Hands are shaken and the key to the city presented.

He watches everywhere for Red and his buddy.

⁂

Before following Lloyd George to a theatre performance in his honour, Hemingway slips in and out of dark alleys and peers into doorways. He stares at a group of men talking in a park.

"I wonder where they are," he says out loud as he turns onto Fifth Avenue. He stops dead when he sees a familiar figure. It's not Red Ryan. It's the face from the wall of the radio room at the *Star*. It's Luis Firpo, erstwhile opponent of Jack Dempsey. At six feet two-and-a-half inches, two hundred and fifteen pounds, Firpo is not hard to spot.

"Señor Firpo," he calls out. "Ernest Hemingway, the *Toronto Daily Star*." Should he mention the defeat at the Polo Grounds? "Are you fighting in New York? I'm a fan."

While his trainer fidgets at his elbow, Luis Firpo extends a hand. "Thank you, son."

Son? Firpo's only four or five years older, twenty-eight or twenty-nine. His grip is strong and his smile is warm.

"Not New York. I'm off to South America. I always keep fighting. It will be another grand tour for fighting," Firpo says. "We begin in Lima, Peru."

"They have bullfighting there?"

Firpo nods. His trainer pulls at his arm and they start to move away.

"You were robbed at the Polo Grounds," Hemingway calls after him as Firpo disappears into the New York City crowd like a convict in a quagmire. "Robbed!"

⁂

Just north of Forty-Eighth Street, he sneaks into Scribner's bookstore looking for the *Little Review, Exiles' Number,* the very late spring edition that contains, with Ezra's help, his work. Things that he wrote before they left Paris. It is there on a bookshelf with Fernand Leger's drawing on the cover, a bird with the hole in its huge belly.

On a polished wooden chair hidden away in a corner at Scribner's, surrounded by books written by other people, he opens the little magazine to find his vignettes and his poem. Six short vignettes, titled "In Our Time," one crafted from a newspaper article he'd read, others from stories told by friends, someone else's war, someone else's attendance at a Spanish bullfight. All refined until you feel you are there, until it is his voice the reader hears. "Everybody was drunk," the first one begins. He worked on them so long he could probably recite them from memory. But seeing them there on the page with his name, satisfaction is soon obliterated by that frightening, familiar weight, the dead weight of the unwritten stories that have died, imprisoned in his brain since he arrived on North American soil. The weight that gets heavier every day he walks through the front doors of the *Toronto Daily Star.*

At the other end of the long shelf of books, a young woman stands on her toes and reaches up to the top shelf. Securing the *Little Review* under his arm, he gets to his feet. "Can I help you reach something?"

She turns and studies him. He is conscious, suddenly, of his rumpled tweed suit, the shirt he didn't hang up last night. "The *S*'s have landed on the top shelf. You'd think they'd keep the popular books closer to the ground," she says, holding up the volume she has coaxed down. *Whose Body?*

Hemingway feels himself blush as he squints to read the author's name.

"It's a mystery," she says, handing it to him. "By Dorothy Sayers. No need to blush. The body in question is dead."

He opens the book, always curious to see what is getting published. Who and what has won over some editor in New York. Although he has no desire to write mysteries, he cannot help but wish that he, too, had a novel on the shelf to impress young women in bookstores.

All the while he has been in Toronto, he has been writing back and forth to Bill Bird in Paris about his new little book, *in our time* — flashes of stories, vignettes.

"Sir." The young woman has touched his sleeve to get his attention. She smells of gardenias and summer nights. "Sir, may I have it back?"

A slight figure, small breasts, long black hair, gold-rimmed glasses sliding down her nose. No wedding ring: perhaps a student?

She pushes her glasses back to a safe position. "I have to go," she says. "My friend is waiting for me."

And it's over before it started.

Someone has left a copy of the *New York Times* in the corner. He picks it up and looks up the sailings to Europe: Cunard, White Star. Maybe tomorrow he'll visit the ticket office. And do what? Buy a ticket and leave? Take a long leap off a high deck? That's been one of Hadley's fears whenever he gets really down. She knows he thinks about death sometimes. It's been that way as long as she's known him.

He pays for the *Little Review* and walks out onto Fifth Avenue, out of the world of books, and back into the real world, heading to the theatre where he will witness another hero-worshipping audience cheer for Lloyd George. Would Red have any interest? Greg told him that during the Great War the government let Red and lots of other prisoners out of jail on condition they enlist. Red didn't last long. He couldn't stop stealing. He and another con named Alex stole from their fellow soldiers. They went AWOL in England and robbed fancy country houses, until they got caught.

Not a very good time to rob anything in Manhattan, there's a policeman on every corner.

At the theatre, before the play begins, he leans against the marble wall of the lobby and reads his work in the *Little Review* again. The bird with the belly on the cover makes him think of Hadley. The baby was a blow.

In 1922, so many good things had happened. A few weeks after they arrived in Paris, he discovered Shakespeare and Company. He met Ezra and then Gertrude Stein. He would walk through the Jardin du Luxembourg. He can still hear the gravel paths crunching under his feet, see the children sailing boats in the bassin. He studied the Cezannes and Monets at the musée.

Though he was writing for the *Star* then, too, most of the time it was on subjects of his choosing unless he was on an assignment. It wasn't all-consuming, not like now. He had time to write or travel with Hadley to Switzerland and Italy. With Ezra's support, he'd submitted poems to *Dial* and a poem and the sketches to the *Little Review*.

But as 1922 was coming to an end, the *Star* sent him to Lausanne. Hadley lost all his work when she was coming to join him. As 1923 began Hadley told him she was pregnant.

From that moment he had convinced himself that for at least the kid's first year he would need a regular paycheque. He'd started writing to John Bone hinting that he might come back. So here they are, in Toronto. Even with the regular paycheque, they still fight about money. The new apartment is expensive and there is a problem with Hadley's trust fund. Some railway bonds have lost their value. They need a better investment or they won't be able to return to Paris when their year in Toronto is done. Hadley hears nothing from George Breaker, her financial adviser and best friend's husband, the man who walked her down the aisle. Breaker just may be a crook.

He is starting to think everybody is a crook.

22

THE REPORTERS COVERING LLOYD GEORGE PASS AROUND A bottle. Hemingway is in the last seat of their railway car, leaning against the window, the *Little Review* in his hands. He puts it down and takes a swig of bootlegged Canadian whisky. Red Ryan met Ed McMullen on a train; Hadley lost his manuscripts on a train: the accidents of fate.

They travel up the Hudson on their way to Montreal. As the train hugs the riverbank, Hemingway can still see the tall buildings of Manhattan, crowded together, reaching for the sky, an excellent place to hide if you are a convict on the run.

The river is wide and majestic, with the land rising to either side. Mansions of the rich and hated. Someone says the robber barons have their own private railway stops along the route.

As they travel along, at every stop Lloyd George stands on the back platform like he is Teddy Roosevelt. The crowds are always large, the speech is always the same.

Teddy Roosevelt was his boyhood hero. Teddy Roosevelt wouldn't have liked working for Harry C. Hindmarsh. "Speak softly but carry a big stick," Teddy advised. Hemingway has been following the first part of that advice but it's difficult when you don't like to speak softly, when you are swallowing your anger, and you have no big stick. Teddy had money, lots of money — he does not.

They make a side trip to Vermont to meet with Abraham Lincoln's son, Robert. Hemingway studies the face of the man who has lived a long life after the tragedy that befell him when he was only twenty-one years old. Close to his own age. Why did fate have it out for him? Young to lose your father and in such a horrible way.

Robert is a country gentleman now, likes to play golf. He's an amateur astronomer. The meeting between the two old men is brief but Hemingway makes notes and sends in another piece to the *Star*.

They cross the Canadian border, heading to Montreal. His stories keep going in, five, six, seven, eight. Lloyd George is supposed to go golfing in Montreal. He could write this stuff in his sleep. Bored out of his mind, he wishes he was still in New York looking for Red.

More and more bottles appear as they travel along. The laughter in the train car gets louder and louder. The jokes get filthier and filthier. He's never been one for dirty stories. In his opinion, all talk usually means no action. Ezra felt that way about writing. "There's Talkers and Doers," he'd say. These days, Ezra would probably use him as a case in point of the former.

The last stop is Ottawa today and then, after the dinner, back to Toronto, arriving Wednesday morning.

⁂

The whisky comes by Hemingway again, but he turns it down because it's nine in the morning and the towns east of Toronto have come into view. He needs to decide. Does he tell anyone what he thinks he saw in New York? Hadley will think he's crazy. Greg will say he had too much to drink. Hindmarsh doesn't deserve to know even what he thought he saw. Ralph and Harriet? He feels all their judgments flying at him already and he's not sure he likes what they have to say.

"You sure, Hemingway?" one of the reporters from the *Telegram* says, tapping him on the shoulder and waving a half-empty whisky bottle in his face. "Last chance."

He shakes his head and the man staggers away. At the far end of the car, the door opens and a porter comes through. "Hemingway," he shouts. "Hemingway." The reporters turn and point to his hiding place at the back of the car.

The porter sways as he walks toward him. He's smiling and holding a beige telegraph form in the air.

++

Hemingway runs his hand through his hair and straightens his tie. The baby had made an earlier-than-expected appearance. As he approaches, a group of nurses standing in the hospital lobby next to a ten-foot potted palm turn in his direction. He doesn't look good, up all night on the train, drinking and stinking of cigar smoke.

The nurses stop talking as he walks by. Maybe they were saying, Where was he when she went into labour? Why did a family friend have to bring her to the hospital? How brave Hadley is. Came through it like a real trooper, a couple of hours in labour and there you have it, Grace and Ed's first grandchild. Little John or James or Victor Hugo Hemingway. Whatever they are going to name the poor little bugger who, for good or ill, has hitched his wagon to the family star.

"Congratulations, Mr. Hemingway," one of the nurses says. "You have a beautiful baby." Poor little bastard will have this city stamped on his life forever.

++

"Come and meet your son, Papa," Hadley says when he lingers in the doorway of her room. He walks to stand at her elbow and looks down at the small bundle in her arms.

"Isn't he handsome? They said I did a very good job."

Tears begin to well in his eyes and form two streams cascading down his cheeks. He is so exhausted from six days on the road with Lloyd George — New York, Montreal, Ottawa, a million whistle stops in between — he can barely speak. He wants to fall on his knees and rest his head on Hadley's lap and have her stroke his hair and tell her about his conundrum. But the baby is on her lap and the bed, and the baby and the room all feel so white and pure and he is so dirty and foul-smelling that he stays where he is.

"You can touch. He won't break. He looks like you, don't you think?"

Hemingway reaches out and touches the baby's cheek. When he does, the baby turns his head. Tears begin to fill his eyes again. He is a father. He looks at Hadley and she says, "I know."

"Are you well?" he says, wiping his eyes with his shirt sleeve and bending down to give her a kiss. "Did it hurt?" he whispers in her ear.

⁂

The next morning the *Star*'s typesetters sing a hymn with joyful voices as if they know about the baby's safe arrival.

> God moves in a mysterious way,
> His wonders to perform;
> He plants his footsteps in the sea,
> And rides upon the storm.

He stops and listens. Last night at the new apartment, he was deadly lonely without Hadley. He didn't sleep very well even though he was so tired he had to use the banister to pull himself up the four flights. He has helped to create another human being. It is a very deep and overwhelming thought. But it's good. The baby is here, at last.

The typesetters' voices blend in a precise and beautiful harmony as the presses rumble to life. He closes his eyes and leans against the building. As the machinery gears up, the typesetters sing louder and louder, like the prisoners that night at Kingston Pen.

He promised Hadley that he would let all their friends know the baby is here, but the thought of his telegrams being opened in Paris makes him sad: Sylvia standing at the front desk of Shakespeare & Co., Alice and Gertrude sitting in their apartment on the rue Fleurus, Bill Bird stopping work on his book of vignettes. They should be there, in Paris. They would have champagne and cigars and toast the baby until they could toast him no more. He is a handsome boy, there is no doubt about that, they would all say. Looks like his papa. And his mama too.

The typesetters pause and then begin to sing again. The presses grind on. Hadley will be in the hospital for ten days, maybe two weeks.

> Ye fearful saints, fresh courage take,
> The clouds ye so much dread,
> Are big with mercy, and shall break,
> In blessing on your head.

He climbs the stone steps and opens the *Star*'s front door. How nice to have such faith. These days, he's not sure God is on his side. He's heard through the grapevine that HCH is unhappy he didn't report to the *Star* before he went to see Hadley at the hospital.

Well, he's not happy about a few things either. Hindmarsh thinks the *Globe* scooped them on a Lloyd George story. Hah, he doesn't know the half of it. There might have been an even bigger story in New York. One that would sell more papers than Lloyd George.

-+-

His eyes have just adjusted to the bright lights of the city room when the worn wooden floor behind him creaks like the hull of an old sailing ship. Every inch of His Royal Hindmarsh's six-foot frame hangs over him like a collapsing building. The reporters look down at their desks.

"I expected you to report in as soon as you arrived," Hindmarsh says. "We've had a letter to the editor about one of your Lloyd George pieces."

"You made me miss my son's birth." Hemingway stares up at Hindmarsh, his steel grey hair secured in place with some kind of pomade. The man does not have a kind face. Full of cracks and crevices like a trench field in the war. A face that he would like to rearrange with his fist.

Instead, he says, "Right now, Hindmarsh, I'm doing everything I can to control myself. I will work for you. I will do the excellent job I have always done but I have nothing but disdain for you and this whole damn place."

That is the polite version of what he wants to say. He wants to say, "Fuck you, Harry C. Hindmarsh. You and your whole goddamn crew can go to hell."

The expression on Hindmarsh's face does not change. "I would watch your words, Mr. Hemingway. I hear you complain that you don't always get a byline. In these circumstances," he says, putting a letter down on the desk, "I would think you'd be rather happy you didn't. We asked you to confirm young Mr. Lincoln's current age. This reader says our 'correspondent' made a mistake about that very fact in his report. Our reader is right," Hindmarsh says, pointing at the reader's objection. "We'll be publishing his letter today." Then, he picks up the letter and walks away.

⁂

Hemingway pushes his chair out and jumps to his feet. He's angry when he's supposed to be letting everyone know the good news. He feels a cold breeze across his back, as if someone has opened a window or a ghost has passed by. Some people say the *Star* is haunted by the spirits of the sad, lost men who laboured there, but did not survive.

It haunts him every day that that first morning when he was studying the assignment sheet at the *Toronto Daily Star* and dreading the day ahead, Red Ryan and his pals were sitting down to their breakfast in the prison dining hall. Nervous probably, excited, giving each other furtive looks, looking forward to their day and what was to come. Today's the day. Today's the day we go over the wall and set ourselves free. They were escaping their prison the same day he was entering his.

23

Red reaches over and finds the switch to turn the headlamps on. They have been driving all day, out of New York, into New Jersey, then Pennsylvania. The sun is a fireball that is about to slip below the horizon and when darkness comes, he doesn't want to get caught for doing something stupid like forgetting to turn on the lights. He changed the licence plates the first time they stopped for gas but he still keeps one eye out for the cops.

Sully has fallen asleep on the seat next to him. How nice for Sully. Have someone else do all the work.

He gives Sully's knee a shake. "Stay awake. We aren't out for a Sunday drive. I want you to keep one eye out for a place to get more gas and the other eye open for the cops."

"More gas?"

"Just do it." When you are driving an unfamiliar car, you have no idea how much leeway there is with the gas. His dad's car would go another five miles when it registered empty. They always knew they were safe. But who knows with this piece of shit?

Sully opens the glove box and rummages around.

"Watch for cops, Sully."

Sully pulls out a little book. "Hey, the manual." He thumbs through it and stops about halfway in. "It says here we should get twenty-three miles to the gallon if we're doing thirty-five miles an hour. I don't think we've been going that fast, do you?"

"Damn it, Sully. Forget the arithmetic and keep your goddamn eyes out for the cops."

"Okay, don't get snappy."

"You know, Sul, there is a way I could get more miles to the gallon. Ditch about a hundred and fifty pounds of escaped con."

"Ah, you'd never do that," Sully says. "You need me. One or two more stops and I bet we could make it to Pittsburgh. Do some business."

Not a bad idea, Red thinks. They have a lot of factories there. And where there are a factories, there are big fat payrolls. He can let Babe and his brother know that's where they're going to be.

He takes his eyes off the road and turns to face Sully and grabs the book out of his hands and throws it in the back. "How many times do I have to say it? Watch for the cops and a place to get gas. And by the way, we're going to help ourselves this time. I don't like wasting money."

"I don't like doing the dash-and-grab."

"That's a funny thing for the break-and-enter artist to say. We'll find some place that's closed. Break in, get the keys to the pumps, fill it up for as long as we dare, and then get the hell back on the road."

"What if there's a dog?"

"Are you watching?" Red says.

"What about a place out in the country? There's always a gas pump at a general store. That would be better than stopping in a city. No police out in the country."

"No police," Red says. "But everybody is nosy as hell, and they all have dogs — dogs and guns."

"There's a place on the left," Sully says, pointing up ahead. "It looks closed up."

Red sees a gas pump standing on its own, attached to a small store: Hackett's Fruit Market, Shippensberg, Penn. James T. Hackett and Sons Props. Est. 1911. The terraced wooden counters stand outside the door waiting to display their wares tomorrow.

He slows the car, drives by, then doubles back, and parks a way down the street. "Okay, Sully, I want you to take a walk over there, and if it looks all right give me the sign. James T. Hackett and Sons, you are about to become part of history."

Sully opens the car door and crouches down behind it.

"Red?"

"What?"

"I need something to smash the window."

"Shit, here," Red says, reaching behind his seat and pulling up the hatchet they got at the barn that night. "We should have brought a blanket from the hotel. If there's a dog, use the hatchet on him."

Sully waits for a car to pass, then crosses the street over to the market. To the left is a house, but there is a tall hedge running along beside it. He heads around the right side of the building.

Red hears the sound of a window smashing.

Then Sully is back out front, waving. His new white shirt is blood-soaked at the wrist. He's holding a set of keys.

Red puts the car in gear, ready to drive into the yard, but Sully signals with his hands, stay away, stay away.

A light has come on in the house, in an upstairs bedroom. A shot rings out.

Then Red hears the growl.

Sully runs toward the car. Red reaches across the seat and pushes open the door. A dog as big as a horse clears the front steps and looks like he is going to pull the veranda off with the chain that's attached to his collar. Red lets the clutch out and pushes the gas pedal down. Another shot gets fired.

"Where's the hatchet?"

"I don't know," Sully says. "I guess I left it on the ground."

"Damn it, Sully."

Red turns onto a side street, then drives back toward the gas station. The lights are off again in the house.

"Give me the revolver."

"What? Why?"

Red swerves over to the other side of the street and rolls down his window. "Just give it to me. Is she loaded?"

Sully reaches under the seat. "Yeah, she's loaded."

Red sticks his hand out the window, scrunches his eye, and gets a bead on the etched glass window in the front door.

Bam! The etched glass shatters.

"Are you crazy, Red? What are you doing?" Sully slides down in his seat.

"Who the hell does that guy think he is, firing on us?"

The light comes on in the front bedroom again and Red guns the car and peels off down the street.

Sully sticks his hand up in front of Red's face. "You see that? I'm shaking, Red. Shaking. I feel like I'm going to puke. Are you trying to get us killed for a couple of bucks worth of gas? You never listen to me. We shouldn't be stealing gas."

"Sit back up and keep an eye out for the cops."

"You said we should think big. This is small potatoes. We should steal money and pay for gas."

"You mean like regular people?"

24

"GUESS WHAT, HEM." GREG SAYS ONE AFTERNOON WHEN they run into each other at city hall. "I heard one of their wives works at Eaton's."

"Which one? I should check it out."

"I'm not sure, Sullivan maybe."

Ever since Hemingway got back from New York, ever since he heard Hindmarsh thought he should have turned in his copy before he went to the hospital, he's decided that Hindmarsh can go to hell. Some of every damn day now belongs to him. An added bonus, Hadley will be in the hospital for another two weeks.

He opens his satchel and pulls out the information he has accumulated about Red Ryan with the librarian's help. He didn't see any connection to New York but that means nothing. He looks at Greg standing across from him in the echoing marble foyer. He's a good guy, brave, decorated in the war. His wife found Hadley her doctor in Toronto. But he's still not sure he wants to tell Greg what he thinks he saw at Madison Square Garden.

Greg reaches out to pick up one of the clippings and Hemingway moves the file away. "I got it all organized. Keep your lily white, fancy writing paws off it."

"Whoa," Greg says. "Don't get cranky with me. Who else is bringing you the latest news while you're out doing Hindmarsh's bidding or hiding down in the library?"

"So?" Hemingway sneers. Does Greg have to rub it in?

"So? What?" Greg says, batting his eyelashes.

"You know damn well so what. What do you know?"

"The word upstairs is Red and Arthur Sullivan went one way."

"To New York?"

"Didn't hear anything about that, just that Red and Sullivan went one way and Gord Simpson and the kid, what's his name, went somewhere else."

"Tommy Bryans."

"Yeah, they think Simpson's gone to Quebec. They don't know where the kid is. But Ryan's at the top of their list after they robbed that bank. He's the one they're after."

"I've made a map of all the places that Red Ryan lived before he got sent to the Pen. He has a sister and a brother here."

"Two brothers, one's legit. Red's been in the news for a while." Greg picks up the map and turns it from side to side to side to side.

"If you were Red, where would you go?"

"Not home to Mama? Come on, Hem,"

"His mother's dead," Hemingway says, holding up a clipping from the obits.

"Cherchez la femme, my friend. What did you tell me about Kansas City? The three iniquities, right? Booze, banks, babes. I don't see fifty-two Carlton on your little map."

Could they still be there, even after the bank robbery? Goddamn it, Greg is probably right. The baby's got him rattled.

"You need to find the girl, Ernie. And I'll bet you the royalties on your first real book she's not working at Eaton's."

✢✢

The streetcar rattles along Carlton Street in the dark; Hemingway stands at the back door until it stops at Church. He crosses Carlton and then he creeps back west again. On the same side as Number 52 now, he stays close to the houses: follows the outline of the porches, and front steps. It's like hunting in Michigan in the summer, only with telephone poles instead of trees and garbage cans instead of rocks.

He creeps across the front lawn of Number 54, staying close to the latticework that hides whatever is under their front porch. The ground is wet. It rained all afternoon.

The cold damp from the ground seeps into his pants. But that doesn't matter, he doesn't want to go back to the empty apartment yet; he wants to sit for a while longer and imagine what he would do if he was the escaping one, or more to the point, what he would do if he actually found Red Ryan. That is not an issue that is resolved in his head. Red's freedom is precious.

There is music coming from Number 52. He can barely hear it but it's there. He wishes he remembered more of what he read down in the basement of the *Star* about the alleged proprietor.

Why would anyone be a *fille de joie* in Toronto, he wonders, when a person could, for the cost of a transatlantic passage, be a prostitute in Paris? The work's the same, probably better, the clientele more interesting in Paris. The French, they have more imagination. The pay might even be better too.

His behind is getting very damp. When he moves, he can feel the water squish out from underneath him. His shoes are soaked. His tweed jacket is starting to smell like a wet dog. He hasn't picked the best night to do this but with the baby who knows whether he'll get another chance. He stands up and pulls his wet pants away from his thighs. On the east wall of Number 52 there is a chimney with two small leaded-glass windows on either side. The light is coming out in two square shafts. Inside, he can see shadows on the ceiling. If he could just find something to stand on, he could take a look. It appears people are dancing, their own little *bal musette* here on rue Carlton.

Down the lane between the houses, he finds two orange crates. He stacks them up and, certain that his own height will cover the rest of the distance, he climbs on top and rises inch by inch until he can see what is happening inside.

When he peers in, no one is dancing anymore. There are men standing in a doorway looking toward another room. Maybe the kitchen, judging by the harsh light that spills out through the door. The line of men separates and he ducks down as a woman carrying drinks on a tray comes to greet them. He grabs a hold of the narrow windowsill because if he doesn't hold on, he will fall off his orange crates. When he looks again, three other women have joined the one carrying the tray. Each one drifts toward a man.

The music starts up again. On the other side of the window, one couple looks like they are on their way to having carnal knowledge of each other right there on the overstuffed Victorian sofa. He studies the back of the man's head, his torso, his legs. Would he recognize Red Ryan from this angle? Hemingway's eyes follow the couple as they get up and make their way toward the stairs, swaying to the rhythm of the song. It's not Red Ryan. The man looks young, although Hemingway can only see the side of his face.

He slips down off his perch and heads for the back of the house. There is an old grey clapboard garage, listing to starboard. He pushes open the side door.

There must be twenty cases of booze stacked against the back wall. Not really any room for a car. One of the rumours floating around by way of police headquarters is that bootleggers had something to do with the prisoners' escape. He didn't hear that in Kingston but maybe it's true.

He can hear their voices, the men and the women. It looks like the rest of the party has moved into the kitchen. The window is open a crack. Someone has turned the music off. He can smell food, roasting chicken. He creeps out of the garage and crouches in the bushes beside the back stoop. The ground smells like gin. Somebody must have dropped a bottle on the way in. He pulls his legs in closer, up underneath him. A branch snaps under his foot. "What was that?" one of the men says from inside. "Did you hear something?"

Hemingway shoves his body past the bushes, underneath the back porch. The farther in he goes the more it smells like skunk. Lying down flat on his back, holding his breath, he can feel the dirt, damp and stinking, against his clothes, his hair, and his head.

"I'll take a look," a woman says.

Through the gaps in the porch's floorboards, he can see a woman wearing bright red high-heeled shoes come out onto the back porch. She is wearing a robe and he can see right up inside it, lacy, pale blue underthings. "Shush," she says about a foot and a half above his head. When she moves, she smells like roses. Her shadow falls across the porch railing and down into the yard. What will they do if they find him? Even if they don't find him, Hadley will be furious when she finds out what he was up to. He doesn't dare move his feet or try to pull his legs up any farther.

"See anything, Babe?" Another woman comes out on the porch.

"Nope."

"Maybe your boyfriend's come back."

"Not yet. According to his brother, they were in New York but they're heading to Pittsburgh."

He knew it. And he spent most of his time traipsing after a has-been English politician.

The woman in the red shoes walks over to the top of the porch steps, stops, then turns around. "I don't see anything," she says. "You're always such a nervous Nellie, Edward."

A man's voice says, "You know I have to be careful, Babe. I have a reputation to protect."

Interesting. Who's that? He finally lets some air out of his lungs when the woman laughs and goes back inside.

He remembers that laugh. Bold and brassy.

Red was here, staying at — what did they call places like this in Kansas City when he was working at that other *Star*? — an immoral resort.

Someone closes the window and the voices fall off to a low mumble. He pulls himself out of the bushes and heads back along the side of the garage toward the lane that runs behind the houses.

Is your boyfriend back, Babe? The words are on a loop in his head. Babe who?

The next day he goes down to the library.

The librarian lifts her nose in the air and pushes her chair back from her desk. "Where the heck have you been?"

"I lost something under a porch. I'm looking for some information on brothel raids, arrests in the last three years."

"Um hum," the librarian says. "Trying to put two and two together?"

"Maybe"

"You're not going to do anything stupid, are you?"

"Of course not."

"Come back tomorrow. I'll see what I can find. Do us all a favour. Take your jacket to the cleaners. You stink."

25

Red leans out the window while Sully steers the car along the river. The air is thick, brown, rancid. Not what he needs to clear his head. They tried to pull a job in some one-horse town along the way, but it didn't go well. The manager was armed. They need a place to spend the night. A place to hide out and plan. Maybe a boarding house. Somewhere private. They stole a couple of suitcases from the front of the hotel on the way out of New York.

"I'm glad we picked up some decent clothes," Sully says, as if he's reading Red's mind. "The ladies like a guy who looks respectable."

"I told you, no ladies. No speakeasies. No going to the fights. We aren't on vacation. We need to do a job, get some more cash, and get the hell out of town."

"Fine by me. Pittsburgh looks like a dump anyway," Sully says as the car rattles over a double set of railway tracks. "Nothing but train sheds and factories."

Red stops by the water and they get out and have a look. Brown rivers fan out like spokes on a wheel. Packed into the space between the water and the hills that surround the city, there are steel mills and freight yards and huge storage tanks. Crammed between the blackened factories are shacks with grit-covered windows and washing hanging between two poles. The trees on the hills are starting to turn brilliant colours, the beauty of the foliage out of place with all the ugliness it surrounds.

While he is looking up at the hill behind them, Red sees a flash of light passing through the trees off in the distance, halfway up. Then another flash. When he gets Sully to turn around, they both stare as a streetcar-like box glides to the top of the hill.

A man with a blackened face strolls toward them, a paper lunch sack in his hand. Red draws his suit coat around him to hide the bulge of his revolver. "Excuse me, sir."

"Yah," the man says with a thick German accent.

"What is that on the hill?"

"Is the Incline, the *Seilbahn*, to take people." The man makes a gesture, raising and lowering his paper sack. "Up and down."

"What's at the top?"

"Houses. Air is rotten down here." The man points along the street at a red brick building. "There, you can take, costs one nickel."

"*Danke*."

Sully stares at Red. "*Danke*?"

"Our neighbours were German when I was a kid. I used to go to their church and sing in the choir."

"Let's go up," Sully says. "I want to have a look."

"We'll check the banks out first and then go for a ride on the whatsit."

They go back to the car and Sully stows the suitcases they acquired in the trunk. Red takes his gun out of the shoulder holster and pushes it into the top of his trousers.

"Man, you are going to blow your nuts off someday."

"Just drive, Sully."

The car coughs when Sully puts it in gear and heads toward a bridge into the centre of the city.

"Now that's a bank," Sully says as they drive along Fourth Avenue. Thick granite columns, two stone lions guarding the entrance.

"Forget this one," Red says, scanning the street. "We need to hit somewhere smaller. Look for a bank closer to one of the factories."

They cross back over the bridge and head east, past the bottom terminal of the Incline. The houses and buildings come and go, a string of villages, each more downtrodden than the last.

"Doesn't look like there's much money out here, Red."

But then Red sees it in the distance, the steel company chimney spewing out smoke into the grey sky and over the street lined with buildings two and three stories high. There is the jeweller, the butcher, the drug store, the Farmers and Mechanics' Bank, the Manufacturers' Bank.

"There, that's what we're looking for," Red says, pointing at the Manufacturers' Bank. "We'll take a quick tour of the area. Make sure there'll be a clean getaway."

Sully parks the car down the street. In the pocket of his new suit, he has a twenty-dollar bill. "Okay. Let's check it out." They head into the bank. Sully straightens his tie and approaches the short blond teller. He's going to say he needs change so he can pay off some lads who were working on his farm. That's his standard line.

While Sully talks to the teller, Red stands to one side and memorizes everything: the location of the manager's office, the location of the vault. They can park around the corner on the side street.

Red hears the teller laugh. Sully could sweet talk the drawers off a prison matron.

"I can't believe you just started working here."

"What got you interested in banking, a pretty girl like you?"

Is she blushing? Red can't hear her answers, but the clerk starts laying out brand new one-dollar bills, snapping each one onto the pile. "That's one, two, three, four ..."

Sully looks back over his shoulder as if inviting Red to watch him go in for the kill. "You know, I don't need all of that money to pay my men, sweetheart. What if I dropped by tomorrow after I settle up with them and took you over to the diner for lunch?"

"Oh, that's too bad," he hears Sully say. "I guess it'll be pretty busy."

"You were right," Sully says as they walk back to the car. "Big payroll coming through first thing tomorrow. She says there's over five hundred men working at the mill down the street and they'll all be coming by to cash their paycheques. We should get at least five thou. We'll be sitting pretty."

⁂

The bright red Incline starts its journey from the brick terminal at the bottom of the hill. Red and Sully face the city as it stretches out beneath them. The car is almost empty. A woman sits on a side bench surrounded by her three children and sacks bursting with packages and groceries. An old man stands in the corner smoking a pipe.

As the city drops away, all across the landscape they see smoke rising from the factories. "I've heard there's a lot going on here, lots of booze business. Other stuff too," Sully says.

Red takes Sully's arm and guides him to the opposite side of the car. "Keep your voice down. We stick to what we know."

"I'm just saying. Those liquor guys live like kings."

Red turns to face their destination. There is another car heading down. The wood creaks as they enter the clapboard terminal at the top. Squeezing ahead of the woman and her children, they walk around the building to look at the scenery. The sun is starting to set.

The rivers stretch out below them, in the middle, to the left, to the right, like a giant slingshot with the city centre in the middle. They watch the barges travel up and down. On the terminal there's a sign that says this is where the Allegheny meets the Monongahela to form the Ohio River.

"The Monon what?" Sully says. "Man, what a crazy name for a river."

⁜

The houses at the top of the hill are large with turrets and wide verandas. The woman from the Incline walks ahead of them with her children, her back bowed with the weight of her parcels. Behind her, the boys are pushing and taunting their sister. The mother puts her parcels down.

Before Red has a chance to stop him, Sully picks them up. The woman smiles. "*Danke*," she says, pointing to a house not far away. Sully carries the parcels up to the front door of a white clapboard house. The children disappear inside but Sully stands on the porch talking to the woman. Not really talking so much as gesturing. The woman bends down and takes something from one of her bags. Sully stands at attention and bows like a Prussian army officer. Oh boy, here we go, another dame.

Sully comes running back. "Catch this," he says, giving Red a shove. "She gave me two bits and she has a place where we can sleep." He rests his head on his hands and closes his eyes.

"You don't need to act it out for me. I speak English."

"It's a boarding house."

"What about the car, and our suitcases?"

"You go and talk to her. I'll fetch the suitcases. According to Anna, she *kocht gut*."

⁂

Red is sitting in the dining room when Sully gets back. Anna is serving sausages and warm potato salad. Next to their plates, she puts down two large mugs of beer. "No probit here," she says patting her ample bosom. "I make like my father in old country."

When they turn in, the narrow beds are soft and comfortable. The sheets smell of laundry soap and fresh air. Their room looks out over the lights of the city.

Sully says, "What did you tell her?"

"I told her we were just passing through Pittsburgh on our way to Boston."

"I'd like to do more than pass through. That Anna, what a chassis. Even after three kids."

"Go to sleep, Sully."

⁂

In the morning they wake to the smell of bacon frying. When they go downstairs, Anna has made them breakfast. After turning down a second helping, Red stands up, reaches into his pocket, and presses a five-dollar bill into Anna's hand. "Full," Red says, patting his stomach. "We are full."

When they finally get away, the Incline is crowded with men heading into work. "We should have left earlier," Red whispers. "There must be twenty-five people on here who could identify us."

"These guys all reading their newspapers, they don't care about us."

The Incline glides into the lower terminal and Sully and Red rush to the exit and find the car.

They drive east again, through the clusters of smoke-stained houses and businesses surrounding the factories. Red sits rolling the cylinder of his Smith and Wesson. He has that feeling in the pit of his stomach, the one he always gets, never sure if it's fear or joy. But in the end, it's always a high pulling a job and then, of course, another high when you're counting the money.

"Slow down, slow down, there it is."

Sully cruises past the Manufacturers' Bank, circles the block, and then coasts to a stop on the street that runs alongside. As they walk toward the corner, Red looks through the window and stops dead. "Jesus, there's something going on in there. Your little friend has her hands up in the air. Some son of a bitch is robbing our bank!"

Two policemen come out of the alley behind the bank, guns drawn. As they run past Red and Sully, a man comes crashing through the front doors of the bank, turns left, and then stops at the corner as if he can't decide which way to go.

"Halt! Halt, police!" But the man dashes across the street.

"Halt! Police!"

Red grabs his stomach at the sound of gunfire. The man falls, a revolver flying from his hand and rattling across the sidewalk. More police come running. A trickle of red flows from the man's mouth down onto the cement.

A crowd forms and sirens blare in the distance. Sully motions to Red. "Let's get back in the car. The cops had this place surrounded. Let's get the hell out of here."

"We can't take off," Red says. "They'll think we're the getaway car."

He starts to walk across the street, toward the fallen man. Sully grabs him by the tails of his suit coat. "Are you crazy?" Red brushes him away and pushes to the front of the crowd.

"Back," one of the cops barks. "I want everybody back." But Red keeps moving.

"Did you hear me, buddy?" the cop yells. "I want everybody out of here."

"Come on, Norman," Sully shouts from beside the car. "Let's go."

"That your black car over there?" the cop says.

Red nods, "My brother's."

"Then get in your brother's car and get the hell out of here."

"Come on, Norm," Sully shouts again.

The man on the sidewalk isn't moving.

"Listen to your brother," the cop growls.

"I'm coming, Art," Red says and walks back to the car.

"Sweet Jesus, that was a close one," Sully says when they are a couple of blocks away.

"Just shut up and drive. Don't stop until we are well out of this stinkin' town."

"Red?"

"What?"

"What if Anna hadn't made us that breakfast?"

"I don't even want to think about it."

Red takes the Smith and Wesson out of his pocket and stows it underneath his seat. It's almost noon and the sun is high in the heavens. The windows of the Incline flash in the light as it makes another journey up the hill.

"Damn."

"What's the matter?"

"I forgot to check at the post office. There might have been some mail."

26

HEMINGWAY STANDS AT THE BACK OF THE ROOM WHILE THE president of the Empire Club introduces a Hungarian count. Hindmarsh acted like he was doing him a big favour sending him on this assignment. Even though he didn't have a chance to go downstairs and see what the librarian has dug up for him, for the first time since he began working for His Royal Hindmarsh, it does feel like the old days in Europe. All of well-heeled Toronto is here, satiated by a gourmet luncheon and fine wines. In a private club, you can have all the wine you want.

Count Apponyi is a tall, cultured gentleman with white hair and a long white beard. He's here to win people over, no small task since Hungary was on the wrong side of the War to End All Wars. The count plays the audience very well: He begins by flattering them and then by describing his meeting with Lloyd George in Chicago. Let bygones be bygones because, the count says, throughout the Great War, Hungarians behaved like gentlemen. Chivalrous and sporting gentlemen to those trapped within their borders after the war and to those they held prisoner. This is proven, he says, holding up two documents, by the signed testimonials of those entrapped and the Report of the Swiss Red Cross on the treatment of the imprisoned.

The count moves on to talk about the Treaty of Versailles. He was head of the Hungarian delegation to the peace talks in Paris after the war. "I will not find fault with the treaty," he says. "Here is what I saw and what I hope the solutions might be."

When the count is finished speaking, the room rises to its feet, cheering and applauding. After the thank-yous are said, Hemingway works his way to the head table and stands beside him. "*Toronto Star*, Your Excellency."

The count turns and offers an outstretched hand.

"Excellent presentation," Hemingway says. "I think it would help my readers understand your position if you would let me study the documents to which you have referred."

The count picks up the two reports from the lectern. "Certainly, my boy, but I will need them back. I have another talk this evening."

After working all afternoon, Hemingway puts his article and the documents down on Hindmarsh's desk, right next to the ridiculous foot-long fountain pen that sits like a Civil War sword on an oak carved stand. A gift to HCH from his mother, Greg says.

Hindmarsh doesn't look up. He's reading what the competition has put out this morning.

"Count Apponyi entrusted me with these."

Hindmarsh picks up the report emblazoned with the logo of the Swiss Red Cross, then puts it back down and goes back to reading the *Globe*. "Thank you."

"I thought you would like to review them. I have to return them later this afternoon."

Hindmarsh nods his head and gestures to a corner of his desk. "Leave them there."

The conversation is over.

-+-+-

By the time he gets down to the library, the librarian's desk is clear, her chair pushed in, and her bouquet of newly sharpened pencils sits in the right corner, at the ready for the next day's requests.

Hemingway reaches down and pulls at one of the drawers but it's locked. He travels up and down the aisles but he knows it's hopeless. He needs his guide for this hunting mission and she seems to have gone home early. He'll have to wait. He doesn't have much choice but to go back upstairs to see if Hindmarsh has approved his piece and get the documents back to the count. He prides himself that his pieces often appear as written.

He can hear the presses starting to come to life, getting ready to print up the evening edition. No more convicts for today.

The metal stairway rings with his footsteps as he trudges back up to the city room. Hindmarsh is off in one corner talking to a group of reporters when he arrives. It's the gang from the *Weekly*. The boss often brings them in when he feels there's something important that could use their literary touch. The staff reporters don't like that. Neither does he.

He walks into Hindmarsh's office looking for the documents.

"Mr. Hemingway, may I help you?" Hindmarsh calls out, holding his hand up to silence the literati from the *Weekly*.

"The documents? For my article? I need to give them back."

"You didn't mention that they were borrowed."

Is there any point in saying, yes, he did?

"I'm afraid they've gone out with the trash."

Hemingway is rendered speechless. Hindmarsh threw the goddamn documents out. He cannot tell the count that Hindmarsh did this. He'll have to make up some other reason for breaking his promise. He can tolerate being treated like a rookie reporter, he can tolerate not getting the story he wants, but damn it, this is his reputation. This is his word.

"I'm sure there are other copies," Hindmarsh says, turning back to the staff from the *Weekly*, seemingly unconcerned with what he has done.

⁓

The metal steps resound like cymbals as he stamps down the stairs, through the lobby, and out onto King Street. He wasn't going to start a fight in front of the gang from the *Weekly* but he's shaking he's so angry. Maybe Hadley can calm him down. But the hospital is blocks away and the King Edward Hotel and his buddy, the doorman, are just on the other side of Yonge Street.

The doorman is nowhere to be seen but Hemingway runs up the front steps and plonks himself down in a velvet wing chair in the lobby and takes a deep breath. The place looks like the grand foyer of a country house. Flower arrangements the size of a fountain at Versailles. Marble everywhere you look. As his eyes do a tour of the lobby, he sees the doorman moving toward him.

"To what do we owe the honour? You have a face that could shred a cabbage."

"The boss."

"Again? Really? You have to let this stuff run off your back. I could get furious every day over something that happens around here. I choose not to."

"Well, good for you," Hemingway says, starting to get up out of the chair.

"Sit back down, my friend. Forget about your boss for a minute. Heard something you might be interested in." The doorman crouches down on the floor beside him. "Those convicts of yours, word on the street is Red Ryan's brother might have a few friends in the police department."

"Really?"

"Wouldn't that just come in handy if you're on the lam?"

"How do you know this?"

The doorman pushes his cap back on his head and with two fingers taps his eyes and then his ears.

"Want to know something else? The chief is getting nervous about the lads from our esteemed daily rags. I hear he's going to issue an edict to his boys about talking to the press. Says some of these overzealous reporters may be interfering with the investigation."

"Is that so?" Hemingway says, reliving for a moment his adventures behind Number 52 Carlton Street.

"A cop got suspended once for letting a gentleman of the press get a little too close to some evidence. Allegedly. It was before the war."

"Somebody from the *Star*?"

"Nope, think it was the *Globe*. He wasn't just a regular cop, he was a head guy, chief of detectives, been a cop for years. Supposedly, he let a reporter look at some documents. Some say he was tricked. Some say it never happened."

"What happened to him?"

"Ended up resigning, I think. Duncan was his name. Look it up. There's the boss. Gotta go. You can go back to being angry," the doorman says with a chuckle.

The doorman has calmed him down and, as Hemingway walks out through the hotel's heavy front door, he wonders if this is the kind of place that Red and his friends are staying in with all their stolen money. Maybe not, because you can tell pretty fast who belongs there and who doesn't. Hindmarsh should have left him on that file. With no byline half the time and this business with the count's documents, he's starting to feel less guilty about New York. Anyway, who knows if it really happened? Maybe it wasn't even them. Maybe it's just as well he kept his mouth shut.

27

It took them a while to find the main post office in Pittsburgh. That's where you have to go for General Delivery. "Too bad we didn't ask Anna before we left," Red said.

"Good afternoon." He smiled at the clerk. "General Delivery, Sam Gower." He has to keep coming up with new names every time he writes.

"Let me check," the clerk said. While Red waited, he wondered how much money they might keep in a cash drawer at the post office.

"What's the name again?" The clerk had come out of the back room.

"Gower. G-O-W-E-R." The wait was making Red nervous.

"Right. Let me double check."

The clerk disappeared again and after about five minutes came back with a large manilla envelope in his hands, the contents pushing out the seams on all sides. "Here it is. Looks important. Got filed in with the *S*'s instead of the *G*'s. New man on today. I'll have to talk to him."

You do that, Red thought as he pushed out through the post office door.

⁂

"You know what," Sully says when they get back on the road. "I'm glad we're heading west. There's no death penalty in Michigan."

"You planning on killing somebody, Sul?"

"No, but let's face it, Red, it could happen."

"Yeah, yeah, yeah, pull over behind that grove of trees and let's see what I got."

Red shakes the contents of the envelope out on the seat between them. "You take half."

"Look at this. The feds are holding an inquiry," Sully says, holding up a clipping from the *Toronto Daily Star*. "They've raised the reward to five hundred dollars and the Bankers Association will pay five thousand dollars."

"That's not good. The more we're worth, the more people will be on our trail."

"Shit."

"What?"

"Remember the farmer who left food for us? He's telling the inquiry all about it."

"That's his problem, Sully."

"Do you ever wonder whether Ed'll talk?"

"Nope. He's a good friend."

Red goes through his pile of clippings again. All the mail is from his brother Frank.

"You got anything in your pile from Babe, Sul?"

"Nope."

⁂

The water of Lake Michigan gleams silver and blue in the sun. Most of the leaves have fallen off the trees.

"There is something sad about the fall," Sully says.

"That's cheery, Sul."

"We've come a long way," Sully says. "Not that much to show for it. They got lots of banks in Chicago. It's a big city. Time to do some business."

"We need to watch cutting in on somebody else's territory. That could be worse than dealing with the cops." Red holds his finger up to his temple and pretends to fire. "At least with the cops, they put you on trial first before they execute you."

"You hope."

"These guys in Chicago will shoot first and ask questions later."

"I'm hungry," Sully says.

Good old Sul, never stays on one topic for too long.

"We'll get you something to eat. I want to find a post office and mail this letter to Babe."

"All this letter writing isn't a good idea. You don't see me firing off letters to my old lady."

"Why is that, Sully? What have you got against your missus?"

"I don't know, Red. Ever since the kids came along, it's like I come second. And she has that job at Eaton's."

"Do you blame her keeping her job when you can't pull a simple B and E without getting caught?"

"Let's not talk about getting caught, Red."

"Yeah, you're right. It's bad luck."

"Do you think they still have people looking for us?"

"Thought we weren't going to talk about it, Sul."

"Well, do you? It's been a while. Could we pay for somewhere to spend the night? It was nice when we stayed in that hotel in New York even if it was a dump. And the boarding house. That Anna was something else."

"Let's save some money until we know what we want to do." Time to stop and make a new plan.

⁂

They follow the shoreline of Lake Michigan, passing through Chicago territory. Welcome to Wisconsin. The farmers had turned over their land to get ready for winter. Nowhere a man could hide if he wanted to.

The wind sweeps dried brown leaves across the road. The sun is low in the sky and it looks like there might be a storm brewing over to the west.

Red points to a grove of pine trees about a hundred feet away. Finally. They could tuck in there, out of sight.

"I don't want to hide out in the woods."

"Just one more night, Sully, then I promise you, we'll pull another job and stay in another hotel."

"Where?"

"Where what?"

"Exactly where are we going to pull this job and stay in this hotel?"

"We could head for St. Paul or try Chicago although it still makes me nervous."

"That's two hundred miles away."

"We could drive all night. Take turns sleeping."

"I don't want to drive all night."

"Then let's pull the goddamn car behind that grove of trees and camp out here for the night."

Red puts the car in gear, turns out the headlamps, and drives across the rutted field in the dark. When he stops and gets out of the car, the ground around them is littered with fallen pine needles. The smell is glorious.

"I'm tempted to sleep outside."

"Are you crazy, Red? It's freezing cold."

"Okay. Back or front?"

"You had the back last time."

Sully climbs in the back seat and Red rests his head against the car's frame and stretches his legs out across the front seat. The moon is rising and he can see the yellow globe of it shining through the trees.

"I don't think they'd ever guess we made it this far," Sully says.

"Hope not." The silence in the pine wood is heavy. Red looks up again at the moon. You long to see these simple things when you're trapped in a prison cell.

The wind shifts and the trees roll and sway. A cloud blocks out the moon. Although they are no longer saddled with Gord's nervousness, the thought of being recaptured is never far from Red's mind. They are vulnerable sleeping like this, where anyone could look in the window, where anyone might think it odd that two men are sleeping in a dusty old car and call the cops. But there are no houses close by. He takes another deep breath. The smell of the pine forest is so wonderful that it is clearing his head. His eyes are heavy. He can feel himself drifting off to sleep. "Good night, Sul." He pulls his new coat up over his shoulders to keep away the cold.

But in his dreams, boots shuffle on the prison's damp stone floor. The cellar is cold. The warden is there. The deputy warden too. Four or five guards and the prison doctor, just in case.

They take off his shirt. The leather covering on the strapping table is dry and cracked, like scales of a reptile crawling over his skin. He twists his hands, his arms are held fast over his head. His legs are spread, wide. Rough hands pull his prison trousers down below his knees. The air is cool on his balls and his behind.

The lash makes a noise like a rifle shot when it smacks down on his skin. Surrounded by guards, he doesn't flinch. The humiliation stings more than the pain.

"One," a faceless voice counts off. The boots shuffle again.

"Two," the same voice says.

"Three."

"Four."

The boots shuffle.

"Five." A different voice. The blow is harder. The pain is sweet almost.

"Six."

"How many strokes of the lash for a prison break?"

"Seven."

He cries out, "That's not right."

His back aches. His ankles are shackled to the table legs. The boots shuffle again. Old soldiers who found work as prison guards after the war, they never tire of marching.

"Eight."

"Nine."

"Ten."

Shuffle, shuffle.

"Eleven."

"Twelve." Then silence.

Is it over?

Shuffle.

"Thirteen."

Shuffle.

"Fourteen."

The blows get harder.

Shuffle. "Fifteen." Shuffle. "Sixteen." They are all taking a turn now.

"Too many," he yells to where he last saw the warden standing. "Too many lashes for a prison break."

"Red! Red, you're having a nightmare."

Red puts his hands together and searches for the leather straps on his wrists. He touches his chest and all he finds is the smooth cloth of his new clothes. His hands travel down his torso; his pants are where they should be. He moves his leg; there are no shackles there. When he opens his eyes, Sully is staring down at him from the back seat.

Still free.

-+ +-

The next morning, back on the road, Sully sorts through the pile of newspaper clippings again. "Look at this one," he says. "It's like the *Star* is fixilated. Don't they have other things to write about? The guy who wrote this says the police have been taking a lot of ribbing because they can't catch bandits with cars. Here, read it."

Red takes a quick look at the ragged piece of paper. "I can't read that and drive the car."

"The title is 'Bandits' — that's us — 'and the Police.' This guy says one day the police will have wireless. And when somebody, say, robs a bank, it'll be hard to get away because the cops will be on the wireless telling the police all over the city about you. Every cop in the city will be on the lookout. That doesn't seem fair."

"Fair or not, Sul, it's coming. If you steal a car, could be the same thing. Once the description and the licence plate number are sent out everywhere, you're done for."

Red thinks of all the times they have stopped to change licence plates since they've been on the road. Sometimes he's wondered if it was a waste of time but from what he's hearing, apparently not. "Always gotta stay one step ahead of the cops, Sul."

"Look at the date. It wasn't long after we hit the Bank of Nova Scotia. I bet the guy who wrote it was thinking about us."

"Maybe. We did kinda make the cops look foolish. They drove right by us."

"Maybe it was the same guy, the guy from New York, who wrote this. He was out looking for us in the bush too."

"You mean Hemmyway?"

"Yeah, Hemmyway. Did Hemmyway write that?" Sully takes another look at the tattered clipping. "Doesn't say."

28

Red watches Sully. He's sleeping again while yet another ancient piece of tin, picked up last time they changed transportation, chugs along the highway. As far as he can figure, they are halfway between Oshkosh and Minneapolis. Sully rolls toward the window and lets out a yelp like a dog having a dream. Ed wouldn't be asleep, that's for sure. Ed could turn on a dime. He'd be helping him plan the next move, just like they did all the planning for the breakout. The prisoner work gangs outside the walls were cheering until the guards raised their rifles.

Sully is okay but he's no Ed.

The cruelty of fate. Ed gets hit but the Bryans kid is fine. Should have made him carry Ed. That damn kid was a last-minute addition when their first choice couldn't get assigned to the wood shop, where they made the ladder. Not sure now why they saw the need to replace him. Just goes to show you. Don't make snap decisions. Don't change the plan. That kid was a pain in the ass. And Gord, the big tough baby, turned out to be afraid of his own shadow out in the woods. Who knows where they are now. Gord probably shed the kid at the first opportunity and headed back to la famille in Quebec.

Next time he breaks out of a prison, no murderers, no petty thieves. It will be all bank robbers. "I could write a book," he sighs out loud. But Sully's still sleeping beside him on the front seat of this shitbox piece of tin.

The person he really wishes he was with right now is Babe.

Babe is smart. Babe knows what's what and who is who. Babe would call him on stuff if she thought he was making a mistake. Babe would have her fair share of ideas.

He will end up someplace nice, somewhere Babe would like, too, maybe California.

One thing he knows for certain is he never wants to end up in a cell again. He doesn't want to spend any more time trapped inside four walls with someone telling him what he can and cannot do.

"That is like being dead," he says out loud.

Sully stretches out in the seat beside him and rubs his eyes.

"What?"

"I said I never want to end up inside again. I'd rather be dead."

✢✢

The Mississippi River spreads out before them as they drive across the bridge into St. Paul. Red steers the car along tree-lined streets with large Victorian houses.

"You know what a guy in the joint told me?" Sully says. "St. Paul is like a ... what do they call it where you hide out in a church ... and they have to protect you no matter what?"

"A sanctuary?"

"Yeah, that's it, a sanctuary, like we're safe here."

"We'll see. Just keep your eyes out for a bank. This should be a payroll day."

"Remember when we were in New York and they put the whole layout of a new bank right in the paper?" Sully says.

"We should have robbed that bank when — whoa, there we go."

The small bank sits where Grand Avenue meets Victoria Street. The door is cut into the corner.

There is a fruit market across the street. Red parks the car in front, walks in, and buys two apples.

While they sit and crunch down on the shiny red fruit, a truck drives up beside the bank. Red nudges Sully in the ribs and puts his finger up to his lips.

"Take a look at that. What'd I tell you? It's Thursday, that'll be the money. Look at that guy doing a scan of the street."

When the truck pulls away, Sully walks across the street and leans against the bank's window, chomping out huge chunks of apple, wiping the juice off his chin. Finally, when it's down to the core, when Red is about to yell at him to get moving, Sully opens the door and steps inside. Red slides out from behind the wheel.

-+-+-

The blond girl in the teller's cage looks frightened when Red points the gun at her. He orders her to keep her hands where he can see them, straight ahead where the cash drawer is. He doesn't want to see any dip to the right. He knows what that dip of the shoulder means. They found that out the hard way. Watch the shoulders. If the shoulder dips, they're looking for the buzzer.

The girl's hands are shaking as she hands over the money. Red almost tells her not to be afraid. Sully has everyone else down on the floor in the manager's office. If this crew is smart enough, they'll realize: Do what you're told, nobody will get hurt.

⁂

"Five thousand dollars, I never thought we'd get that much." Red and Sully sit in the car on the outskirts of town and count out the money: twenty, forty, sixty, eighty, one hundred, again and again. Five thousand dollars.

"Payroll," Red says. "I told you."

"Where we going to stay tonight?"

"Nowhere, we got to hit the road."

Sully opens the car door and gets out. "I'm putting my foot down, Red. Right here on County Road Five. I've had enough of this, travelling and sleeping in the car. What's the point of stealing the money if we aren't going to spend any of it? What are you saving it for anyway?"

Red pulls a brochure out of his pocket. "See this, the 1923 REO six-cylinder." He unfolds the paper and holds it up so Sully can see. "The Phaeton," he says. "I don't want a crummy Ford. I'm the kind of guy who should be riding in a car called the Phaeton."

"You think I'm a Ford guy?"

"I don't know, Sully. Another man can't tell you that. It's like women. You gotta decide for yourself what model you like."

"All models," Sully says, squaring his shoulders and looking at his reflection in the rear-view mirror.

"You shouldn't have a problem then, if you're happy with anything."

"That's not true. You know I like a girl with class."

"Look at this," Red says, holding up the brochure again. "You wanna talk about class. Power for every kind of driving, it says."

"How much for that car?"

Red stares at the long low lines of the car and the woman and her noble-looking dog standing by the hood. "One thousand five hundred and forty-five dollars," he says, "plus tax."

"The girls would fall for a man driving a car like that."

"Nickel-plated bumpers. Cigar lighter. Unusually efficient cooling and lubrication."

"Lubrication," Sully says. "Hello, ladies."

"Get your mind out of the gutter," Red says, waving the brochure in Sully's face. "It's going to be red. I don't want any other colour but a nice bright red."

"I like red."

"I might let you ride in it sometime, if you watch your p's and q's." Red folds up the brochure and puts it back in his pocket.

"Unless we get a bath, nobody's going to think we're very classy. The two of us stink."

Red lifts his arm and takes a whiff. Sully's right. He smells like he's been on a work gang in the quarry breaking rocks.

"Come on, Red. Let's go across the river and find a place to stay. Have a bath and a clean shave."

⁜

The Minneapolis Athletic Club stands tall and straight looking down over Second Avenue. Red runs his fingers across his face. Maybe he should grow a beard. Harder to recognize him and he wouldn't need to find a way to shave every day. They have cleaned themselves up as best they could, opened the trunk and pulled out the suits they helped themselves to in New York.

"What's our story?" Sully says as they approach the solid oak front doors.

"Arthur and Norman Miller, two salesmen."

⁜

The wood that lines the lobby walls smells of lemon oil. Huge arrangements stand in pots that look like they came from China. The pattern on the tiled floor makes him dizzy. "Good afternoon," Red says to the clerk. "My brother and I need a room for this evening."

When the clerk turns around to collect a key from the board, Red has another look at the lobby. Through an arched doorway, he can see a dining room with starched white tablecloths. But not tonight. They'll go out. Don't want to be too familiar a face around the ritzy old club.

⸭

Always sit with your back to the wall. That's what one of Red's brothers told him and that's what he does. They take the table in the back of the restaurant that nobody wants. That way you can keep an eye on everything. Tell if a cop walks in the door because pretty much anyone with a brain can spot a cop anywhere. And there isn't a restaurant in the world that doesn't have a back door. Might surprise the cook on the way out but that's fine.

"I don't know if I like Chinese food," Sully says.

"I bet they make great Chinese food here in Minneapolis."

A young woman comes in and they stick this poor dame at the back of the restaurant too. "It's not fair," Red says, trying not to stare. "Restaurants don't like women on their own. They think it makes the place look like a pickup joint or a hangout for working girls."

The young woman looks self-conscious. Her hand straightens her lace collar and then her blond hair.

Sully gives Red a nudge with his elbow. "That's no working girl."

"Lest you forget, a bunch of working girls saved your sorry behind in Toronto."

"I didn't mean anything by it, Red."

"Whatever you meant, forget it, Sully. We're just here to have dinner. That's it."

"Okay, okay," Sully says, studying the menu. "What is this stuff, Red? I don't know what the hell to order."

"It's what all the hipsters eat. Babe told me." He hasn't told Sully but he's not too happy with Babe at the moment. He expected to hear from her more often than he has.

"Look," Sully says, tapping his finger on the table. The girl is giving her order. "What the hell is Moo Goo Guy Pan?"

Before Red can stop him, Sully leans over. "Excuse me, miss. My friend and I don't know too much about Chinese food. I wonder if you would help us order."

"Of course," she says.

Sully stands up, stretches out his hand, and introduces himself. "Art Miller."

The woman looks in Red's direction and smiles. Sully picks up a menu, sits down at her table; he and the woman study it together.

Red leans in her direction. "I'm sorry, miss. Is my brother bothering you?"

"This is my ... uh ... brother, Norm," Sully says.

The young woman laughs and shakes her head. "I'm Irene. You better join us, Norm, and be part of the food decision."

She points out the dishes she likes to order, and the next thing Red knows they are having dinner together. When Irene goes to the ladies room, Sully says, "I really like her."

"There's a surprise. You like anything wearing a skirt."

"I think we should offer her a ride home."

"No."

"Why not?"

"What do you mean, 'Why not?' You know why not. We need to keep a low profile. We shouldn't have sat with her in the first place."

"She's a classy dame. She works at the Athletic Club. Do you believe it?"

"She works there, Sully, she's not a member. There's a difference."

"You still have to be classy to work there. Come on, Red, admit it. They're not going to hire just anybody. I want to ask her out."

"No. For chrissake!"

Sully stands when Irene returns from the bathroom. She has put on a new coat of dark red lipstick.

The Chinese man who runs the restaurant comes over and puts down the bill. "We'll take care of that," Sully says. He turns to face Irene. "Where do you live? Can we offer you a ride home?

"Art," Red says. "Aren't you forgetting we have some business to take care of?"

"Maybe another time," the young woman says. "I'll catch a taxi."

Red watches Sully walk Irene to the front of the restaurant and head out onto Lake Street. Irene is scribbling something on a piece of paper. Then she holds up her hand and a cab swerves over. He can see Sully studying her as she climbs inside.

"You know what, Norm?" Sully says, sitting back down at the table and slipping a book of restaurant matches in his pocket. "You are not what I call a fun guy."

⁂

"I wasn't up for entertaining young ladies tonight. I have a lady," Red says, taking off his clothes and slipping in between the crisp white sheets of his bed.

"She was something else. I can't get her out of my mind."

"Go to bed."

"Got any smokes?"

"Nope."

"We should've stopped for smokes somewhere."

"We'll get some tomorrow."

"I'm going out." Sully opens the window and leans out. "It's dead quiet out there. I could use a walk. Don't worry, I won't ask the desk. I'll do it the old-fashioned way," Sully says, wiggling the fingers on his right hand in the air. "I won't get caught."

"We just broke out of a prison full of guys who thought they wouldn't get caught."

"Yeah, like Ed McMullen."

"Ed got injured, not caught," Red says.

"We had to ..."

Red throws the covers off and stands up. "We had to what?"

"Nothing," Sully says. "We had to do nothing except what we did. I'm going to go get some smokes. If you ask me, you could use a smoke. Might calm you down."

Sully opens the door and walks out into the hall. Red locks it behind him. From the window he watches Sully work his way across the lawn and down the street zig-zagging along the sidewalk, staying in the shadows.

There is a Bible on the night table. Red closes his eyes, opens it, and jabs his finger onto the onion skin page. Might as well see what the Almighty has to say about things. "Be strong and courageous. Do not be afraid or terrified." He rips the page out, walks over, and sticks it in his suit coat pocket, a handy thing to remember. He goes to the desk and pulls out a piece of writing paper and a pencil. "Dear Babe," he starts to write.

Dear Babe,

Dear Babe,

He doesn't know what to write next and crumples up the paper and throws it in the wastepaper basket. He wants her here with him. He wants his REO. They need to make a plan. Hit the road again, get some more cash. No more hotels, maybe rent a proper apartment, stay in one place. This isn't why he risked life and limb to bust out. Maybe Babe's not getting his letters. He's sending them to her mother's address like they agreed. Maybe her old lady opens up every one, reads it, and throws it out.

He finds what's left of the whisky the rum-runner gave them for the road. Down to half a bottle. Damn, Sully's been at it. He looks at his watch. Where the hell is Sully anyway? He's been gone for half an hour.

He never should have let the guy out of his sight. He would bet some of his hard-stolen money the horny bastard isn't after cigarettes — he's out hound-dogging for that piece of ass they met.

He opens the door to their room and looks up and down the hall. He stands at the top of the dark oak staircase and peers down into the lobby. No one. At the end of the hall, there is a door out to a balcony. Red pushes it open and walks out into the night. He can see St. Paul through the mist rising off the Mississippi River. No sign of Sully.

Back in the room he makes another try at writing to Babe but the more he thinks about her, the harder it is to put any words down on the page. He doesn't like that she is still working at Carlton Street. She could end up in jail. She could fall for someone else. You never know.

He goes out on the balcony again. The street is eerily quiet. One of the streetlights at the end of the block sizzles and flashes like the fireflies in the swamp. While he stands there watching, a figure appears from behind a house, presses up against the cream-coloured clapboard, and ducks into an alcove at the entrance.

Two headlights appear farther down the block. Red goes back to their room, turns out the light, and then returns to the balcony, lying down flat on the wrought iron floor. There is a terra cotta pot wrapped for the winter in the corner. When he peeks out from behind it, he can see that the car coming down the street belongs to the police.

He lies there for a moment trying to decide what to do next. There is a huge spotlight shining out of the car playing against the houses as it drives along. They are looking for somebody and he bets he knows who. Better go back inside.

When he opens the door to their room, Sully is sitting on his bed, a long pole in one hand, and a paint can in the other.

"I had to do some angling," Sully says. "But look what I got." He dumps the content of the can on one of the beds: a tin of tobacco and some wrapping papers.

"The police are driving down the street."

"I know," says Sully. "I gave them the slip. Came in the back door."

"Where'd you get the pole?"

"Around. There was a shed. I know where to look."

"Who the hell leaves their windows open in Minnesota in November," Red says, "so you can go fishing for smokes?"

"Some fool. I think he was drunk. He was sleeping about a yard away. He woke up just as I was pulling the stuff back out the window. The can hit a figurine on a table and it smashed on the floor. A woman started yelling from another room."

Red gets up from the bed and stands in front of Sully. "I don't want you doing shit like this again."

"Sure, Red, sure."

"I mean it. I want you to promise me."

"I promise. Now let's have a smoke."

Sully pulled out two papers and rolled two cigarettes. They each sat on their bed and lit up.

Sully takes a few more drags, strips down, and gets under the covers.

"I keep thinking about Irene, Red."

"Go to sleep, Sully," Red says. "You can think about that dame from the Chinese restaurant in the morning."

Sully starts to snore but Red lies awake looking at the flowered wallpaper. It reminds him of that first night in the swamp when they were all sleeping, except him.

It's already November. He should get back to Toronto before the snow flies and convince Babe to come with him on the road. There's a map down in the car. They need to start heading east.

29

At the end of the week, Hemingway was invited to go hunting, but he didn't go. Friday, Curly Wilshur was taking on Benny Gould at the Coliseum. Featherweights. His money was on Wilshur. That, of course, jinxed Wilshur right from the start and gave Benny Gould a chance to win which, in fact, he did. The fight was good. The place was packed, about three thousand people, everyone screaming, cheering on one side or the other. Hemingway had scoured the faces, searching for another glimpse of Red Ryan, but why would that even be a possibility? New York, maybe, but Toronto? Too risky.

From the sound of it, he wasn't the only one who'd bet on Wilshur. He'd already clobbered Gould once. But it was a different Gould who showed up. Not overweight and soft. Third, fourth, fifth round, he was leading and even though Curly put on the steam at the end, it was too late.

-+-+-

Too late, that's what he worries about, about waking up one day and realizing it's too late. Hadley is home with the baby now.

Harriet Connable collected them. It's hard to work in the apartment so he's back at the paper. The baby cries and eats and sleeps and stares into your eyes. It's unsettling. He's a smart little bugger. Has their number already.

Last night when he got back, the baby was crying, keeping Hadley awake. She is looking tired and wrung out. Her breasts hurt and things at the *Star* are getting to her too.

But sore breasts and crying baby notwithstanding, she'd insisted on reading the pieces he'd written the last two weeks for the *Weekly*. "I'm glad they're letting you write for them again," she said, handing the baby over to him.

The first piece was about bullfighting, the second one about their trip to Pamplona in July.

"I don't think I will ever forget Pamplona," Hadley said, a mischievous smile on her face. "The fireworks, the music, the people, drunk and singing, the strong coffee from the café. You brought me some every morning to bring me to life so we could watch the running of the bulls. I'm happy to see I made an appearance."

"Of course you're there," he'd said, putting his arm around her. "You were a damn good sport. Five bullfights is a lot of bullfights for anyone, let alone someone expecting a baby."

"If you can keep writing for the *Weekly*," Hadley said, "we'll have more money when we go back to Paris."

"I'm not sure how it happened but there had to be some behind-the-scenes manoeuvring after my blow-up with Hindmarsh."

"Maybe Mr. Hindmarsh felt guilty about tossing the documents."

"I doubt it. Maybe Greg said something. He is the features editor up there. Or" — he'd said, looking her in the eye — "did you complain to Harriet? I know you women have your ways."

"Ernest!"

"Hadley, did you say something?"

"Do you think I had to say something? Harriet knows you're run off your feet, so does Mr. Connable. They love you, Ernest. Ralph Connable and Mr. Atkinson do belong to the same club and Mr. Connable does spend a lot of his advertising money at the *Star*."

"Who knows. Maybe they had a little chat. Mr. Hindmarsh may be Mr. Atkinson's son-in-law but Mr. Atkinson still owns the paper. And you didn't say anything?"

"Ernest. Really? Go write something else for the *Weekly*. Give me back the baby. He's starting to fuss."

"Whatever the reason, I'm very glad, even if I still have to work for Hindmarsh sometimes."

"I know, Tiny, I know."

He watched Hadley open her dress and put the baby to her breast. He was very happy with the pieces he wrote about Spain. In the *Weekly* or in a story, you don't have to start the same way every time like in the paper, with the most important facts.

-+-

A woman runs for a streetcar as Hemingway looks out the window of the *Star* building. She is tall and slim, her face obscured by a black umbrella. King Street has two streams of water running along the sidewalk. It's been raining all day. The office smells of the damp. Around the window water pools on the floor. Somebody will clean it up in the morning. He walks to the stairwell and turns off the light. It's so dark now in the late afternoon. No hymn singing coming from the basement. Must be taking a prayer break. The money from the *Weekly* is improving his mood but he needs to write more for them, pick up the pace. He can't waste time.

Who said "Lost time is never found again"? He can see it, written somewhere, some church bulletin, some high school textbook, some prison wall.

Four months since he and Hadley were in Spain, almost three months since they left Europe. Three months since his *Three Stories and Ten Poems* was published. *in our time* is in the works. Bill Bird is working on the cover.

Like a prison sentence, full-time journalism has cost him, diminished him, set him back. He opens his umbrella and walks along King until he gets to the King Eddy but his pal the doorman is too busy to chat. He's finding cabs and holding doors in the rain for the hotel's well-heeled guests.

There is something nice about walking in the rain, like it's washing your troubles away. Paris always looked beautiful in the rain.

If he is honest with himself, he doesn't feel like going home. Not yet. His steps take him farther east, up Sherbourne, in the direction of the Selby.

South of Carlton Street, three old boys sit under an old army tarp they've hitched up to a tree on the east side of Allan Gardens. They pass something in a brown paper bag back and forth. The greenhouse glows behind them, off in the distance, with its humid, dripping windows and its forest of exotic vegetation.

The statue of Robbie Burns looms above them. Robbie Burns with his dishevelled hair, his flowing cloak, his britches, and his knee-high boots. Like Ezra, he has the wild-eyed look of the poet right down. Hemingway starts to hum to himself as he walks along.

"Should old acquaintance be forgot ..."

Hadley told him that Harriet Connable was playing "Auld Lang Syne" the night she went into labour at their house. He is in a melancholy mood tonight.

One of the drunks starts to whistle along with him and then holds the bottle out in Hemingway's direction as he passes by. He sits down on the damp ground under the tarp and listens to them talk about where to get a free meal in Toronto and who in Rosedale doesn't lock their doors at night. The bottle goes around, once, twice, a couple more times. The liquor tastes like cheap French brandy. And like cheap French brandy, the more you drink, the better it tastes.

"Something on your mind, young feller?" one of the old guys says to him.

"Just work troubles."

"I had a job once," the old guy says. The bottle makes another round.

"Can I have some of that?" says a voice from behind Hemingway. He turns and with the help of the street lamp sees a pair of legs in dirty blue overalls. The knees bend and a young kid wearing a ripped red sweater slips into the damp darkness under the tarp. He has long dark hair sticking out from under a tweed cap and a scraggly beard over skin that is an eerie shade of pale.

"You just in from the farm?" one of the old guys says.

"Never seen a farmer with hair like that," someone says.

Hemingway laughs, a little too loud. With cheap French brandy, the more you drink, the wittier your companions sound.

Two men move over so the kid can join the circle. Whoever has the bottle hands it over and the newcomer holds it up to his lips, taking a long drink.

"Hey," says one of the old guys, "we're meant to be sharin' that."

The kid looks at him and then lifts the bottle back up and takes another drink.

"Hey!" The old guy pulls out a flashlight and shines it on his face.

The kid drops the bottle on the ground and for a moment no one moves as they watch half the precious contents flow out onto the grass.

"We aren't fertilizing the grounds with that stuff, kid. Get lost, farmer-boy."

Hemingway picks the bottle up and wipes the mouth of it off with the corner of his jacket. He holds it up. Not much left.

The kid looks at him, scrambles to his feet, and starts to stride away. "To hell with you," he calls back over his shoulder.

"No one gives a damn," another old guy yells. "Get out of here."

The kid is already halfway across the rain-soaked lawn between them and the path, but he's still yelling, "To hell with you guys," through the rain.

Hemingway stands up and cranes his neck but loses sight of the kid when he rounds the corner of a church at the edge of the Gardens' wide lawn. His skin sure glowed ghostly white under the beard in the glare of the flashlight, like he hadn't seen the sun in weeks or maybe years. For weeks after he did the story about the prison break, he carried the wanted poster in his pocket. He was wishing he had it now but it's back on his dresser. Could this long-haired, scraggly-faced kid be Tommy Bryans? The height was about right.

He hands the bottle back and starts to run. That kid took off when he got a look at Hemingway's face just like what happened at Madison Square Garden. Could Bryans possibly know who he is? Could the squat little jerk possibly be one of the four? When he reaches the church and steals a look around it, he can see the short figure farther down, on the north side of Carlton. Maybe he's heading to that house. There's a slight stagger in his gait. He stops every now and then, looking up at the houses, like he's checking to see if anyone is home.

At Jarvis he turns north. Hemingway hurries to the corner but he sees nothing. No one. He's the only person around.

Inside the window of a Chinese laundry, a faded black clock clangs the quarter-hour. *Hemingway, you jackass, you're as bad as the good people of Kingston, convict sighting here, convict sighting there.*

He takes another look up and down the street. *Go home. Hadley is waiting.*

Nothing happening here. All quiet. Just Toronto on another Saturday night.

⁜

On Sunday evening the Connables send their car because of the rain. Harriet Connable opens the door herself; her perfume mingles with the smell of Sunday dinner coming from the kitchen.

"I hope you like roast chicken, Hadley," Ralph says. "It was one of Ernie's favourites when he stayed with us."

When the beautiful chicken, golden brown and smelling of lemon and thyme, is placed in front of him at the dining room table, Ralph stands up and raises a sterling silver carving knife. "Once Harriet had to cook with a knife that killed a man."

"Ralph!" Harriet says. "Carve the chicken."

⁜

When the maid starts clearing their plates away, Ralph rises. "Follow me to the library," he says. "There's something I want to show you young folks."

In the library Ralph runs his finger along a bookshelf until he finds a tattered photograph album. He opens it and points at a faded picture. "Hope you don't think we've always lived in a house like this, children. Far from it. That was our house up in the wilds of Minnesota."

"Mr. Connable's family was in the fish business," Hemingway says.

In the picture Harriet and their daughter, Dorothy, stand outside a rough-hewn shack.

"I used to walk the payroll through the woods from one camp to another. I had a few close calls with people after our money. Makes me think of those convicts you were writing about. I wonder how they made out."

"Ralph, darling, they're criminals," Harriet says. "Who cares how they made out?"

"Ernest cares," Hadley says. "He went looking for them in the woods north of Kingston. He's always looking for them."

"Ernie's like me, always up for an adventure and a good story," Ralph says with a wink. "Minnesota is where the bad guys went to hide out, always been that way. You had to keep your wits about you. It was dangerous. I would pretend I was two people walking through the soggy woods at night with the payroll."

"That you, Jack?" Ralph says in a low, rough voice. "Over here, Ted," Ralph says in another, slightly higher voice.

"Better save it for another night, darling. Let these folks get home. I'll call for the car."

⁂

"You're crazy, Tiny." Hadley says when Hemingway suggests they walk home instead through the ravine. But she agrees to come along. After hugs with Ralph and Harriet, they hike down the hill. The leaves are gone, and the ground is soggy from all the rain. Hadley covers the baby's head with his blanket. The wind blows and shakes water off the trees.

"I feel like we're reliving Ralph's story," Hemingway says, stopping to look up into the creaking branches swaying in the wind. Eddies of dead leaves swirl about their feet. "I hated being alone in the woods when I was a kid."

"That you, Jack?" Hadley says in a low voice. "Over here, Bill," in a higher one.

"Why did you tell Ralph about me looking for the convicts?"

"I don't know. You are kind of obsessed with them. Does it matter?"

"I hope Red Ryan never gets caught," he says, picking up his pace.

"What?"

"You heard me. I hope he never gets caught."

Hadley grabs his arm. "Stop. With the baby I can't keep up. Why do you feel this way? You told me he shot a horse."

The wind swirls again and Hemingway turns to look at her. "I don't know," he says. But he does know. The wind swirls again and the baby starts to cry. He reaches up to get rid of a dead leaf that's gotten caught in Hadley's hair.

⁂

As soon as they get inside the apartment, Ernest sits down at the desk and pulls out a piece of paper.

"Are you working now?" Hadley says.

"Shhh. Let me think."

"Ernest?"

He doesn't answer.

"Do you have to work now?"

"It's not for work," he says over his shoulder. "You go to bed." For the first time since they got here, he is letting a story escape from his head and onto paper.

Hadley whispers to Bumby as she takes him off to bed. "How did this happen to us? We are in the company of adventurers and writers."

Scrape, scrape, scrape, his pen moves across the paper. He's breaking his rule. Beginning a story he may be too exhausted to finish, letting it start to come to life. A story about a boy, alone and frightened in the dark woods at night.

30

"What's the matter with you, Red? Your head is off in the clouds."

Red takes his foot off the gas and steers onto the side of the road. There aren't many people around. He is getting used to the midwestern landscape, wide and open, then populated, then wide and open again. They've travelled through Wausau, Green Bay, and Oshkosh. Now they are just outside Milwaukee with the houses bunching together like the menfolk at a wedding.

"Look at this," Sully says. He found a copy of the *Chicago Daily Tribune* in the library at the Athletic Club and he's been rustling through the pages ever since. "I'd like to take some of our money, stay at another fancy place, and have a nice dinner. I saw an ad for the LaSalle Hotel. We can stay over, have dinner, and take a close look at a bank or two while we're there."

"Frank's Detroit associates told me the LaSalle's the best hotel in the city."

"Who are these associates and when were you talking to them?"

"Better that you don't know, Sul. Just some friends of Frank's in Detroit."

"Are they the guys who want us to work for them?"

"With them, not for them."

"Okay, with them. If I'm going to rob a bank with someone, I like to know their name."

"Let's worry about that when we're in Detroit. I would like a good meal," Red says. "That was one thing that drove me crazy at the Pen, food most farmers wouldn't use as slop for the pigs." He chuckled to himself as Sully went on rattling the pages of the newspaper. After they escaped he'd written a letter to the prison explaining that was one of the reasons they'd gone over the wall. Couldn't take the food.

In the letter he also said they were in Niagara Falls. One of his rum-running friends mailed it. They were still on Carlton Street at the time, where the food, he had to say, was just fine. And so was the company.

He puts the car in gear and pulls back onto the road. He hasn't heard from Babe in weeks.

"Put that paper down and keep your eye open for a bank, we're getting closer to the city."

Sully taps him on the elbow. "Slow down. Look at that."

Up ahead Red sees the sign for Grosvenor State Bank. Sully points to a girl who has just walked out the front door. She is slight, maybe five feet, tiny waist, long dark hair. She clutches a bag close to her body. She is cautious, looking up and down the road. In the doorway of the bank, a man in a three-piece suit stands watching her.

"It's a payroll she has in that bag. I'd bet my bottom dollar," Red says.

Farther up the road he can see the phoney-looking grand facade entrance of a factory. In the doorway stands another man looking toward the girl.

"Let's make some easy money, Red."

They are going to have to act fast. The distance between the bank and the factory is not very long.

"Slow down and I'll jump out and grab that bag."

"I don't know, Sul."

"We want a fancy place to stay and a good dinner, don't we?"

Red moves the car slowly toward the sidewalk. The girl is looking straight ahead. Sully can grab the bag from behind. But when he stops the car, the brakes squeak a little and the girl begins to run.

Sully jumps out and runs after her. He catches her hair and throws her to the ground but she won't give up her precious bag. Must be a lot of loot.

While they struggle, the bag opens and money and coins fall onto the sidewalk. Red jumps out of the car.

The man from the bank comes running and the other man races out of the factory's front door. Red and Sully collect as many bills as they can on the windy street. Lucky for them, the two men appear to be more worried about the girl than about studying their faces or writing down the licence plate number of the car. Red and Sully jump back in and barrel down the street.

"Whoa," Sully says counting out the money. "Let's get out of here and get to Chicago."

The sky is a light winter blue with only one small cloud. They head out into the country. But soon, open fields give way to factories, then the factories to houses. The sun shimmers off the surface of Lake Michigan. They're almost in Chicago.

++

Red and Sully get off the elevator and walk through the lobby of the LaSalle Hotel. This time they aren't sharing a room. They have connecting rooms. They are bathed and shaved and wearing their new suits, pressed in the hotel's laundry and returned to them this morning.

The lobby is panelled with ornately carved dark wood. "It's like a gentleman's club," Sully says. "They have a room just for writing letters."

"Don't get too attached to it. I promised we'd be in Detroit by December."

They approach the door to the Palm Room. It is beautiful with a soaring ceiling and columns painted to look like marble. There is a magnificent fountain, and after Red slips the maître d' some money, he seats them in its shadow.

The sound of water is soothing. Red sits back in his chair and looks around the room while Sully studies the menu. The large painting on the wall just past the fountain is a picture of a nude reclining outside on a garden wall. The way the woman rests upon the divan, her full breasts and her shapely legs, remind him of Babe.

How wonderful it would be to have her here with him. He and Babe could tour the country together in his REO Phaeton. They could head for California.

"Listen to this, Red. It all sounds so good. Rib-eye steak or roast turkey. Pumpkin pie, mince pie, plum pudding." Sully devours the menu with his eyes.

If Babe came, would he keep Sully around? He's been a good friend. He's been calm when they pulled a job. He's honest, at least so far. There's just one thing, bird-dogging the broads. He can hear Sully correcting his thoughts: not broads, classy dames.

The maître d' walks by with a young girl, followed by her mother and father, and seats them at the next table. The girl is about the same age as the one they robbed yesterday. How she fought back. He hopes the men took good care of her. They shouldn't have let such a slight young woman do such a dangerous job in the first place. Cowards. He has young sisters. He would hate it if someone did that to them. He would kill anyone who did that to them.

"What's the matter, Red?"

"That girl."

"So?"

"I have three sisters. One about the same age as that girl we hit on. After my Ma died, they were all alone except for my sister Irene. She had to care for them. She was just twenty-three."

"I'm sorry, Red."

"Shed more than a few tears when my Ma died. When my Pa died, not a one. He was mean and nasty, tried to beat me into submission."

The waiter comes and pours some water and leaves a basket of rolls and a plate of celery and olives. "May I take your order?"

"Roast Tom Turkey and cranberry sauce with baked sweet potatoes," Sully says. "Home cookin', that's what I'm having."

"I'll have the rib-eye," Red says.

When the waiter's gone, Red reaches over and takes a roll out of the silver basket and rips it in two. "I don't like picking on little girls," he says, slapping on the butter.

"Not a bad haul, though." Sully lifts his hand and motions to the luxurious surroundings of the Palm Room. "Look where it got us."

"We acted too fast. Do something without thinking it through, you could regret it. Like bringing Tommy Bryans with us, I regretted that from the beginning. I don't want to make any more stupid mistakes."

Sully motions with his head toward the family at the next table. "Shhhh."

"You know what else I regret? Leaving Ed behind."

"What's the matter with you, Red? Keep your voice down. I think they're trying to listen."

Red looks over at the family and they all stiffen in their chairs as if they'd been caught passing notes in school. Then they start to chatter again and Red can hear snippets about schoolwork and church and young gentlemen callers.

He leans toward Sully and whispers in his ear, "Babe was the biggest mistake of all. Shouldn't have left her behind either."

He and Sully sit in silence, each with their own thoughts, waiting for their dinners to arrive.

"Will you write to me, Red?" Babe had said to him the night before they robbed the Bank of Nova Scotia. "Let me know you're all right?"

For the first time, he'd thought, maybe it wasn't just business. She really did care.

"If you do," she'd said, "I promise I'll write back."

So far, the plan isn't working out too well.

Red pulls his napkin from his lap and throws it on the table. "I'm not waiting any longer. I'm going to buy that car. Frank knows a guy who can get you a real deal on a new REO."

"A new and hot REO?"

"I'm going to pay for it."

"Doesn't mean it's not hot. You know how it works."

"I want to drive a decent car. I want to find a place to live. I want Babe to come with me. I'm going to send her some money, show her how well we're doing now."

"Okay, okay. Keep it down. Remember where we are."

"I want to marry her. I'm going to buy her a ring." Red pulls his wallet out and holds up some ten-dollar bills. "I'm sending her some of our loot. I'll tell her to be careful. They're probably marked."

"Red, will you shut up."

"She could take them to Eaton's, where your wife works."

"Let's leave my wife out of this. Babe might tell her where we are. I don't want her traipsing after us. Showing up when we least expect it. Where are you going to buy this ring? Does Frank know a guy in Chicago?"

Red leans over to Sully. "No, I'll buy it in Detroit after we pull the job with that gang."

"Okay, okay," Sully says, tilting his head toward the family at the next table.

"But first, Sul, I'm getting the car. We can head for Lansing."

"What's in Lansing?"

Red sticks his hand in his breast pocket. He waves the Phaeton brochure under Sully's nose. "Lansing is where they make these beauties. You drive me to Lansing. I pick up the car. I go back to Toronto, talk to Babe, and you make your way to to Detroit.

"Red, will you please shush."

⁂

Red wishes the man would stop talking. He's going on and on about how well he knows Frank and how glad he is to do Frank a favour. Red is about to pull his gun on the guy just to get him to shut up. Sully, who for some reason is showing no interest in the car whatsoever, walks around the man's grey and greasy shop like he's doing an inventory of possible B and E tools. Red can't take his eyes off his beautiful REO Phaeton.

Finally, the man says, "Have you got the money?"

While Red counts the bills out into the man's hand, Sully coughs and finally comes over. "I think we better get going, Norm. We have a bit of a drive ahead of us."

"This is a wonderful car for the road. It can go up to fifty miles an hour."

Somebody please tell the guy he's made the sale.

"That steering wheel is made out of the finest American walnut."

"We really need to get going."

"Certainly, certainly, the missus says I talk too much about these cars, like they was my kids or something."

Red does the thing he has been dying to do for forty-five minutes. He opens the door and gets behind the wheel.

Everything is as promised in the brochure. The cushions are deep and comfortable. The leather, he can tell, is of the highest quality. He turns the headlamps on and off and looks into the rear-view mirror.

"Start her up," the man says.

The engine comes to life and Red smiles at Sully. His dream has come true. One of his dreams.

"Need me to get rid of this piece of junk for you?" the man says pointing at their borrowed car.

Sully and Red exchange glances. "No thanks," Red says. "We're keeping both of them for now. But what I do need is a telephone."

"Where you boys headed anyway?"

"I wouldn't ask too many questions if I were you," Red says, patting the spot where his gun is tucked into his belt. "My buddy's taking that car. We're headin' our separate ways. That's all you need to know. Now where can I find a phone?"

Red walks with Sully over to the old jalopy. "You ditch this thing once you get to Detroit. Make like you arrived by train. You know where to go. You'll like the Statler Hotel. It's even classier than the La Salle. I'll be there in a couple of days. You take off. I'm going to call Babe."

⁂

If she was surprised to hear from him, Babe hid it well. "Here's the plan," he'd said. "When I get to Toronto, I'll head to the

King Eddy and get a room. I'll say I'm from … I don't know, somewhere."

"I don't think that's wise," Babe said. "There's still stuff about you in the papers."

"What kind of stuff?"

"I'll get the room. We can meet out back, corner of Victoria and Colborne, around three o'clock on Tuesday. That should give you enough time to get here. The deliveries will be finished by then. I'll warn Lillie I may need to take a night off."

As Red turns the car toward the Canadian border, his head fills with thoughts of Babe, her hair spread out on a pillow on a big soft bed at the King Eddy Hotel.

31

HEMINGWAY SITS IN THE LAST STALL OF THE MEN'S WASHroom on the *Star* building's fourth floor. The heavy bathroom door creaks and he listens while the interloper takes a piss. Whoever it is, is now humming as he washes his hands. What the hell is this guy singing for? Hemingway wants to scream at him. *Hurry it up! I'm trying to think.*

The interloper coughs and Hemingway hears the rotation of the linen towel through the rack. At last the man opens the door and leaves. Hemingway unlatches the cubicle door and walks out into the echoing white light. Hard surface after hard surface. He needs to go for a walk. Clear his head.

When he steps out into the hall, Greg Clark comes running up to him. "There you are. I've been looking for you. Where've you been hiding? You're not still smarting about your run-in with Hindmarsh? You shouldn't let him get to you."

"Easy for you to say."

Greg reaches into his suit coat pocket and pulls out a small envelope. "This was sitting on your desk."

Hemingway looks down at the small beige envelope, his Paris address crossed out, the address of the *Toronto Daily Star* written in. "Everybody knows I'm here. Who would write to me in Paris?"

"How the hell do I know? Open it."

The envelope has English stamps. Then it hits him. There's only one person who might think he's still in Paris. He grabs Greg's arm. "I think it's from Edward O'Brien. I met him in Italy. I wrote to him months ago."

"So open it and find out."

"I'd rather be by myself if you don't mind. It could be bad news. You don't want to see a grown man cry."

"Okay, I'm going back up. If you need me or my hankie, come and get me."

As he moves toward the stairwell, Hemingway scours the city room looking for the bulky shape of Hindmarsh but the coast seems clear. The sounds of hymn singing–voices start to drift up from the typesetters' inky domain. He descends one floor, then another, round and round the straight metal staircase. He opens the door to the lobby.

⁂

It is late in the afternoon and the sun is soaking all the buildings along King Street with yellow light. He walks east, with the sun behind him. His hand is in his pocket clenched around the letter. He wants to know and he doesn't want to know what Edward O'Brien has to say.

In May he had asked O'Brien, the editor of the *Best American Short Stories* anthologies if he had any advice on how he might get himself published. O'Brien had read his story "My Old Man" when they met and suggested he send it to the *Pictorial*. The editor at the *Pictorial* seemed to think Hemingway was trying to pull something by mentioning O'Brien's name. Regular rejection letters were depressing. Rejections letters after there's been a recommendation are worse.

Even so, when *Three Stories and Ten Poems* came out in August, he'd sent O'Brien a copy because publication is one of the rules for inclusion in the anthology.

When the doorman at the King Eddy Hotel calls his name, he is surprised to see that he has already travelled that far east.

"Hello, Hemingway, scouting out new arrivals?" The doorman never lets him forget that his first morning at the *Star*, he'd been sent to hang around the King Eddy to find out if anybody important was in town.

"No. But I wouldn't mind the use of the hall for a few minutes."

"Just keep ya boots off the furniture."

Hemingway laughs and walks up the stone steps, waves at the lads on the front desk, and finds himself a comfortable velvet wing chair in a corner. He takes out his pocket knife and slits the envelope open.

"Dear Hemenway," the letter begins. Can no one spell his goddamn name right? He reads the letter through. It's not bad news, it's very good news. O'Brien wants to publish his story "My Old Man" in the *Best American Short Stories of 1923* and to dedicate the anthology to him. He wants to know how many short stories he's got. Enough for a book?

Not very many is the answer to that question unless the stories that are about to make his head explode count.

O'Brien apologizes for taking so long to write back.

"I need to go see my wife," Hemingway calls to the doorman, waving the letter. "Hail me a taxi."

"Good news?"

"The best."

"What is it? You can tell me."

"Nope, the wife gets to know first."

The doorman blows his whistle and a cab appears from around the corner. "Fifteen ninety-nine Bathurst Street," Hemingway says.

⁂

Hadley cries when he shows her the letter from Edward O'Brien. Cries, then kisses him. Kisses him in a way she hasn't kissed him in a long time. He takes the baby from her arms and puts him in his bassinette.

"I just fed him," Hadley says. "He'll sleep for a while."

He sits down beside her and when he kisses her again, she puts her arms around him and draws him closer. His hands caress her face, her cheeks, her neck. He can feel the fullness of her breasts pressing against him. When he moves his hand farther down her throat, she grasps it and brings his fingers to her mouth. The soft touch of her tongue on his fingertips makes him think of Paris, of making love in Paris. Of lying in their bed, windows open, listening to the noise from the street below, Hadley leaning over him, her arms, her breasts, her belly.

Ever since they found out about the baby, most days she is a self-contained unit of calm. As if she is practising being a mother. As if she knows she will be the force, the head, the matriarch, and he will be but "the father." Broad of beam and round of face, she cut her hair. Until today, he saw no desire in her eyes. Desire had transformed into a fondness for him, a tolerance of him. Like he was the petulant but much-loved older child.

⁂

He thinks about that kiss in the middle of the night as Hadley sleeps beside him. Unable to sleep himself, he walks out into the kitchen to get a shot of brandy. He rereads O'Brien's letter again and again. He turns off the light to go back to bed but then he turns it on again and reads again. Just to make sure he didn't dream what it says. The words "publish" and "dedicate" and his misspelled name are still there. It's not a dream.

What if this had happened earlier? With the baby coming, would they have stayed in Paris?

32

THE DRIVE FROM LANSING TO PORT HURON IS ONE OF THE best drives Red has ever had. In his own car. Legit. Well, mostly legit. The signs for the car ferry send him north of the city. The line-up is short. It's the last run of the day. There's a man taking money just before they wave you on board.

Once one of the crew puts blocks under his front wheels, he steps out of the Phaeton and lights a cigarette. This is a lot better than the last crossing, half crouched in the rum-runners' launch, not knowing what to expect on the other side. It's been quite a journey, over two months since they robbed the Bank of Nova Scotia. There've been some ups and some downs but they have another job coming up in Detroit, a big one. At last he will have some good, solid money.

The car ferry's engine revs up and they start to glide across the water. There's a light wind and it's warm for a night in late November. It's not a long trip. The lights of Detroit shine off in the distance.

He's going to stick with his good luck alias, Norm Miller, on the other side. It's worked for him so far. But as the Canadian shore moves closer and closer, he starts to get a nervous feeling in the pit of his stomach. The ferry clangs into its berth and the crew scramble to fasten the ropes around the thick metal cleats on the worn wooden dock. Engines around him rumble to life and the cars begin to file off. He watches. Do they stop? Is anyone checking on who you are and where you're going? But the cars don't stop, they just proceed up the road. No one patrolling the border today. So far luck is on his side. He is on his way. When he comes back, maybe Babe will be with him.

It's nice to drive along by himself. A chance to think. A chance to plan. The roads may be bumpy but they're quiet. It rained yesterday so there's little dust. He is observing the speed limit — nothing to see here: just a well-dressed, respectable man in his good-looking car. But every time headlights appear behind him he tightens his grip on the steering wheel until the car either turns off or passes him in the dark.

In London he stops at an all-night diner and orders the all-day breakfast. Every meal he's had in the last two months has been a joy. Fancy or just plain cooking. God, the food was crappy in the joint. Why do they have to do that to a man? Isn't being imprisoned enough? In the burning light of the diner, chatting with the night cook, he relishes every sip of real coffee, every bite of scrambled eggs that taste like they came fresh from the hen house. He devours the biscuits that taste like his mother made on her good days.

When the night cook starts into another story of the Great War, Red makes his excuses and gets back in his car. On the outskirts of town, he pulls over behind a stand of trees and closes his eyes. This is a lot of hours on the road, but it will be worth it. The sun wakes him in the morning and after taking a piss he heads back to the main roadway.

⁂

Once he hits Toronto city limits, he turns south and drives along the water with the railway tracks keeping him company on the way in. The lake is beautiful with the sun shining silver on top of the waves. This, too, makes him think of the prison, so cruelly built next to such a beautiful body of water. He bets there's a view of the lake from the King Eddy. The taste of fine accommodations and good food has gotten under his skin.

From Lake Shore Road, he turns onto King Street. At a stop sign, a man points to the car and gives him a thumbs up, a sign of approval. It happens again, a few blocks later. This is something to think about. The beautiful, classy car may be too visible, too unique. This car, in this city, may be a liability. Might be a good idea to park the Phaeton while he's here so they don't get identified with one another, just in case a fast getaway is required. You never know.

Just east of Bathurst Street, there is a garage on the north side. It looks like a no-questions-asked kind of place. When he inquires about a short-term storage arrangement, the owner points to an empty spot on the lot just beside the outdoor privy. "Just back her in."

When he comes back into the garage, he slides a two-dollar bill across the counter. "There's another one of those for you if she's in perfect shape when I get back."

The man picks up the money and pulls a cigar box out from under the counter and drops it in. "She'll look better than when she got here," he says.

"Just one more thing," Red says looking around. "I need to make a quick phone call."

He picks up the receiver and turns his back to the garage man while he waits for the operator to connect the call. Then waits again while someone goes to find Babe. "I'm here. I'll be there at three." That's all he really needs to say once she's on the line.

The garage owner gives Red a knowing wink when he tosses his extra set of keys and a nickel down on the oil-stained counter to pay for the call.

"Sorry about the privy, my lady," he says, returning to give the car's left bumper a pat before he heads across the street. "You won't be here too long."

The streetcar clangs at a group of boys taking their time crossing the tracks, then stops for him. Some of the passengers look up when he climbs on board and suddenly, he is very conscious of his face. His infamous face and his big Irish head seem like a balloon resting on top of a cashmere coat. But as they sway along, the other people don't seem to give a damn about him and his face once he takes a seat that isn't next to them.

The businesses along King Street flash across his vision as they glide by. This used to be his territory. Things haven't changed that much since he was sent east. He fingers his coat. Cashmere. Babe will be impressed. He looks like a man of substance.

As the streetcar moves toward Yonge Street, he sees the offices of the *Toronto Daily Star*. He wonders if that Hemmyway fellow is still working there. It's been quite a while since they saw him in New York.

⁂

When Red gets off at Victoria Street, Babe is standing on the street corner south of the hotel. When he reaches her, she puts her fingers to her lips and hands him a piece of paper with a hotel room number on it and a crude drawing of the hotel's innards.

"I'm not sneaking in through the kitchen," he says, making a move to take her in his arms.

"It's not the kitchen, it's the laundry," she says, stepping aside. "Just go in the escape door, follow the hall until you get to the stairs, then start climbing. The room is on the fourth floor right next to the stairwell."

He grabs her hand and tries to pull her into a doorway.

"None of that my lad, not yet," Babe says. "Are you listening?"

Truth be told he is not listening, he is looking at her long red hair, her bright green eyes, her perfect figure. She is dressed like a society matron in a modest navy-blue suit, not her usual wardrobe. But it's not hard to imagine what is underneath.

"The floors are plainly marked. You'll find me. I'm going in the Ladies Entrance. There's a special door so none of us have to run into the likes of you," she says, giving him a push. He studies her in her well-fitted suit as she walks away and disappears through the tall oak door.

It is a heady thing to be standing on a street in downtown Toronto, free as a bird, looking good, about to spend the evening in this beautiful place with a beautiful woman even if he does have to sneak in. A question better not asked or answered flashes through his brain. How is it that Babe is so knowledgeable about the inner workings of the King Eddy Hotel?

++

He opens the door from the stairwell and peers back and forth along the hallway. All clear when he reaches the fourth floor. The first door on the right, she told him. The door is slightly ajar and when he pushes it open Babe is lying on a settee by the window. Past her, he can see Lake Ontario stretching to infinity, like an ocean. This is the way a man should be looking at a body of water, from up high, not from down low, imagining it from a prison cell.

Babe has changed her clothing. No longer looking like a Rosedale matron on her way to afternoon tea, she is wearing the same thing she was wearing the first night they met.

She stands up and the turquoise blue kimono with a red-and-black fire-breathing dragon embroidered down the front slides off her shoulders and onto the floor. She reaches up and starts to unbutton his coat.

"I want you to come back with me," he says.

"We'll talk about it later," Babe says.

His new cashmere coat slides off onto the floor. She takes his hand and leads him to the foot of the big brass bed. "You'll have to finish the rest yourself," she says with a grin, lying back on the crisp white sheets. "I'll just watch."

++

The clothes stolen with such care from the Manhattan gentlemen's shop now lie in a heap beside the bed but he's not going to worry about that. He'll get them pressed at the hotel in Detroit. What he is worried about is Babe telling him he has to leave by midnight. It's almost eleven. She still hasn't given him an answer.

"So? What do you think?" he says, playing with a strand of her hair. "I drove all the way from Michigan."

"I can't just walk out on Lillie on a moment's notice. She has a business to run. I have clients, regulars."

Why is she reminding him of the thing he does not want to think about? That here, in Toronto, she is with other men, many other men.

It makes him angry. He wants to say "Lillie can replace you. Girls like you are not hard to find," but he knows that's not true. He's been with lots of girls. She is special. Different and smart. Very talented in more ways than one.

"I've got money. I want us to get married."

"Whoa, Red, honey, let's not get ahead of ourselves."

"I thought you would write to me more often?"

"We had a good time but ..."

"But what?"

"I make good money here."

There's that picture in his head again.

"You wouldn't have to work anymore. We just took a big haul. We got another one coming up in Detroit. Planned out this time. Not just me and Sully. The biggest haul yet."

Babe gets up and goes over to the settee where her kimono lies in an aquamarine tangle. Wrapping it around herself like a towel she walks back over to the bed and stands, lifting his face to look straight into his eyes. "You want me to be honest?"

"Yes."

"The cops are working on this night and day from what I hear. I'm not sure I want to be on the run all the time. Or die in a shootout."

"Once I get some money, we won't be on the run. Maybe I'll go into the booze business. Those guys are living pretty high. We'd be legit."

"The booze business? I know a lot about that already, from the house. That's how we got to know your brother Frank. It would be a pretty good business to be in, particularly in the States."

She is thinking that one over. "The booze business," Babe says again, letting her kimono go, leaning over and kissing him on the mouth.

"You should see the car I'm driving." He gets up and reaches into the pocket of his coat searching for his brochure. "Look at this, we'll be living high."

"Just a couple more jobs," he says, pulling her back down on the bed. It is almost midnight. "Do I really have to go?"

33

The late November air is not kind but Hemingway needs to blow the smell of the *Star* building, the stale tobacco smoke and the printers' ink, off his skin. The story he started writing the night they walked home from the Connables is hidden in a drawer. It's under Hadley's old blouses, her breasts too full to wear them now. Morning, noon, and night, John Hadley is hungry for his mother.

What he knew would happen, happened. The story's gone. Will he get it back?

He pulls the scarf Hadley bought him in Paris tighter around his neck and walks west along King Street. It will take a long time to get home but he warned Hadley he might walk to clear his head. As he goes by Bay Street, he can see the makeshift cenotaph from the Armistice Day celebration is still up in front of city hall. The cold burns his face and makes his eyes water. The bell on the city hall tower tolls the three-quarter hour. Bong, bong, bong.

He still has nightmares about the war, fewer now than he used to, but still vivid and terrifying, ripped flesh and blood-soaked ground, staring death in its disfigured, grinning, lustful face.

It was the women crowded at the base of the cenotaph that held his gaze on Armistice Day, not the veteran soldiers. Some stood alone; others clutched the hands of children. The children were young, four or five, conceived, perhaps, before their fathers left to fight in Europe in the last months of the Great War. The women wiped away their tears; the children fidgeted and let their eyes wander. Spared mourning the loss of someone they never knew.

He heard the names of the battles whispered among the mothers and wives and sweethearts: the Somme, Ypres, Vimy Ridge, Passchendaele. The places where their loved ones had died or lost a leg or an arm or the ability to love them.

War moves from one place to another and leaves sad stories of the body and the mind everywhere, love letters, broken hearts, leather pouches full of shrapnel pulled from your invincible body, kept safe where they can't hurt you just like your unfinished story in a bottom drawer.

Someone had fashioned a ridiculous machine gun made of flowers that day and attached it to the top of the wooden cenotaph. The flower gun, thusly secured, pointed out at the crowd. He'd moved out of its range, uneasy and fearful, even in a floral line of fire.

A delegation of the Toronto police had marched in, led by Chief Samuel Dickson. The chief sat next to the mayor, his eyes going back and forth as if he, too, was accustomed to looking for Red Ryan at every public gathering. Hemingway remembers what Greg told him: Red had a bit of a war record. The government let the prisoners out to serve. Governments, he guesses, are just like people. They come up with some stupid ideas when they are desperate. Pardons all round, as long as you don't mind being a guinea pig for the efficacy of gas masks. Red did mind. He and another released convict went AWOL.

⁂

As he turns onto Bathurst Street, an icy wind comes up from the lake. It hits with a brutal force, creeps into his back, wraps around his legs, blasts through his worn winter coat like shrapnel. He thinks again of war, about Edward O'Brien, about chance, about how his own life had almost ended in Italy when he'd felt it had just begun. Right after the war, they all believed in "live while you can." Squalls from the lake travel up Bathurst Street and blow around him.

As he pulls his collar up against the wind, two polished brown shoes appear on the sidewalk in front of him. A figure has stepped out of the shadows and blocked his path.

The figure is tall, equal to his height if not more. Hemingway notices it is no Salvation Army retread coat he is wearing. The damn thing is cashmere. Camel coloured like the boys on Bay Street wear on their way to one of the banks downtown. But it is not one of the young Bay Street gentlemen who stands before him. "Hemmyway?" the figure says from underneath a fedora.

The figure in cashmere looks to the left and the right. There is a small opening about two stores up. It's Red Ryan.

Red says, "Could we get off the street?"

Perhaps he should say no. Perhaps he should not acknowledge that he knows who stands in front of him. But he's been dying to get his hands on this guy from the moment he got assigned to the prison escape. He follows Red about four feet into the opening, careful not to let the escaped con get between him and the way out.

"I'm not going to hurt you," Red says.

Hemingway hopes that's true. It's very dark in the alley. There aren't many people on the street. No illumination from the street lamps or the small windows that are many feet above them.

During his four days in Kingston, how he'd wished that he would be the one to find Red Ryan, that he would have just such an opportunity as the one currently presenting itself.

Be careful what you wish for, he hears Ezra laughing. Nobody wants to read the headline "Star Reporter Found Dead in Alleyway."

In Kingston, back when he cared about such things if he's honest, at first he wanted to find Red to impress the hell out of Hindmarsh and get his goddamn byline back.

As if Red is reading his mind, he says, "Why don't you write about us anymore?"

"Boss took me off the story. Called me back to Toronto."

"You remember that day you were out in the woods," Red says, "and the guards caught you? I thought you might write about that."

Hemingway tries very hard to maintain a poker face. How the hell does Red Ryan know what happened? The rumours about a mole in law enforcement just might be true.

"Who told you about that?"

Red looks him dead in the eye. "I have my sources."

"Really? The cops?"

Red laughs. "No. We were about twenty feet away. You saved our soggy behinds."

So that's how they knew who he was that night in Madison Square Garden. That's why they took off. And again, as if Red is reading his mind or the look on his face, Red nods. "That's right. That's how we knew it was you at the fight in New York that night."

A streetcar goes by clanging its bell. Red stops, leans past him, looks out toward the street, and pulls Hemingway farther into the alley.

"We saw you the next day, too, very early in the morning. And now here you are again. It seems our paths are destined to cross."

In spite of himself, Hemingway laughs, an anxious, girly laugh he stifles right away.

"Don't be nervous. I told you, Hemmyway, I'm not going to hurt you."

So many things are running through his mind. Could he take Red Ryan if he had to? The guy is pretty damn big. And it doesn't look like he's been starving out on the road. In fact, he looks exceptionally good. All those hours he spent trying to put himself in Red's place, to imagine himself as an escaped convict, he never imagined himself looking like this, in a goddamn cashmere coat.

"Hemmyway," Red says, a note of annoyance creeping into his voice. "What I don't understand is you didn't say anything."

"About what?" Hemingway says. Should he tell Red it's Hemingway, goddamn it? No, not down a dark alley. He'll just add Red to the list of people who mispronounce his name. Unlike the others, Red might have a gun.

"About seeing us in New York," Red says. "I hear there was nothing in the paper and the cops don't seem to have known about it."

"That's a long story." He can't believe he's about to tell Red Ryan what he's about to tell him. "I'd asked my boss not to send me to New York because my wife was expecting a baby." He can feel his anger at Hindmarsh bubbling up inside him again. "But he did anyway and she had it while I was gone. I was mad. I told him off. I thought I was going to get fired. I guess I forgot."

A dark cloud seems to come over Red Ryan's face. "You forgot."

"Well, I wasn't sure it was you and there was a lot going on."

"You forgot?" Red sounds very disappointed, like he'd thought the omission had been a personal favour.

Red pulls a package of cigarettes out of his pocket. The cigarettes are American. The smell of sulphur fills the air as Red strikes a match on his thumb. Hemingway becomes conscious that he is staring, eyes riveted on every part of the cigarette lighting ritual, the first draw, the first exhale, because he can't write it down, because he fears this apparition will disappear if he so much as blinks.

"I wasn't completely sure it was you," he says again.

"Right," Red says and holds the cigarettes and matches out in his direction.

"No thanks," Hemingway says. "Never did." The matches, he notices, are from the LaSalle Hotel.

"What?" Red says. "You don't smoke?"

"So, you were in Chicago?" Hemingway says, nodding at the matches. "Know it well. I was brought up not far from there." Now just why in the hell would he say a stupid thing like that? The information is flowing the wrong direction here.

He needs to get a little sang-froid, as the French would say. "Why are you here?" he asks.

"Had some business with a lady friend," Red says. He reaches into his coat again and for a second Hemingway thinks, *this is it*. But it is not a gun that emerges, it's a clipping from the *Toronto Daily Star*. "She reminded me about this. Told me she heard you wrote it even though your name's not on it. You were there when Ed got captured?"

"No, I got there the next day. How the hell did you pull it off? You took a big risk."

Red unfolds the clipping and holds it out.

"I know what's in it," Hemingway says waving it off.

"You talk about Warden Ponsford finding Ed like you were there. You say how Ed looked, all the guards pointing their rifles. You say it like it's Ed talking when he says he's going to play it smart. Knew it was stupid to try and run. But you weren't there?"

"Nope."

"Why doesn't the *Star* say you wrote it?"

At the mention of the *Toronto Daily Star*, with no bylines, its brutal hours, and the boss who seems to think he's a rookie,

Hemingway can feel the familiar anger rising. Focus, damn it, focus. He tries again. "You took a big risk. How did you have the courage to go over that wall? You are one brave son of a bitch. You could have ended up dead."

"A man wasn't meant to live like a rat in a cage. It's worse than being dead."

Jesus, isn't that what Ezra always says? Only Ezra says it about marriage.

"Kingston Pen is cruel. You're trapped inside but out in the yard you can see all that blue sky over the river and you can smell the water and see the birds flying free, the seagulls and the geese in the fall going away for the winter."

"Weren't you afraid you'd get shot?"

"We got jobs in the carpentry shop. We built a ladder. Some of the guards didn't like Ponsford. We got some money to spread around. We decided to change the odds, or at least control the odds as much as possible."

More and more of the things he has been hearing on the street or from Greg are looking like they just might be true. Were the guards, or some of the guards, on the take?

"How do you get money into prison?"

"I'll never tell," Red says.

"Wasn't Ponsford sent in to clean things up?"

Red takes another drag on his cigarette.

"I guess rum-runners are the guys with money these days." Hemingway tries again but Red's not rising to the bait.

"We made a break for it, that's all," Red says. "It was worth a shot. It was worth getting shot."

Hemingway stares at this man who has a price on his head, who will probably be used as target practice if the police ever get near him, and all he can think is he has nothing but admiration for the son of a bitch.

"I don't understand. Were you following me?"

Red looks down at him. "I wasn't following you. I was going to pick up my car."

He has a goddamn car.

"I saw you stop to pull your collar up against the wind and I thought, you know, someday, someone will write a book about me."

"What?"

"Someday, someone will write a book about me. Maybe it will be you."

The ego on the guy. It's unbelievable. "Not doing too much writing these days, except for the *Star Weekly*," he says.

There are two old barrels at the end of the alley and Red pulls at his sleeve and says, "Let's sit down."

Maybe he should leave now while there's still a chance. Who knows what the police know. They could know Red's here. They could be following him. They could storm the alley with guns drawn or guns blazing. Maybe he shouldn't be standing this close to a potential target. Maybe he shouldn't trust this guy? He's a criminal for chrissake. He shot a goddamn horse.

Red signals again to come. "I told you I wouldn't hurt you."

A criminal and a goddamn mind reader.

"What do you mean you aren't doing much writing?"

"For the paper yes," Hemingway says, dropping himself down on the barrel next to Red, "but for myself, nothing."

"Do you think you're wasting time writing about guys like me?"

"No, no. That's not what I meant. It's not you. It's the paper. People read it and forget it. You would make a hell of a story. A real story. I've always thought that."

Red stands up and stamps out his cigarette. "You know what? If you're wasting your time, then do something about it. Believe me that's what we were all thinking in Kingston Pen. We saw our chance to remedy our situation. It was a big risk, but we took it."

"I take risks. Look at this." Hemingway pulls the letter from Edward O'Brien out of his pocket. "I'm nobody but I wrote to this guy, Edward O'Brien, asking for advice. He's famous. I only met him once. Writing a letter is not as fast as setting a fire and going over a wall but it still takes nerve."

"But you didn't mail it."

"I mailed it," Hemingway says pointing at the cancelled stamps. "This is his answer."

Red is starting to piss him off.

"What did he say?"

"It took a long time for him to answer. He was sick. He liked a story I wrote and now he wants to publish it. He asked if I had any more."

"And do you have more?"

"My job takes up all my time. The paper drives me hard."

Red laughs, "Yes."

"I need the money."

"Um hum," Red laughs. "Don't we all."

"Why are you back in Toronto? You got free. I don't get it. It's dangerous."

"I wanted to see my girl. Things that really matter are worth taking a chance for."

"Did you see her?" The memory comes back of unladylike laughter on Carlton Street, loud and brassy. "Who is she?"

"I'm not at liberty to say."

"How come?"

"Because, my boy, it is none of your business. At least not right now."

Hemingway stands up, the better to make his case. "I have to think about my wife and the baby." What would his parents think if he chucked his job and took a great big chance walking off a fucking cliff now? He heard enough times from his mother about family and responsibility, how she gave up a career as a singer to raise them.

"You have a baby," Red says. "You told me."

"It is better now that I'm writing for the *Weekly*."

"Yeah, well, I've got to get going," Red says, shrugging his shoulders and heading toward the street. Near the opening of the alley, Red turns around again and looks back. "Maybe I was wrong about you, Hemmyway, I thought you got it but maybe you don't."

"It's Hemingway, damn it."

"What?"

"My name, it's Hemingway."

They both freeze at the sound of a siren off in the distance.

"You stay where you are and keep your mouth shut."

Hemingway sits back down on the barrel and watches Red walk through the alley's opening. The street lamp leaves a hazy glow for a second around his silhouette. Then he's gone.

Hemingway pulls his scarf up around his face as if he is the one who has something to hide and heads back out to Bathurst Street. The northbound streetcar is approaching the corner of King. It must be the last run of the day. To hell with walking home. He runs across the street to catch it.

The driver clangs his bell when a woman dashes across the street in front of them. Hemingway leans his face against the cool of the window as the streets go by. What the hell just happened?

⁂

When he gets back to the apartment, Hadley is asleep. Just as well because he needs to process this. Right now, he's sure he looks like a man who's seen a ghost, which in some ways he feels he has.

"Well, Hemingway," he says to himself as he unbuttons his shirt, "just what are you going to do about this?"

He can hear Red's voice. "All you're doing right now, man, is standing in the prison workshop thinking about building the ladder."

As he drifts off to sleep, for the first time he is starting to believe maybe, like Red Ryan, he will bust out. In his dreams he sees the two huge limestone columns that guard the grey facade of Kingston Pen. He pulls the chain. The heavy wooden doors of the front gate swing open.

"State your name."

"Ernest Miller Hemingway."

Inside, the male prisoners cheer for him. The women in long dresses laundered celestial white cheer too.

In the middle of the yard, Warden Ponsford stands with Harry Hindmarsh by his side. Ponsford points at the great dome of the penitentiary with its huge brass bell. Hindmarsh says, "The bell sounds, you work. The bell sounds, you eat. The bell sounds, you sleep. Sleep, eat, work. Work, eat, sleep, until I say stop."

Red Ryan comes out from the keeper's cottage. "No," he yells, "that's bullshit." He twirls and makes a veronica with his cashmere coat, grabs Hemingway's hand, and pulls it up like a boxer's triumphant salute. "Don't listen to them," Red says. "Stand with me, Hemingway."

"We are the bullfighters," Red screams. "We are the bullfighters."

34

"SIR." THE CLERK AT THE STATLER HOTEL TAPS THE KEY ON the polished mahogany front desk and swivels the hotel register around for Red to sign. "Your brother is in Room Five Seventeen. Lovely view of the park." Red hesitates before he writes Norman Miller with the clerk's green fountain pen. He hopes Sully remembered to use their alias.

When he turns around, he sees Sully disappearing into a haberdashery shop just off the lobby.

"Here's my brother," Sully says when Red follows him in. While Sully tries on a jacket, Red sits in a leather chair and looks around the store, glass cases filled with watches and cufflinks and displays of men's shoes. Sully's telling the salesgirl a very big lie about returning from a hunting trip upstate.

The Statler has all the markings of a fine hotel: the wood panelling, the rich red carpets, the marble floors, the beautiful crystal chandeliers. This is what he wants — to surround himself with the finer things in life.

⁂

Their room is large. Twin beds with satin coverlets. Everything in it, the towels, the glasses, the pillowcases, the little tray on the dresser, all bearing the Statler's crest, the gold *S* on the blue-and-gold shield, speaks of luxury. Red picks the little dish up. It's light, a sign of fine china. "I'm saving this for a souvenir," he says, putting it in his coat pocket.

Sully stretches out on one of the beds and leafs through the hotel's book for guests. "Hey Red, guess what they have in this joint? A library. Just like prison. That's a laugh."

Red looks over at his partner in crime. He's a simple guy. He hasn't even asked how the trip went.

"The drive from Toronto was easy. No one checks at the border if you don't look like a bootlegger. And I did get to see Babe when I was there, in case you were wondering."

"Good, I'm glad."

"She's thinking of meeting me after we pull this next job. I saw somebody else too. Remember that reporter from the woods? The guy at the fight? I ran into him on the street."

Sully drops the Information for Guests book on the rug. "What?"

Ah, now I have his attention, Red thinks. "Don't worry, I kept my wits about me. You never know, someday he might come in handy."

"Handy for what?

"He's a good writer."

"What if he tells the cops? What if he puts it in the newspaper?"

"I don't think he's going to tell the cops or the paper. He's got other things on his mind."

"I don't know, Red. Doesn't feel like a good move to me." Sully bends down, picks up the guestbook again, and goes back to flipping through the pages. "Look at this restaurant," he says holding the book up. "I think I might just put on my new shirt and check out the waitresses."

"First of all, Sully, they won't have waitresses in the Grill, they have waiters. You saw the white linen tablecloths and I don't think we should be careless about money."

"But you can buy a fancy car and take a side trip and end up talking to a reporter?"

"I know what I'm doing."

Sully gets up off the bed and walks over to the window. "Okay, okay, no dinner in the restaurant. Can we at least go to the movies or something? I say we read the paper. If we aren't in it, let's have some fun."

"I'll look at it," Red says walking over and picking it up beside the room's overstuffed chair. He starts flipping through the pages, his eyes going from side to side reading the headlines.

"Whoa!" Sully says. "Look at the back page. Never mind the movies, let's go dancing."

"We're not going dancing. I need to figure out what our next move will be after the bank job."

Sully opens a long white box and pulls out a tie. "I know what my next move is going to be. It's Boy Meets Girl Night." He points at the ad that takes up almost the full back page. "At the Graystone Ballroom. We drove by it when we were here before. A big old place out by the Ford Factory. I'm going dancing and I'm going to have a good time."

"No, you're not, because I'm going with you. I need to keep my eyes on you."

"At least I'm not chatting up some stupid reporter."

"I said drop it, Sul."

++

While they wait for the elevator to come, Sully takes out his pocket knife and slices two roses from the bouquet on the hall table and hands one to Red. "Here, put this on. We'll look like proper gents."

"What about the car? I guess you should've called down. We could walk."

"No, I want the car nearby, just in case."

The parking attendant pulls the Phaeton up in front of the hotel steps and hands Red the keys. "Have a wonderful evening, sir," he says.

Red slides his hand under the seat. The guns are still there. He has to remember never to do that again.

⁂

There are cars lined up on either side of Woodward Avenue. Red makes a U-turn and parks on the other side of the street. "In case we need to make a quick getaway."

They can hear the music playing and Sully starts humming along.

"That's a dumb song. 'Yes, We Have No Bananas'? What's that supposed to mean?"

Red stands on the sidewalk and studies the five-storey building. There are balconies all across the second floor. The buildings on either side butt up close but there's some open space. "You go in. I'm going to scout around. If anything happens, the balconies look like the best way out."

"We're going dancing, Red, not robbing a bank. You need to relax."

They walk across the street and push open the heavy front doors. The music is louder and Red can see the gigantic ballroom is filled with couples.

Standing in the doorway with Sully, he feels like he's in the stag line at St. Peter's Church Hall, face scrubbed, nails clean, hair slicked down. The girls, lined up, waiting to be asked to dance, their dresses pressed and starched, like the kewpies on display at the exhibition. On those Saturday nights, he always wondered if the girls got the same talk from the nuns as the boys got from the priests, the dire warnings about dancing too close, igniting the temptations of the flesh.

The ballroom is beautiful, vaulted ceiling and a huge pink dome. They climb the stairs to the balcony that circles the entire room. There must be one, maybe two thousand people dancing.

"I bet they take in a bundle at this joint," Red says.

"We aren't turning this into a job. Enjoy yourself for once. I think that dame over there is giving you the eye. Why don't you ask her to dance?"

"I've got a girl back in Toronto."

"You don't have to marry her, just give her a few whirls around the dance floor," Sully says smiling in the woman's direction.

"Jesus, Sully, now she's coming over."

The blond woman walks toward them, the smooth fabric of her dress sliding back and forth across her swaying hips.

"No need to look so frightened, boys," the woman says when she reaches their place at the wrought iron balustrade. "I'm just looking for a dance. I don't bite."

"That's good," Sully says, taking her arm.

"Unless, of course, the situation requires it."

Red scowls when Sully laughs too loudly at this silly joke. "I'm sorry, Miss, but my brother and I were just leaving."

"Brothers, huh, you two don't look that much alike."

"Different fathers," Sully says.

"Half-brothers then," the woman says, studying their faces. "I'm sure Mom wouldn't disapprove of you having just one dance. Two different fathers, she sounds like a fun lady."

"She was widowed," Red says, insulted at the insinuation on behalf of their imaginary mother.

"Come on, Norman, loosen up. I'm going to dance with this beautiful lady." Sully takes the woman's hand and walks toward the stairs down to the dance floor.

Red waits until he sees Sully and the blond woman dancing on the floor below and then he makes his way down the stairs to the exit for a smoke. He'd go back to the hotel but he doesn't trust Sully not to turn one dance into many dances or into more than just dancing.

The air outside is cool and he turns the lapels of his suit coat up to protect him from the chilly night. The music drifts through the glass windows at the back of the dance hall. He hears the crowd applaud as the orchestra starts to play a song about lost love that Babe liked to play on the Victrola at Carlton Street. He looks at the men and women shuffling across the polished wooden dance floor. Being here is starting to feel good.

From behind him comes the sound of a cornet. Red turns to see a young kid caressing his instrument, producing notes sweeter than the ones coming from the horn player on the stage inside. He finds himself humming along. He closes his eyes and tries to picture Babe's face. The sooner they put together a big stash of money, the sooner he can get her to come.

Inside, the crowd applauds again when the orchestra stops playing. Red applauds the young fellow with the slick-backed hair.

"That was beautiful. Where'd you learn to play like that?"

"My daddy taught me. He has a band back in PA. He plays the horn too."

"All my daddy ever taught me was how to cut tin. How old are you, kid?"

"Eighteen, this month."

When he was eighteen, he was doing his first stretch in Kingston Pen.

The orchestra starts up again and the kid cocks his ear to one side. "Hey, listen, you know what that's called? The 'Tin Roof Blues.' Must be playing it for you and your daddy."

The door to the ballroom opens and a young girl comes out.

"Come inside," she says. "They're letting your brother sit in with the band."

The girl holds the door open and all three stand at the back of the dance hall. The kid leans over and says, "That's my wife."

The girl looks about sixteen. These kids have everything he wants.

Red gazes at the swaying couples but Sully is nowhere to be seen. He picks his way through the dancers and the kid and his wife follow behind. As they get closer to the stage the kid grabs Red's coat. "That's my brother." Another wet-behind-the-ears boy with slicked back dark hair stands and plays his clarinet. As good as the kid was on the horn, his brother is just as good on the clarinet.

The brother finishes his solo and another man steps to the front of the stage and raises a trombone. Red has never heard this song before but he is starting to think he will never forget the 'Tin Roof Blues' because for the first time in years it feels like an ordinary night.

The kid leans over and whispers in his ear, "I'm better than that guy. Someday me and my brother are going to be famous."

Red wants to say, "Me and my friend, we're already famous."

The kid's hands slide an imaginary trombone while his young wife holds his cornet. She leans over and whispers in Red's ear, "They're trying to get a job here."

Once the solos are over, Red stands up to his full height trying to see across the crowd. Still no sight of Sully. There is a woman standing next to Red and he is almost tempted to ask her to dance. To pretend for one night that he is who he wants to be. But another man takes her hand, which is just as well. It probably wasn't a very good idea.

Red taps the kid on the shoulder and says, "I'm going to look for my friend."

It's hard to push his way through all the bodies moving to the band's rhythms. There's no sign of Sully. When he goes out the ballroom's back door, he finds Sully and the blond woman locked in an embrace.

"Art," he calls out, but Sully doesn't look away. The woman looks at him over Sully's shoulder. Just as Sully disentangles himself from the blond, the two young brothers come crashing through the doors.

"I said I'd do the talking."

"When were you planning on doing it? I didn't see much talking going on."

"You can't talk when the band is in the middle of a set."

"They were taking a break."

"No, they weren't."

"Yes, they were."

"It looked to me like they ..." the young wife starts to say.

"I don't care about the way it looked to you."

"Now boys," the blond woman says.

"Stay out of this," the brothers say in unison. They start to wrestle on the ground.

"Let's get out of here, Sully, before somebody calls the cops."

"Fight! Fight!" a tall man yells from the other side of the windows.

"I'm serious, Sul. We need to get the hell out of here."

The dancers start to push toward the back doors.

Red bends over and grabs the two brothers by their collars. "Quit the ruckus. Nobody's going to hire two junior assholes who get in a fight in the back of his dance hall. Smarten up."

He looks toward the hall again and seeing a large, stern-faced man who is too big for his suit walking across the dance floor toward them, loosens his grip and the two brothers fall back to the ground. "You boys'll get out of here, too, if you know what's good for you."

Red grabs Sully by the arm and heads back out to Woodward Avenue, the two brothers, the wife, and the blond woman following close behind. They cross the street and move behind a bread truck parked in front of a bakery.

"Where you wanna go now?" the blond woman says.

"Get rid of her," Red says tightening his grip on Sully's arm. But Sully says nothing. Panic spreads from Red's stomach up through his chest.

"Okay, folks," he says. "Nice to meet you all but me and my brother have to get back to our hotel."

"Where you stayin'?" the blond woman asks.

"The Statler," Sully says.

"Oh, very swanky," the cornet player says, pushing up the tip of his nose with his finger. "Real high class. I bet they have their own orchestra there."

"Well, you keep practisin', kid," Red says, "and maybe someday you'll get to play there, but right now we have to go. We're leavin' town first thing in the morning."

The blond woman smiles and gives Sully a kiss on the cheek. "Oh well, maybe next time you're passin' through." She pulls a lacy handkerchief out of her bosom, hands it to him, and then, to Red's great relief, turns and walks away.

Before something else starts, Red steps forward and shakes the older boy by the hand. "It's been a real treat to meet you and your brother and, of course, your beautiful wife, but we have to go."

"Okay, man. No need to panic. We'll take a hike. Keep cutting that tin." The boy raises his cornet in a salute.

"Why'd you say we were leaving tomorrow? Blondie and me were getting along real well." Sully holds her handkerchief up to his nose and takes a deep breath.

"Sully, unlike you, I never forget we are two escaped convicts on the run." He wonders when that won't be true.

They walk in silence back up Woodward to the Grand Circus. At the hotel elevator, Sully says, "Red, what were you going to do about the car? It's still back by the dance hall."

"Goddamn it, Sully, you are going to be the death of me."

35

THE MORNING LIGHT IS BRIGHTENING UP THE KITCHEN AND Hemingway sets his typewriter down on the table so he can enjoy the feeling of the sun's warm rays on his back. The baby is sleeping in the living room and Hadley is frying bacon and making him scrambled eggs. The smell of frying bacon always reminds him of being out in the woods, of trekking across Michigan with his pals or of hunting with his father. It wasn't about Michigan but two weeks ago he wrote about *la chasse* for the *Weekly*. That's what they call hunting in Europe. And he wrote about trout fishing in Europe. He can write about any damn thing that takes his fancy, like the old days. Readers like stuff about Europe. He wrote about the gargoyles on Notre Dame. There was a local piece too. Water levels have been falling in the Great Lakes. Four pieces in one edition. The next week it was six.

Ever since he walked into that alley off Bathurst Street, he's been restless. His brain going in many directions. He's been talking to himself sometimes. Hadley has caught him more than once. She thinks their money problems and the goings-on at the paper are still getting to him.

"Aren't you happy about the letter from Mr. O'Brien?" she asked him last night. "It took you a long time to write back. Why was that?"

"Because he asked if I had more stories and I don't have more stories," he'd said, ripping a page out of the Corona and throwing it in the wastepaper basket. "I have to keep writing for the *Star*. We need the money if we want to go back. I write so many pieces for the *Weekly*, they should call it the *Hemingway Weekly Star*."

Hadley laughed. "What are you writing about this week?"

"This week," he said, "it's just one very long piece, a very detailed study of bank robberies and what banks do to try and prevent them. I call it 'Bank Vaults versus Cracksmen.'"

"You just can't let it go, can you?"

One time Hadley caught him mumbling about building ladders, but he still hasn't told her about his encounter with Red.

"Let me get back to the task at hand," he'd said, pulling out one page and putting another sheet of paper into the typewriter.

✢✢

The baby starts to fuss and Hadley scurries from the kitchen to the little guy's side and the next thing he knows he has gotten up and is standing next to her. The baby stops crying, looks at them, and then starts to cry again. His face is bright crimson. He is getting himself in a state; his little body has gone rigid. Hadley carries him to the white rocking chair, unbuttons her dress, and slips her camisole off her shoulder. The baby begins to forage for her breast. That kid wants what he wants when he wants it.

He knows the feeling.

"Hemingway men aren't keen on routine," Hadley says with a wink.

The doctor told her routine was important but neither of them liked the idea. Hadley is tired of the every-four-hour feedings. She's not sure the baby cares for the schedule either. It's too rigid. Kind of like him at the *Star*, seven to midnight, seven to midnight. It's constant. Seventeen-hour days, more than he cares to count.

"Why can't babies eat when they're hungry, like everyone else," Hadley says, taking her eyes off the baby's face for a moment to look up at him.

Greg Clark thought he was crazy when Hemingway told him yesterday that he was thinking of resigning. Work on perfecting the *Star Weekly* style was Greg's advice. He doesn't get it. But Greg doesn't know what happened in the alleyway either. Hemingway hasn't told another living soul except the baby when they were alone. Hadley was down in the basement doing a washing. The baby was no help whatsoever with his dilemma.

No matter what Greg says, he doesn't want to perfect the *Star Weekly* style. He likes his own style just fine. So do they — they've published enough of his stuff. As he sits and watches Hadley and his son, he knows what he has to do. Just like the baby, he wants what he wants when he wants it.

Let the other aspiring novelists slave under Hindmarsh. He writes better than most of those guys and the *Star* knows it. Hell, he could count the real writers at the *Star* on his fingers and that includes him. Greg is definitely one and there is a young fellow down at the paper he likes. Writes very well. Stories. The kid's only twenty years old. Callaghan's his name, he's a student at the U of T.

Red reminded him of something he already knew. You have to go after what you want, full tilt. You don't have to be who they want you to be, who they tell you you are, or who they think you should be. That is bull. You've got to have the faith of your convictions, even if it scares the hell out of you. Some things, as Red said, are worth going over the wall for even if you might die or fall on your ass in the attempt.

He looks over at Hadley. "Hash," he says, "I've been thinking."

"You're going to resign, aren't you?"

⁂

Hadley approves of his letter of resignation. It is short, five lines to say he is going to leave effective January 1, 1924. A month's notice. That seems fair. Five lines cut down from the lengthy hand-scribbled draft setting out all his complaints. He notes in his resignation that it is only the staff reporter job he is leaving. Who knows? He might need more foreign correspondent work in Europe. "Good," Hadley said when he showed it to her. "No point in burning your bridges."

He addressed it to John Bone, the man who gave him his foreign correspondent's job at the *Star* in the first place, not His Royal Hindmarsh.

There, he's made a decision, solved one problem. He'll keep sitting on the other one. After all, the whereabouts of Red Ryan is not his responsibility.

36

RED ADMIRES THE LARGE CAR THAT PULLS UP TO THE CURVE. The Phaeton has been safely tucked away on a side street. He and Sully hop in. There are four other men, Frank's friends, guys he trusts.

The car makes its way through the streets of Detroit until they see the sign "Hamtramck." The city is like an island in the middle of Detroit.

The jobs have been divided up in advance, at their first meeting. One of the new guys will drive the car while the other five go inside. One assigned to the manager, one assigned to the tellers, one to handle the customers, one to stand guard, firearm at the ready, and one to scoop the money.

They drive past a place called the Venice Café. *It takes guts to open an Italian restaurant in a Polish town*, Red thinks. But from what Frank told him, the guy who owns it pretty much runs this place. The town is a mess: the mayor's on the take, the cops are on the take, and the Venice Café guy is getting protection money from all the blind pigs and brothels in town. The city council hates the mayor and the mayor hates the city council. The papers in Detroit are all over it.

"How much you reckon we'll get?" Sully asks one of their new partners in crime.

"Should be a pretty good haul."

"Five thousand?"

Their new partner laughs. "I don't get out of bed in the morning for five thousand bucks."

Sully and Red exchange looks. "How much are we talking? Seven or eight?" Red says.

"You guys haven't done much bank robbing, have you?"

"We're from Canada."

"Yeah, Frank mentioned something about that. Well, welcome to the USA, boys."

Red can tell that Sully is about to tell these guys that they've robbed lots of banks in the States but he silences him with a look. The deal is meet up, do the job, split the loot, get out of town.

Last night he wrote to Babe and told her what was happening, that it wouldn't be long. Then he wrote to his old war buddy Alex, now residing in St. Vincent prison, and offered to help him out if he needed it. The big help him out. Right out of St. Vincent. When you have money, you can make things happen.

They drive by the bank and all looks quiet. They circle the block, no sign of the police. Sully's doing the three-sixty scan now.

"Get ready," one of the guys says. "We move fast."

It's a sunny winter day. The windows of the bank reflect the light back onto the street. A woman with a baby carriage comes out the front door and Sully says, "That's good," under his breath. "I'm glad she's gone."

One of the guys slips out of the car and walks by the bank. He makes a signal with his hand, holds up four fingers, meaning there are four customers in the bank.

Red's heart starts to beat as it always does. The driver pulls the car up beside the front door. They know what it looks like because the gang went on a scouting mission a couple of days ago. Red and Sully studied the crude drawing, the same way they studied the one Red drew of the Bank of Nova Scotia.

The main guy gives the signal and they all leave the car, one, two, three, four, five, all in a row. Red pushes the heavy oak door open.

"This is a stick-up. Don't move and you won't get hurt."

A woman over to Red's left grasps for the counter as she falls to the ground. Just as well she has passed out, no trouble from her. The man assigned to the manager sticks a gun in his face as he emerges from his office.

The two tellers look terrified. One of them is shaking. Good. Terrified and compliant is what they want.

"Hands in the air," the one assigned to guard screams. "I don't want anyone reaching for no buzzers."

The two young women do as they are told. Red vaults over the counter. "Open the cash drawer," he says to the tellers, "then stand back."

As his accomplice comes over and begins to scoop out the money, Red moves the women, prodding them in the back with the barrel of his gun, until they arrive at the manager's office.

"You are going to open the vault."

When the manager resists, Red grabs one of the young women.

"What's your name?" Red says.

A new look of fear comes across her face. "Barbara," she says in a whisper.

"What?"

"Barbara."

He turns to the manager. "Do you want Barbara to get hurt?"

"You won't get away with this."

"That wasn't the question. I said, 'Do you want Barbara to get hurt?' That's what's going to happen if you don't open the vault."

The manager's face turns white. "All right, all right."

As they leave the office, Red says, "No funny business or Barbara and her little friend here will be in big trouble."

Now it's the manager's hands that are trembling as he enters the combination for the vault. The first attempt doesn't work and Red pokes his gun in the small of the man's back. "We're not stupid, open her up."

"He's stalling for time," Sully says.

"Better not be because if any coppers show up here they won't get a good reception and you, my friend, will be bleeding out on the floor."

The manager hunches over the lock and they hear the tumblers falling. The women gasp. He reaches up, turns the wheel, and pulls the heavy steel door open. As it swings by him, Red can see his reflection in the polished metal, standing there, gun in hand. A real bank robber.

The accomplice pushes the manager inside. "Money and fast." Red keeps his gun hand pointed at the women and holds the open leather bag with the other. His accomplice stuffs in stacks of wrapped bills.

They escort the manager back to his office and another guy brings in the tellers. The black leather bag is bulging with money.

They tie everyone's hands behind their backs and run out the front door, jumping into the waiting car.

Three blocks away another car is waiting and they ditch the first car and jump into the second.

Soon they have left Hamtramck and are cruising down Woodward Avenue toward the river. The driver turns down a side street and in behind a warehouse. They sit and count the money. Between the tellers and the vault, it amounts to eleven thousand dollars.

"Hey," Red says, scooping up their share of the take, "it's been great doing business with you but you gotta get me back to my car."

-+ +-

"That's thirty-six hundred dollars between the two of us, Red, almost thirty-seven hundred," Sully says, rolling down the window of the Phaeton. "Enough to travel back out west in style."

"Goodbye, Detroit. Next stop, Minneapolis. When we get there, we'll find a nice place to stay, an apartment maybe. I'll write to Babe and tell her that's where we'll be."

"We aren't driving all night again, are we?"

"You can sleep in the back seat, I'll drive."

As they reach the shore of Lake Michigan, Red suddenly slams his hand on the steering wheel. "Damn it, Sully, I forgot to check the post office before we left. Too late now. I'm not going back. I'll get my brother to do it."

"But speaking of mail, Red, I have something to tell you."

"Listen to that engine, man. It's singing to us."

"Remember Irene?"

"The girl from the Chinese restaurant? Yeah, what about her?"

"I've been writing to her. I told her we'd be coming back."

37

William St. Pierre Hughes, Superintendent of Penitentiaries, paces his office while his friend, Special Inspector Walter Duncan, sheds his winter coat.

"I enjoyed my walk over from the finance department," Duncan says, sitting in the chair next to the window. "There's something about these cold, crisp Ottawa mornings. The sun is shining, the sky is blue. Better than a trip to Florida."

St. Pierre Hughes stops his pacing. "I need your help, Walter. I haven't spent thirty years in the prison service to be made a fool of by this band of hooligans."

Duncan twists the end of his handlebar moustache and waits for his friend to go on.

St. Pierre Hughes slides a pile of papers across his desk. "The Toronto Police have been trying to catch Red Ryan and his gang since they robbed that Bank of Nova Scotia. The RCMP sent notices to police forces all over North America, England, Australia, and beyond, without much result."

"What is it now, three months since they scaled your wall, Bill?"

"Not funny, Walter. Look in that file. Copies of letters. The Toronto police have been intercepting letters, but when they try and follow up ... nothing. I'm starting to wonder —"

"If they have a man on the inside?"

"All I know is it isn't working. I thought of you, Walter, because you seem to get along well with the U.S. authorities."

"We do have a good working relationship with them at Finance. The Americans want Canada to make bootlegging a crime."

"Good luck on that one." St. Pierre Hughes laughs. "Do they want the country to go bankrupt?"

Duncan takes a sip of the sherry that St. Pierre Hughes's secretary puts down in front of him as the clock on the mantle chimes twelve.

"Do you think you could work with the Toronto police again?"

"Where do they make this stuff, Hughes, in the basement at Kingston Pen?"

"I'm not in the mood for jokes, Walter. Seriously, how do you think you'd get along with the Toronto boys?"

Duncan smiles at his old friend. It would feel damn good to catch these bastards when Chief Dickson and his Toronto crew could not.

"I want you to take over the investigation. I want it out of the hands of the locals. Rob Tucker, Deputy Warden at the Pen, would be a good man to help you out. He's ex-RCMP. You'd have a connection there."

"And I'm to be the connection to Dickson and Toronto?

"It's your U.S. connections I'm interested in. Toronto can just fall in line. They're too focused on that damn bank robbery. Red Ryan and his gang escaped from my prison before they robbed that bank."

"Give me a day to think it over."

"Good. While you do that, I'll draft a letter to your boss requesting a secondment."

Duncan downs the last of his sherry and stands to shake St. Pierre Hughes's hand. Capturing that bunch would be another milestone in the redemption journey of Walter Duncan, former Inspector of Detectives, Toronto Police.

There's a calendar on the wall, a lovely scene of Ottawa in the snow. It's Wednesday, December the fifth. Tucker, from what he can recall, is a good man. Hughes just gave him an early Christmas present.

⁂

Red Ryan's a man on a mission that's for certain. No thought about who he takes down with him. Surely, he knew any guard that helped him would get fired or punished. Probably knew it better than they did. St. Pierre Hughes told him he had people looking at the guards' bank accounts almost immediately.

The rumour is some ex-con went to work for Red's brother in Toronto. He wasn't too good at the bootlegging business. He ended up getting arrested. Red's brother goes bail but the guy jumps it and ends up back, guess where, in Kingston Pen. Now the brother's got a man inside. Clever, Duncan has to admit. Money wouldn't have been a problem. Prohibition is making a lot of people rich. The amount he's heard bandied about is eight thousand dollars spread out among a few guards and some people on the outside.

⁂

"I want you to drive me out to College Street," Walter Duncan says to his new assistant, Deputy Warden Tucker. "Doesn't one of Red's brothers live around there too?"

"Yes, sir, north of College, on Lansdowne."

"The one they suspect was wrapped up in all this?"

"No, this one walks the straight and narrow."

"Okay, then just take a drive by College Street. Not too fast. Not too slow. Don't want to arouse suspicion."

Duncan leans forward when Tucker shifts down. Through the corner of his eye, he studies 1302 College Street. According to St. Pierre Hughes, the Toronto cops found out Red has been writing to a Babe Mowrer at this address, where the broad's mother lives. The post office seizes the letters, gets the kettle on the boil, opens them up, types up a copy for the police, then sends them on their way. The police thought they were going to bring Red down in Detroit, but he never showed up.

"The P.O. giving the letters to the Toronto police has to stop, Tucker, agreed?"

"Agreed, sir."

Duncan starts scanning the street. He doesn't see any sign of a police presence. Although, if they're doing their job right, they should be invisible. But not to a fellow cop.

"Let the post office know I'm in charge now. I want copies of every letter."

"Yes, sir."

"They are to keep it under their hat, agreed?"

"Yes, sir."

"We don't want anybody getting nervous or jealous."

"I understand, sir. The letters are to come to you. This is clearly a federal matter."

"I'm not sure the locals see it that way."

Tucker pulls over and lets the streetcar go by. He creeps across Dufferin and slowly drives by the house. It's an ordinary looking place, the same as thousands of houses in the city, a large dormer, a wide front porch.

"In some ways, Robbie, I can't believe Red is that dumb to be writing these letters."

"Maybe he's lonely, sir."

Duncan laughs. "With all the money he's collecting perhaps he should pay someone to make him feel a little less lonely."

That's the thing with most criminals, Duncan thinks. *They believe they are smarter than they really are.* Wily, yes, but smart? Not always. But who knows, maybe the letters are decoys. God knows Red's tried that one before.

"We'll catch 'em, sir. I have every confidence."

"First, we have to find them, Robbie, my lad. First, we have to find them."

38

Red studies the plaster ceiling on the landing while Sully says good night to the girl they met in the Chinese restaurant. He tries to close his ears to the whispered words, the giggles, and the sound of kisses. He can still smell her perfume a flight of stairs away. It smells like roses or lilies. Some kind of flowers. He looks out the window down onto the street. The marble windowsill is cool to his touch. The walls in the stairway are painted a soft grey. The floors are so clean you could eat off them, as his mother would say. There are pictures of mountains and lakes hanging on the walls. You can tell Irene is a respectable girl, living a respectable life here on Second Avenue, in Minneapolis.

Last week, after the Detroit job, he wrote a letter to Babe.

> Hello sweetheart,
> It was great to meet my brother's friends in Detroit. Things are going well. His friend George Ramburg has some great business ideas. He's a real go-getter. He wanted me to stick around but time to head west, maybe Minneapolis.
>
> I miss you.
>
> XO

He wonders what she's doing tonight, back in Toronto, back on Carlton Street.

-+-+-

At last he hears the apartment door close and Sully comes whistling down the stairs. It was nice of Irene to invite both of them over for dinner. He hadn't had a home-cooked meal for a while. It was good. Roast beef with mashed potatoes. Apple pie. So good that Sully burps as Red pushes the door open into the night air.

"Not much snow for December," Sully says.

Red studies the two- and three-storey apartment houses that line Second Avenue. There is a park down the street. The tall trees sway gently in the winter wind. They must have been there for a hundred years.

"Irene is my kind of girl. She's got class. She wants me to go to a play with her tomorrow night."

Sully kicks a can across the street. The streets are clear and dry. It's been so unusually warm the snow has been melting as fast as it falls. "I'm serious about Irene. Ever since I met her, I can't stand to be away from her."

"You met her? I was the one who chatted her up in that Chinese place."

"I've been thinking Red, we've been getting pretty good hauls and maybe we should ..."

"You're not talking about going straight again, are you?"

"Irene says she might be able to get me a job at the place where her brother works. Or maybe at the Athletic Club."

"Let's talk about this tomorrow, Sul. I'm tired."

The grounds of the park are raised above street level. As they walk along, they can see into the apartments across the way. Lights glow from behind the curtains in the front windows. Red can see shadows, a woman here, a man there, families moving about in their parlours. The crunch of the gravel reminds him of shuffling around in the prison yard when it was time for exercise. The memory makes him shiver. "Stay away from the light, Sully," he says as they near a lamppost.

In one building someone has left a window open despite the cool evening. "Listen. Can you hear that? A piano. My mom used to play at home and my dad played the mandolin if he hadn't been drinking too much. We'd all sing along."

"Irene certainly can cook, I'll say that for her."

"I don't know, Sully. There's more to life than cooking. Babe can't boil water. Do you want to live in Minneapolis for the rest of your life?"

"Fresh start, south of the border."

"What about your boys?"

Sully stops, leans against a tree, and lights a cigarette. "They hardly know me. I've been inside most of their lives."

Red watches as a car drives slowly along Second Avenue and rounds the corner of the park. "Put that thing out. I don't want to draw anyone's attention."

Sully drops the burning cigarette on the ground and grinds it out with the toe of his shoe.

"I like the way things are now, Red. I like how we look. Look at the shine on that shoe. Look at your car. It's like you said before, we look respectable. I like having a nice girl."

You can never argue with a guy who thinks he's in love.

"You're jealous because I have a girl and Babe is still back in Toronto."

The car passes and when its tail lights disappear around a corner, Sully lights up another cigarette. "Red?" he says, after his first draw.

"What?"

"Do you think the cops are tailing us? It's been over two months."

"I dunno."

"What about the feds?"

"Ha, they never had a clue. I hear they're too busy investigating the guards."

"Do you think Ed talked?"

"Maybe. I hope not. But he only knows about how we planned to bust out. It's the guards who ought to be nervous about Ed, not us."

They come to the place where they parked the car. Never leave your vehicle near your destination, unless you're robbing a bank.

"Let's go, Sully" Red says, opening the Phaeton's smooth, shiny door. He loves this car. It's fast and powerful. The engine roars to life and he heads back toward Lake and Park. They're renting the second floor in an old house. Not as nice a neighbourhood as Irene's place but better than a hotel or a prison cell.

39

WALTER DUNCAN STANDS BACK AND LETS ROB TUCKER WALK ahead of him through the door of Minneapolis City Hall.

"Welcome, welcome," Minneapolis Chief of Police Frank Brunskill says. "Please have a seat."

"We appreciate your co-operation," Duncan says. "These boys have been leading the local police on a merry chase." He likes to remember that Robbie is ex-RCMP.

"But you aren't an officer, are you?"

"Inspector Duncan has a great deal of experience working on both sides of the border."

Why thank you, Robbie, my lad, for jumping to my defence.

"Inspector Duncan is very experienced," Rob Tucker says.

"Yes, so I've heard."

Duncan feels all the muscles in his body start to tighten. The chief sounds like he is a notch away from saying ... it takes one to know one.

Robbie comes to his rescue again. "It would be very helpful to meet the detectives who are going to assist us."

"We've already been working on it," Brunskill says. "We've put surveillance on all the banks in the city."

"Banks?" he and Robbie say in unison.

"Yes. They've robbed a bank here too."

"I thought it was in St. Paul. Is that part of your territory?" Duncan says.

"We are most anxious to meet the team that is going to help us." God bless Robbie, doing his best to keep this meeting from heading into rough waters.

"We haven't shared everything with you," Duncan says. "There is some reluctance to put everything in writing just in case there are any leaks."

Brunskill looks offended. "There won't be any leaks at this end."

"It's just a precaution, sir," Robbie says. "My superior, Warden Ponsford, at the penitentiary, is having all relevant correspondence come directly to him rather than through the regular channels."

"Well, let's get my boys in here," says Chief Brunskill.

While Brunskill is out of the room, Rob Tucker turns to face Duncan. "Don't let him get to you, sir. You've been a police officer. He's just sussing you out."

"He's not getting to me. He better put his best men on it."

Brunskill comes back in, followed by four men. He introduces them as Detectives Meehan, Marxen, Forby, and Lally. It is clear from the beginning that Meehan is the man in charge. "Detective Meehan, like you, Inspector Duncan, has worked on investigations outside of formal police work."

"Got my start working for the railways," Meehan says.

"I bet he's knocked a few heads together," Duncan says under his breath to Rob Tucker. "Pleased to meet you," he says to Meehan, extending his hand to the middle-aged man.

"Likewise," Meehan says, pumping his hand with a grip so tight that Duncan concludes this is not so much a handshake as a power display.

"I've arranged for you to have a room so you can brief my men," Brunskill says.

"Yes," says Meehan. "I want to hear what you've got."

"We think our boy may be heading here from out west."

Billy Meehan runs his hand down his pasty cheeks as if he's stroking a beard and stares first at Duncan and Tucker and then looks over at the other three detectives. "Oh, you do, do you? Well, we think otherwise."

Rob Tucker reaches down and grabs his leather valise, packed full of letters and memos that have been flying between Ottawa, Toronto, Detroit, and numerous other places. "We have these," he says, laying the letters out on the table. Red to Babe, Red to his old pal, Alex Courtney, Red to his brother. "If he tells them where he's going, we think the deal is they write back to General Delivery. This is the most recent one."

Al Marxen reaches out and picks up Red's last letter to Babe. "Minneapolis, I see. General Delivery. That would be the main post office, Third and Washington."

Meehan nods but he doesn't pick up the letter or any of the documents. "Okay, Duncan, we know what to do."

40

If you visit the Hemingways' apartment, you take something with you when you go. They'll be breaking their lease. As December rolls on, more and more of their possessions disappear, hidden under coats, packed in hat boxes, wrapped in blankets. Sometimes they are just brazenly carried down the stairs and out the front door. Hadley said if she could find some way to do it, she would keep her little white rocking chair where she nurses the baby. "Leaving that behind," she said, "hurts."

From everything Hemingway hears at the paper, Red did exactly what he said he was going to do — went for one last big haul in the States, added another notch to his belt, another chapter to that book he wants someone to write. The bank robbery was in Detroit so what does it matter that Red was on Bathurst Street two nights before? It's old news, resolves his dilemma. He'll concentrate on earning the money they need, wherever he can, to get the hell out. Right after he resigned, he bought tickets on the *Antonia* in January.

Last week the euphoria of his resignation wore off and the practicalities set in. Hadley was upset about George Breaker's last letter, although she refuses to admit it. George said he will explain everything to them in February, in Paris. That's no good. They need to know what their money situation is now. "It must be some kind of misunderstanding," Hadley keeps saying. She often sits and reads everything that has passed between her and George, looking to see if there is some past unintentional slight that now has caused him to ignore her questions. What is going on with their investments?

It makes Hemingway furious. He sat down with a sharp pencil. There is money missing. It's all highly suspicious.

When he was young, stupid, and about to be married, he worked for this place called the Co-operative Commonwealth. He thought he was lucky to get the job. There were hundreds of thousands of veterans out of work.

It was a newsletter for farmers, widows, and the small-town businessmen who invested in the Co-operative Society of America. He was the writer-editor. It was hack writing and easy money.

Whatever article was needed, he produced: the high cost of shipping cowhides on your own, the high quality of the products in the co-op store, the priceless bond of the co-operative brotherhood.

But the principals had set up a phoney securities company and were siphoning off all the dough. Like he said to Hadley, "Not all the crooks are on the inside. One is married to your best friend."

"Another one escaped from Kingston Penitentiary," she said, "but for some reason, to you he's a hero."

* *

He has decided to go to Oak Park at Christmas without Hadley and the baby, to say a quick goodbye. She thinks it's mean not to let his family meet the baby when they are taking him so far away.

"We should all go. We'll be fine," she said.

He shook his head. "We can't risk it, Hash."

"Your parents said they'd pay for it."

"It's not about the money."

But it's partly about the money because soon they won't have any. He stops working at the end of December. That's two weeks away. They will be living off his wits and what is left of Hadley's trust fund. But the trust fund is up in the air and so far, his wits have not been producing much.

"Ernest," Hadley said, unwilling to let the matter drop.

"I'm going alone. What if something happens to your milk supply? What will we do on the ship?"

"This isn't about the baby's welfare," she said. "It's about you and your parents. They've been so kind and you won't let them see their grandchild. They'll have milk on the ship. We'll give him a bottle."

"No!" He jumped to his feet. "It's not safe. Haven't you read that book the government gave you?"

"Stop shouting, you're going to upset the baby," she said, looking up at him. "I read and re-read that book to try and find out when the nursing pain might stop."

He found the book in a drawer and stood over her, flipping through the pages until he found what he wanted. "Read that," he said.

The baby, distracted by all the commotion, had stopped nursing and bawled red-faced in Hadley's arms. She moved him up on to her shoulder and started rubbing his back. "You read it to me if it's so important."

"It's the father's job to understand about breastfeeding: about the benefits, about the dangers of not." He took a deep breath, "A baby could die."

"Die!" Hadley wrapped her arm a little tighter around the warm, sweet-smelling bundle. "What are you talking about? He's not going to die."

"No, he's not," he shouted, "because he's breastfed. It's an eight-to-one ratio, Hash. Five times as many bottle-fed babies die before they are a year old."

The baby started crying again. Hadley grabbed the book and threw it on the floor. "I don't want you talking about babies dying. He's beautiful and healthy. I will never let anything happen to him."

"I'm just going for a day. You can't do that with a baby."

He thinks sometimes that they are trying to kill him before he can get out of here, all of them: Hadley, George Breaker, the tiny creature to whom he now owes his allegiance, Ezra, Greg, the *Star*.

The *Weekly* is taking up all of his time. He is writing features, he's writing Christmas pieces, night and day. Not just one piece, always two, and this Saturday, four.

Gertrude wrote a review of his little book and called his writing intelligent but he doesn't feel intelligent. If he was that goddamn intelligent he wouldn't have come here in the first place. He had the ring in his hand and he opened his fingers and let it drop away.

Hadley's refuge is her piano. She plays Ravel and Brahms and tries to stay in a happy frame of mind. She does believe in him, he knows that. But it feels like they are walking off a very high cliff.

What if they are making another mistake? Greg Clark thought he was crazy to give up a good job. He got upset and said some very unkind things about Greg, who has been nothing but a good friend. He's nervous but he won't admit it.

Red made it. He has a cashmere coat and a fancy car. Red's voice is in his ear. "You're just quitting a job you hate. It's not like someone is going to be hunting you down with a gun, pal. If they don't want to give you a chance, take it."

41

Red can smell the perfume of the woman ahead of him in line at the post office. Like roses, like his mother's garden in June, like Babe, like Irene's the other night when they had dinner. Every time the woman shifts the parcel she is carrying from one hip to the other, the scent floats over him again: summer roses on a cold day.

He reaches up to brush the melting snow off his new fedora. His elbow touches the back of the woman's fur coat and she turns around. "Sorry," he says. "I just bought this."

"Very nice," she says and turns to face the front of the line again.

George Ramburg is his name today. He's hoping there's a letter from Babe.

He shouldn't have come so late in the day on a Friday. Everyone has an armful of parcels they are mailing for the holidays, only ten more days before Christmas. The line is long. Half of Minneapolis is in here.

There's a squad of janitors mopping the floor, moving back and forth across the marble with brooms wider than an elephant's grin. Over in the corner, a group of painters in overalls studies the ceiling. The place is a cavern; the ceiling must be fifty feet above them.

The line moves slowly but at long last the lady in the fur coat places her parcel in front of the clerk. It has a large red sticker that says "Fragile," and the clerk gently places it on the post office scale. And just as the clerk says, "That will be seventy-five cents please," Red hears a shuffle behind him. When he turns to see what is going on, one of the painters locks his gaze on him, then the painter's eyes move to the woman in the fur coat and then along the rest of the post office line. Red realizes the painter is judging the distance. His heart starts to pound as he reaches into his pocket and puts his hand on his gun. Another painter starts to walk in his direction. Red knows now that these painters aren't painters, these painters are cops. He's heard things about the cops in Minneapolis. They're tough.

The lady in the fur coat finishes her business and shifts to the right, resting her pocketbook on the marble counter. The painter-cop closest to him reaches out and touches his elbow. "Don't move, Ryan." Red backs away, bumping into the woman in the coat. She steps aside in another cloud of rose-scented perfume.

Red faces the cop. They both pull their weapons and fire. Somehow, he misses and so does the cop. But then from somewhere off to his right comes the sound of gunfire and something rips through his arm, a sweet, painful burn. It knocks him down and when Red looks up there are four revolvers pointing at his chest.

The four policemen grab him and shackle his hands and feet. Cops appear from everywhere, holding back the Christmas crowd.

They move him toward the door. Through the glass he can see Sully waiting outside beside the car, looking down at the street, hat tilted to hide his face. As they drag him outside, Red calls out, "Go. Take the loot, get out of town."

Sully looks up and then takes off on foot, followed by a couple of cops, guns drawn. Shots ring out. Red sees Sully flinch. Looks like he might have been hit in the face. But he looks back, hand at his nose, and keeps on running around the corner with two policemen in hot pursuit.

"Never you mind." A cop puts his hand on Red's head and pushes him into the police car. Just as the cop's about to slam the door shut, more shots ring out. Then Red hears, "Officer down, officer down," as one cop comes running back from around the corner.

The one in charge of his arrest slams the car door, rattles the handle, and pounds his fist against the window. "Your buddy shot a police officer," he screams. "Every patrolman in the city will be looking for him."

42

HEMINGWAY STANDS ON THE BALCONY LOOKING OUT ACROSS the ravine. There is a strong wind blowing from the west although the weather has turned warm for mid-December. But the warm days are short and the dark nights are long. The clouds roll over his head and follow along the ravine that days ago lost its glorious colour and now is nothing but workmanlike shades of rust and brown. He hears Hadley moving around inside and goes in to wish her good Saturday morning.

By some miracle the baby is still sleeping and Hadley has already made coffee and collected the paper from the hall. It sits on the kitchen table. The bold black headline states Berlin will have to pay if given control of the Ruhr. He may have written a seven-part series in the spring about Germany and France's fight over the Ruhr, but the story doesn't hold his interest anymore.

He feels irritated today and he can't put his finger on why. It feels like something is wrong. He should be happy but time seems to be dragging its feet. Knowing he will be a free at the end of the month has almost made things worse, not better. Despite writing for the *Weekly* most of the time, working for the *Star* in general seems as unbearable as ever. And Ezra is angry because

Hemingway's late with his copy for Ford Madox Ford's new magazine, the *Transatlantic Review*.

He is confronted with the one thing he had been complaining he lacked: time. Now he has to deliver.

The weather forecast sits where it always sits at the bottom of the *Star*'s first page. The warm December will continue. The baby cries and Hadley pours his coffee before she scurries off to answer Mr. Bumby's latest demand for her breast.

He opens the paper and the picture of four men on page two hits him like a strong left hook. It's Red goddamn Ryan and his fellow escapees. It's the pictures from the wanted poster that he carried in the pocket of his tweed jacket for weeks, months.

Red Ryan captured. Where?

In a post office in Minneapolis late yesterday afternoon.

The article describes Red as "resourceful, brainy, with cool nerve."

Hemingway can see him standing in the dark alleyway off Bathurst Street in his cashmere coat, tall and strong. Handing out life advice to this disheartened wannabe writer whining about his existence.

Suddenly, it feels like the walls of the apartment are closing in around him. He folds the newspaper under his arm and calls out to Hadley, "I'm going out for a walk."

The four flights of stairs seem to echo his mood, descending round and round, down and down. He cannot bear to think of Red beaten down and trapped, clutching the cold bars of a cell. He walks behind the building and half slides down into the ravine. His pants are wet and the jacket he grabbed as he walked out the door is too light. The clouds block out the rising sun and he shivers as he walks along the ravine's beaten-down path.

When he's travelled about half a mile, the sun comes out and he finds a fallen log to sit on and read the story again.

Life has given Red a sucker punch right to the gut. Life will take you down just when you thought you were on the way up.

He hears Ezra saying, "Come on, Hem, I can't believe this Ryan guy didn't think getting caught was a possibility."

"Maybe he did but I didn't." A young boy walking with a small black dog says, "What, Mister?" Hemingway waves him on. He thought Red was home free.

He reads through the details and then reads them again. A name jumps out at him. Walter Duncan. Why does he know that name? Then he remembers. It was the day the Toronto cops contemplated restricting press access. The doorman at the King Eddy told him there was some ancient history. "Look it up," the doorman had said. "Duncan was the chief of detectives. He ended up resigning."

The paper says the Penitentiary Service only brought Duncan in on the case a week ago. Being a detective must be like being a writer. You have to fall right into your character to figure out his next move. It appears Walter Duncan did just that.

He stares down at Red's face. Red has had the thing he wanted most taken away from him. Freedom. The story says Red's downfall was writing letters. The police were intercepting them. Was this the investigative tactic the cops didn't want to disclose? The story says Red gave away what he was about to do or worse, where he was going to do it.

"Never mind him," he hears Ezra asking. "What is your next move? We aren't going to sit around forever in Paris waiting for your copy."

Why the hell did Red do that? Was he lonely? Was he bragging? He was doing pretty well from the looks of him that frigid night just two weeks ago. "Pride cometh before the fall," his mother always said. Was that it?

Life can have a cruel way of shooting you down when you're flying high. He sure as hell knows that. You are in Paris, you're hanging around with James and Ezra, Gertrude and Alice, they are even starting to publish your stuff. Then, change of plans. Hadley is expecting a child. You feel you should get a real job, for a year at least. The *Star* was too easy a place to do that.

That *should* have got him three months of hell at the *Toronto Daily Star*. Precious time lost from his writing career. The thing he wanted the most, to write, taken away from him. And it's not proving that easy to get it back.

Red's downfall feels like a bad omen. It's unsettling. He doesn't like it one goddamn bit.

43

INSPECTOR WALTER DUNCAN PULLS THE CURTAIN OF THE window in his hotel room aside and looks out at the city of Minneapolis. They got him. St. Pierre Hughes'll be glad to hear that. It didn't take long.

He starts to compose the telegram he knows he will never send. It's not to St. Pierre Hughes in Ottawa, but to Dickson, head of the Toronto police. "I got your man for you STOP No need to thank me STOP"

There's a knock on the door and when he opens it Rob Tucker is standing there, hat in hand. "They have a lead on Sullivan."

"Sit down, Robbie. Have a drink. The sun's almost over the yardarm. What's going on?" If they get Sullivan too, the feather in his cap will be even larger.

"A cabbie reported that he drove a fellow to the Athletic Club, where he picked up a blond."

"What makes them think it was our guy?"

"The cabbie said the fare caught his attention because he kept dabbing his nose. It looked like it was bleeding. He didn't think anything of it but when he read the reports of the shootout near the post office, he thought this guy might be the one the cops are looking for."

"Who's the blond?"

"According to the Athletic Club, her name's Irene Adams. She's a waitress in their dining room."

"Got anything on her?"

"Nope, she's clean. Meehan's bringing her in."

⁂

The Minneapolis detectives escort a young woman into an interview room at headquarters. "She looks like a decent enough girl, Tucker," Duncan says. "How'd she get mixed up with these two?"

Through the glass Duncan watches as the detectives speak with her. He can only imagine what is happening, the pressure that is being put on this probably innocent young woman. The cops stand up and loom over her. She raises her hands to her face and wipes tears from her eyes. But in the end, because Duncan has done it so many times himself, he can tell that his two Minneapolis associates have beaten her down. The cop he has come to call Billy pulls out a handkerchief and hands it to her as she starts to rise.

The door opens and Billy Meehan escorts the young woman to the front entrance of the central police station. Once she's outside Billy says, "Tail her," to his fellow detective.

Meehan comes over to where they are sitting. "It's him all right. She knows both of them. Norman and Arthur Miller, just a couple of salesmen travelling the Midwest. Sullivan's been writing to her from all over the place."

"Isn't he married?" Rob Tucker asks. The three other cops burst out laughing.

"Oh, Robbie." Walter Duncan shakes his head.

Tucker stands up and squares his shoulders. "You let her go?"

Meehan pulls out his revolver and slaps it against the palm of his hand. "Your boy Sullivan hit one of our men square in the chest. They had him trapped in a store. He shot his way out. Jumped right over our man lying bleeding in the street to get away."

"The young lady's going to call him," Detective Forbes says. "Invite him over."

"And when loverboy shows up," Meehan says, "we'll grab him."

44

WHEN HEMINGWAY ARRIVES AT THE *STAR* LATE MONDAY morning, the place is abuzz with news of the capture. From all he can see, nobody knows too much right now. Apparently, a cop was shot when they tried to capture Red's accomplice. Was that the guy he saw with Red in New York? They say the cop might die. Red's accomplice got away.

He picks up the morning edition and turns to the travel section. Maybe they should get out of here sooner in case fate decides to jump up and ruin all of his plans, like it did to Red. There are ships leaving earlier for Europe but sailings right before Christmas are expensive. That's not going to help their bottom line. They are saving as much as they can for Paris. He had four pieces in the *Weekly*: "European Nightlife," "Goiter and Iodine," one about Americans, and one about Canadians. For next Saturday he needs to write even more. No matter what's happened to Red he has to keep going. And there's his parents and the younger kids. He needs to make the trip back to Oak Park even if it's just for a day.

The morning passes into afternoon without any more news. He sits in the city room tapping his pencil on a pad of yellow paper. Next week's edition will be right before Christmas. He can usually write a thousand words about anything, but the words aren't coming. He can't stop thinking about Red.

The reporters have started a game of poker in a corner of the city room but when they call him to come over, he says he doesn't want to play. With every round they get louder and louder. The paper says they are having a warm spell in Minneapolis, record-breaking.

At two o'clock he decides to go home. He heads toward the stairs and, as he reaches the bottom of the second flight, the door above him flies open and bangs against the plaster wall. Greg's voice, "Hem, Hem," echoes through the metal stairwell. "Wait up. The guys told me you'd just left."

He leans against the wall and waits. When Greg arrives at the second-floor landing, his eyes are blazing.

Hemingway sits down on the stairs and looks up at his friend. For Greg, the news about Red's capture is just newshound exciting. For him, Red's capture is a demonstration of how fast and how loud the gods can laugh in your face.

Greg sits beside him on the stairs. He's a good friend. He has the clear blue eyes of a teller of truth. "More news about your friends, the bank robbers."

What is it? Maybe Red couldn't take it. Did he kill himself? The thought makes him feel sick. He still sees Red standing in the alleyway in his cashmere coat, looking like a million bucks, taunting him to get off his ass and write if that's what he thinks he was born to do.

"I've got to get back home. Hadley's trying to finish everything up."

"Don't you want to know?" Greg says.

"No."

"What is it with you and that guy? Journalists are supposed to be objective."

"Well, maybe that's a sign I wasn't meant to be a journalist. I'm not objective. If something terrible has happened to Red, if the cops have beat the crap out of him, I don't want to know."

Greg gets up and turns to head back up the stairs. "Okay, fine. You go home, Hem. Finish packing. I'm going back to work. But you and I both know you're going to read the paper when it comes out."

45

RED STANDS UP AS THE BEEFY DETECTIVE ENTERS HIS CELL. IT'S Meehan, the man who shot him in the shoulder at the post office.

"Good morning, Mr. Ryan," Meehan says. "How's the place where we nicked you?"

"It's feeling better," Red says, touching his wound.

"You'll be seeing Sullivan today," Meehan says.

Damn, Red thinks, *they got Sully.* He looks at the cop. The self-satisfied son of a bitch is almost grinning. Red would like to knock the stupid half-smirk off of Detective Meehan's face.

"Is he down at the station?" Red asks, trying to look past Meehan. "Is he up here in the cells?"

"No," Meehan says, "he's over at the morgue."

Red puts his hand out looking for the wall of his cell, then sits down on his bed, "In the morgue?"

"Yep, your buddy's dead. The officer he shot when he was trying to escape just might make it though. Thanks for asking."

Sarcastic bastard. Red clenches his fists trying to decide whether it just might be worth it, no matter what happens, if he punched Meehan right in the mouth.

The detective pulls a set of handcuffs out of his suit coat pocket. "Get up. We need you to come and identify the body."

Red slowly gets to his feet and holds out his hands and Meehan snaps the handcuffs on and puts shackles around his ankles.

"I bet you're wondering how we caught him."

"Doesn't matter if he's dead." Red feels a knot the size of a bowling ball forming in his stomach. He doesn't want to hear about Sully being shot in the street like a dog.

Meehan gives him a shove toward the open cell door. "It was that woman he's been seeing, the cute little blond. She says she knows you too, Mr. Miller."

At the mention of their alias, Red feels the knot grow larger. His head starts to spin. "Could we stop for a minute, Meehan? I'm not feeling well. These shackles are hurting my legs."

"No funny business, Ryan, or you might find yourself lying on a marble slab."

"Just let me sit on that bench for a minute."

"You think I was born yesterday? Nope."

Meehan grabs his arm and they continue along the corridor. "Yep, your buddy could have been home free. But he couldn't pass on the broad. Blondie co-operated and we surprised him when he showed up at her place on Second Avenue. When he saw us, he went for his gun. Never a wise move."

They reach the morgue and Meehan holds open the door so Red can pass through. Meehan gives the attendant a sign and he pulls the sheet, not just off Sully's face but all the way down to Sully's feet. Red's eyes fill with tears as he looks down at his comrade's naked body. One clean shot straight through the heart. At least it was fast.

"I was the one who dropped him when he went for his gun," Meehan says. "Right in the doorway."

Only a few nights ago, they were having dinner in Irene's apartment, walking through that same doorway, Sully talking about settling down.

"Do you confirm this is Arthur Sullivan?"

"Yes," Red says in a whisper.

"Louder, Ryan, we can't hear you."

"Yes," Red growls, "it's him."

⁂

"How are you, son?"

Red looks up at the man in uniform that bears no small resemblance to Warden J.C. Ponsford of Kingston Penitentiary. Hair parted sharply on one side, wire-rim glasses perched at the end of his nose as he looks down at Red on his jail cell cot.

He doesn't trust the police. He's already heard that Ed McMullen sang like a birdie to Ponsford after Ponsford promised him clemency. You can't trust a warden or a cop. Ed should have known that. He got a longer sentence for the escape and for stealing that shitbox of a car.

Red swings his legs over the side and rises slowly to his feet. The officer sticks out his hand. Four gold stripes, one gold star, it's the chief.

"Frank Brunskill, Mr. Ryan, I'm in charge of things here in the city. I hear you've been upset about your friend."

Red takes the chief's outstretched palm. Although the handshake is firm, he can detect a slight film of perspiration on his palm and those long fingers with their manicured nails. Brunskill is a little nervous. Always good to know, between the two of you, which one might have the upper hand.

"You've been causing a peck of trouble," Brunskill says. "All over this country. But now you're causing me trouble. Ever since the word got out that we have you, I'm getting calls from every town that ever had somebody rob a bank. Oshkosh; Cleveland; Flint, Michigan, for chrissake. If you're the guilty party, you and your buddy sure moved around. Don't see much logic in the itinerary myself. Pretty circuitous. You know what that word means, son?"

"Are you going to send me back to Canada?" Red asks.

The Chief sits down on the cot and motions Red to join him. "Well, son, I don't know the answer right off. There's more than one lawman who would like to get a hold of you. But never mind that right now. I'm here because your buddy's widow wants to talk to you. They're coming to collect his body."

"They?"

"Her and your friend's brother."

The sound of other inmates snoring comes rattling down the corridor and through the bars. Red sits at the other end of the cot and drops his head into his hands. "I wish I was dead."

Chief Brunskill laughs. "No you don't."

"I can't stand the thought of going back to prison. I can't face Sullivan's wife. It's my fault he's dead." His eyes begin to fill with tears.

Brunskill reaches over and touches his arm. "She wants to collect his things and take his body back to Toronto."

Red looks back up at the chief and wipes his eyes with his shirt sleeve. The chief reaches into his pocket and pulls out a brilliant white handkerchief with the initials FWB in one corner. Red holds the fine, snowy linen in his hand before applying it to his eyes and blowing his nose. Monogrammed handkerchief, he'd been thinking of getting some of those. They're classy.

"All right, I'll see her," Red says.

"Good. We'll bring his stuff from your rooms. I'm warning you she may want to know something about that dame he was running around with."

Chief Brunskill walks over to the bars and calls for the guard. There is a crease in his trousers and a shine on his boots. It's almost midnight, Red reckons, but this guy looks like he's just starting his day.

"Chief," Red says, "it's awfully cold in here."

"Well, that's this old building in the Minneapolis winter."

"Do you think if you are sending someone over to our rooms to collect Sullivan's stuff, they could pick up my coat?"

"I'll see what I can do."

Red watches Brunskill follow the guard down the corridor and stop at the watch desk to talk to the other officer in charge.

The guard comes back toward Red's cell dragging a chair. He sets it across from the door, sits down, and offers Red a cigarette.

"What are you doing?" Red says.

"Suicide watch, my friend."

"What?"

"Did you put your head in your hands and tell the chief you wished you were dead?"

Red sticks the cigarette between his lips and leans forward until the bars are pressing into his face. The officer stands up, lights a match on his thumb, and holds it out. As Red takes the first drag, the guard says, "Well, did you?"

Red nods his head. Goddamn it, yes, he did.

"Not a wise move, my friend. The chief don't like no trouble in here. Now you're on suicide watch. Twenty-four hours a day."

++

The next afternoon Red takes his cashmere coat from the guard's hands and throws it around his shoulders. "Thanks, boys."

Once the guards leave, he checks to make sure the little files he sewed into the hem are still there. Always think ahead.

Always have a way to improve your situation, no matter what it is.

His watcher sits back down on his chair and wishes the other guard a pleasant evening. Soon it will be lights out in the Minneapolis city jail.

After the lights go down, Red runs the blade across the window bar, cupping his left hand around it to muffle the sound. His cell is on the fifth floor and through his cell window he can see out across the city. City hall is red granite, red like prairie dust, with a bright red terra cotta roof. From the outside it looks a lot like the city hall in Toronto but in Toronto they keep the prisoners down in the basement. That would be easier than a five-storey drop.

The guard gets up and Red slips the file back up his sleeve.

"How you doin' tonight, Mr. Ryan? They treat you right today?"

"Yeah, they brought me my coat."

"Feeling better?"

"Yes, much warmer."

"I never been up to Canada. Is it bad up there?"

"It's all right." Red holds his sleeve tight up against his body so the file won't move.

"You got a girl in Minneapolis?"

"No, no girl."

"Good thing or you might be on the slab with your friend Sullivan." The guard chuckles and returns to his chair in the corridor.

In five or six hours, the sky will get that before-dawn glow. Red lets the file slide back into the palm of his hand. The steel is cold against his skin. He starts to draw it across the window bars again. He'll get the guard to give him some chewing gum so he can hide the crack he's creating in the bar. He'll make a rope ladder out of bed sheets. If he can postpone the extradition long enough, he just might pull it off. But he's tired. Sometimes, as he draws the file across the bar over and over again, he thinks maybe Sully was the lucky one.

46

HEMINGWAY SETS HIS SATCHEL DOWN IN THE GREAT HALL of Union Station. Hadley is right, this is a bit crazy, going home to Oak Park for a day. A crazy end to a crazy, sad week.

He may have spent more time in the offices of the *Toronto Daily Star* this week than during any other work-filled week since he got here and that's saying a lot. It has been a marathon of writing to earn money for Paris while trying to find out every piece of news that comes in about Red. Hanging around the telegraph room until they tell him to get out. He winces every time he thinks of shackles on Red's legs, of him sitting in a cell, watched twenty-four hours a day.

Duncan is playing it close to the vest, saying he doesn't want to reveal police tactics as they have the other escaped criminals to catch. The cops used to say that in Kansas City, too, but most of the tactics were such old chestnuts that any kid who'd ever played cops and robbers could probably tell you what they were.

How come Red didn't know the cops would be on to this letter thing? Why did he take such a dumb risk? *"Cherchez la femme."* Duncan must have thought that too.

Inspector Duncan may not want to talk about tactics, but he does like to point out how fast he caught Red. The Toronto cops had been chasing him all over the U.S. for three months and Duncan finds him in a week.

On Monday Red's story was in the middle of the front page. He smokes continuously and paces his cell. He says crazy things like he lives in Detroit. He won't admit he robbed the Bank of Nova Scotia, but he confesses to robberies all over the States. The guy's no dummy, it's to avoid extradition.

⁂

By Wednesday the *Star* has pictures, one of Red standing outside the morgue surrounded by cops, Duncan looking very natty with his handlebar moustache. Crowds are lining up to view Sullivan's body. Red says he's broke. He has no money to hire a lawyer. No one believes that.

By Thursday the paper is calling Red a coward.

By Friday it looks like Red is just flailing. He's talking, then he's not talking. He's still fighting his fate.

⁂

Saturday, Hemingway sits in Union Station. It's full of people going home for Christmas, their bags bursting with presents. Children cling to their mother's hands, not wanting to get lost in the crowd. The trip home to Oak Park will be another box ticked even though he still has a lot of work to do. He's behind with his piece for the *Transatlantic*. Ezra is annoyed. It's not easy, all of this. You can only fight on so many fronts.

The train to Chicago is late. The hall reverberates with the chatter of the waiting passengers. He catches sight of a small woman, handkerchief in hand, passing through the arrivals door. She clutches the arm of a man that looks familiar, the long face and the thick wavy hair. A face that stands out in his mind. And then he remembers. The wanted poster he studied like it was the handicap sheet at Woodbine. That guy looks like Arthur Sullivan, a.k.a. Brown, Red's partner in crime, that the Minneapolis police dropped with one shot to the heart. This must be a relative, probably his brother, they look so much alike. And the little mouse beside him is probably Sullivan's wife, the wife who works at Eaton's. There's something going on today. That's why his Chicago train is late.

When he looks around the station anew, his reporter's eye notices that there are a lot of policemen in the station, some in uniform, some not. It's clear this is no ordinary day. A cop approaches the little woman and points in the direction of the baggage check. She and her companion disappear behind the counter.

Hemingway leaves the hall and walks out onto Front Street. Police cars are lined up all along the sidewalk.

While he's standing there, a black hearse goes by and turns into the station's yard. Of course, they won't bring Sullivan through the station. Of course, they won't let his wife travel with him. He'll be retrieved out back like a piece of freight, a piece of baggage.

Arthur Sullivan is making a last trip home, too.

-+-+-

The Oak Park visit goes better than he expected. Marriage and fatherhood seem to have earned him some respectability in his mother's eyes. His father looked tired though, worn down. The respectable suburb of Chicago looked pretty much the same.

There is a wistfulness to memories of days spent in the old places where you were a different person from who you are now. The war changed him. Paris changed him. Red Ryan changed him. Hadley changed him. She is love and support, not demands and criticism. Not always falling short, like at home. Not full of religion, like at home. He feels sorry, in a way, for the young ones who are still there, still controlled by his parents' old-fashioned ideas.

He brought his sister Marcelline a copy of *Three Stories and Ten Poems*. She will be shocked, no doubt, like the librarian at the *Star*, by some of what she reads. Ezra says when you start to worry about what people might think that's a sure sign you should keep going.

The train rattles and shakes as it heads east, a hell of a way to spend Christmas Eve. He was tempted to ask about the fare to Minneapolis instead of going back, but he didn't. He'll be watching Red's story play out from afar.

He thinks about the visit, his family, Hadley and the baby, Ezra and Gertrude, as the landscape goes rushing by. The Michigan forests and rivers, rushing out of his life but not out of his head.

His mother sent Hadley a novel and he starts to leaf through the pages as the train rolls along. He needs to write a novel. According to the book's back cover, the author, a lawyer, abandoned the law and moved to New York to write. Maybe, in her own backhanded way, his mother is trying to encourage him.

The language in the book is dense. Not the way he wants to write. Old-fashioned, last century, Victorian, like his mother. A tale told but not a picture painted. A sensitive young boy who is regularly beaten by his father threatens to leave home. The father is a sportsman, but the boy's artistic mother understands him. *What is my mother trying to say?*

The same boy, now a man, has been studying the newspaper account of an attack on a woman. Hemingway reads the paragraph again. After the hero reads about the attack, he pictures himself as the victim, fantasizing about being raped. He says he wants to experience the womanly feeling of surrender. Hemingway cannot believe what he is reading in a book of which his mother appears to be so fond.

Ezra's voice is in his head. "Why are you surprised? No writer should ever forget: 'There are more things in heaven and earth than are dreamt of in your philosophy.' No writer should fear any part of the human condition."

He's tried to explore what it feels like to be female. Not sure he succeeded. What will his mother think if she reads "Up in Michigan." Even Gertrude wasn't keen.

⁂

When he gets back, Hadley has hung mismatched stockings on the mantel. Before he can even take his coat off, she smiles at him and says, "I have something for you."

"But we said we wouldn't buy each other gifts."

"It's not from me, close your eyes."

He hears the sound of rustling paper and when she says, "Open," she is holding seven copies of *in our time.*

The book seems so small, this thing in which he has invested so much, one of six volumes that make up Ezra's examination of the state of contemporary English language prose. *in our time* has eighteen chapters, some from the *Little Review*, vignettes about the Great War, soldiers, civilians, or bullfighting, or the fallout from another war, the Greco-Turkish war. As in the *Little Review*, "Everybody was drunk," is the first line of the first piece.

"I like the way we set them up," he says. "When you read them all, they say something that isn't written on the page. Makes the reader think."

"Which one is your favourite?" Hadley asks.

"Maybe the one about the executions."

"Executing a man who's so sick he can't stand up to die like the others, with honour. It's heartless."

"In front of a hospital," Hemingway adds.

"Dying and yet they are going to kill him anyway," Hadley says. "In the pouring rain. My heart ached."

He smiles. "That's what I wanted. I wanted something unlike the newspaper report it came from, something that made you feel what you would feel if you were there."

The baby falls asleep in Hadley's lap and she gets up and places him carefully in his crib. "Well, it worked," she says. "Get some rest. We're having Christmas dinner with the Connables."

47

"You know why Ryan's doing this, don't you?" Walter Duncan sits in the hotel dining room enjoying an early breakfast with Rob Tucker. "He wants the Yanks to keep him here. He's telling them he's robbed every bank we suspect he's guilty of and then some. He'll do anything to avoid going back with us. The Yanks are talking about setting bail."

Rob Tucker stops moving his coffee cup in the direction of his lips and puts it back down in its saucer. "That's no Christmas present, getting circles run around us by Red Ryan."

"Don't worry, Robbie, I didn't haul my behind all over the Midwest to have some janitor who got elected judge let Ryan out on bail. We'd never see him again."

"The press swarm around here like a hive of bees," Tucker says, taking a sip of his orange juice. "They're getting in to talk to Ryan. I don't get it."

"I don't like it." Duncan pours himself another cup of coffee from the silver carafe. "Red's complaining to the press about the food in Kingston Pen. Says that's why he had to get out. That's rich."

"They better keep an eye on him."

Duncan puts down his coffee cup and stares into Rob Tucker's eyes. "A penetrating glimpse into the obvious, Robbie."

Rob Tucker's face falls and he starts to get up. "You know, Walter, just because I don't understand the ethics of a prison guard who takes money to look the other way or forget to fire his rifle for five minutes doesn't mean I'm naive. Warden Ponsford warned all the guards to watch him and look what happened."

"Sit down, Robbie, sit down. Finish your breakfast. I'm just teasing you. Any word on what they're doing to those guys back in Kingston?"

"Lots of investigating but no decision. It's bad for morale. You can't have every guard looking at every other guard wondering whose side he'll be on if something goes down."

"True enough, Robbie. That's always the dilemma. Who to trust? It's mighty lonely when you don't know the answer to that question."

The maître d' approaches and coughs. "Excuse me, Mr. Duncan, there's a message for you."

Duncan reads the message, then gets up and taps the table beside Tucker's arm. "It's the chief. I'll go find out what's up. You order yourself another sweet roll."

He walks out into the lobby, sits down beside the telephone, and asks the operator to connect him to the chief of police. He can see Rob Tucker watching him from across the dining room floor.

"What's up," Duncan says when the line connects in response to the chief's "Brunskill, here."

"Well, that's just great," Duncan says, slamming down the telephone. Rob Tucker is up and walking toward him, napkin still stuffed into the top of his pants. With his long stride, it doesn't take long before he is standing next to the telephone desk.

"That son of a bitch has hired himself a lawyer, Robbie," Duncan says.

The maître d' looks in their direction, disapproval on his face. "Sorry," Duncan mumbles. He takes Rob Tucker by the arm and guides him back to their table in the dining room.

"He's hired two lawyers. Damn good lawyers, according to the chief. We need to get this extradition happening. Ottawa better get their act together. And you know what else, Robbie?" Duncan says, shaking his head. "They want to throw us a dinner."

"A dinner? I don't know how I feel about that. A man died."

"Either one of them would have killed us if he needed to."

"It was such an ambush."

"The locals were upset, laddie, he hit one of their own," Duncan says. "Guess where they want to throw this dinner? You won't believe it."

"Not the Athletic Club? Are you serious?"

"Deadly serious," Walter Duncan says. "The girl won't be there. The club fired her for hanging out with undesirables."

"She didn't know."

"They don't call them cons for nothing."

"Are the feds trying to butter us up? Is it the reward?"

"Over a five hundred dollar reward?"

"Not five hundred, Walter. What about the five thousand dollar reward from the Bankers Association?"

"What about it?"

"You told the Minneapolis Police about it, didn't you?"

"And why, my friend, would I do that? Who found these guys? Wasn't the Minneapolis Police, it was me with some help from you."

⁂

The next day, when Walter Duncan arrives at Minneapolis City Hall, Chief Brunskill is waiting for him. They have a deportation order from Washington and bail has been set at five thousand dollars.

"Five thousand dollars is easy to come by when you have a brother in the booze business," Duncan says.

"I know, Walter," Brunskill says, "but we have our orders. They've decided to move him to the county jail."

The two men wait for the filigreed elevator cage to arrive and they ride in silence up to the fifth floor. The guards stand straight when they see the chief. They walk down the corridor to where Ryan is being held. "He's been a model prisoner," Brunskill says.

"As I said to Robbie last night, they don't call them cons for nothing," Duncan says.

Brunskill turns to him and laughs. "Really, Walter? Well, fiddle my moustache."

When they arrive at Red's cell, he is sitting on the bed. If Duncan didn't know him better, he'd think their boyo looked a little nervous.

"Collect your things, Ryan," Brunskill says. "We're taking you to the county lock-up."

Duncan notices that Red's eyes flick for just a second in the direction of the cell window and then back to Chief Brunskill's face. *Jesus*, he thinks, *he's not going to make a run for it, is he?* That would be unwise. He's already seen how trigger happy these Minneapolis cops are.

Duncan walks over to the barred window and looks outside. It's a good five stories down to the ground but any con worth his salt would have made himself a —

Duncan turns to Brunskill. "Search his bed."

"What?" one of the guards says. "Search for what? We've been watching him twenty-four hours a day."

Duncan runs his index finger up the side of one of the bars. Nothing. Next one nothing. Next one, he feels something, a slight bulge in the metal. He wraps his fist around the bar and gives it a sharp yank. The bar comes off in his hands. He can see that at the edge where it's been sawn, chewing gum was holding the two parts together. He turns around to show Brunskill but the chief has found something too. He has one knee on Ryan's bed, and in his hand he has a long length of knotted sheet.

"Well, Mr. Ryan," Brunskill says, "what have we here?"

The guards look like they are ready to bang Ryan's head into the wall. "Leave us, boys," Brunskill says. "I'll deal with you two later."

Red stands beside his bed, hangdogged, like a small boy who has been caught raiding his mother's penny jar.

"You'll excuse us, Mr. Ryan." Brunskill says. "I'm going to speak with the inspector."

Duncan has to hand it to Brunskill; he's a cool son of a bitch. After Brunskill secures the cell door and instructs the desk sergeant to keep an eye on things if he still wants to have a job in the morning, they slip into a small interview room.

"They can set whatever bail they want. He's gone," Brunskill says.

"You mean deported?"

"I mean he's gone, just leave it to me. You go down to my office. I'll have them make you a coffee or maybe pour you a Scotch."

"It's ten o'clock in the morning."

"Really, Walter?"

Duncan waits while a guard opens the barred gate to the main corridor. When he looks back, the chief is heading to Ryan's cell. He probably should go along. He'd hate to lose him at this point but by the look in the chief's eyes, that won't be a problem.

Instead of going down to wait in the chief's office, he sits on a bench by the elevator. After about twenty minutes, a young woman comes up the stairs holding a small file folder. Duncan recognizes her as one of the stenographers who work for the chief. She presses the buzzer and the guard admits her to the cell area. About five minutes later, she comes back out, walks over to the bench, and stands before him.

"Inspector Duncan?"

"Yes."

"I told the chief you were sitting out here. He asked me to tell you that if you would be so kind as to wait about ten more minutes, he will come out and talk to you."

"What's happening?"

"I think it's best if I let the chief tell you."

Duncan closes his eyes and takes a deep breath of the city hall air. Brass polish and floor wax, he concludes, applied recently. Water and vinegar used to clean the windowpanes.

He hears the lock on the cell gate release and opens his eyes to see the chief burst out, waving a paper in his left hand.

"It's done," he says. "You can take him back. He's signed a waiver."

48

For the first time, Red feels a noose tightening around his neck. But the fighting is rounds and that was only round one. He took a long shot and he lost.

Wait until his lawyers hear about what happened. He signed the chief's waiver but he knows enough about the law to know you can't threaten a guy into doing something, whether he's a criminal or not. That's not fair. Of course, he has run across a few cops in his time who don't subscribe to fairness as a philosophy but these guys in Minneapolis seem like straight shooters. No sooner had the words passed through his brain than the mental picture of Sully taking one right through the heart does too. They're straight shooters, all right.

His brother is hanging around Detroit just in case they try to take him back. Always have to have more than one plan in case the first one fails. His brother has a lot of favours he can call in among his rum-running friends.

Red Ryan hasn't come this far to go down without a fight, he says to himself. Not after four months of freedom and Sully dead. This isn't the end. The lawyers are coming to see him tomorrow, right after breakfast.

He lies down on the narrow cot. They've moved him to another cell. The windows are up near the ceiling. The winter light coming through is a pale shade of grey. He and Sully were looking forward to their first Christmas on the outside. The new cell is cold, colder than the old one. After they shoved him in, they threw what was left of his blanket in with him. They've taken his cashmere coat for evidence, although the chief promises he'll get it back — when hell freezes over.

49

On Friday night the snow started and the news started coming in with it. Red, you have to admire the crazy bastard, sawing through the bars of his cell and making a rope ladder thirty feet long. Never say die, that one. When it was discovered, as far as Hemingway can tell, due process died an untimely death. Red was, shall we say, urged to sign a waiver by the Minneapolis chief of police. They shackled him and put him on the train to Montreal. Not a great way to begin the new year.

Not a great new year for some guards at the Pen either. Two were fired. One was allowed to retire and five others were fined. The superintendent with the fancy name of St. Pierre Hughes said, "As an act of kindness, the disciplinary actions should not occur until December thirty-first. Merry Christmas, boys, and Happy New Year!"

The Saturday paper is full of the news too. He cannot believe this is how the story ends.

⁂

When Hemingway steps out onto Bathurst Street, it's a cold and blustery Sunday morning. It's still snowing, snowed all day Saturday, snowed all night. He may have to walk all the way to Union Station to see Red come in. At least it's downhill. Hadley is busy sorting through the last of their things.

The sun on the mounds of snow is almost blinding. No one is out. No one is clearing the roads. The city has come to a standstill. In the United States, people are dying of the cold: temperatures around thirty below.

He reaches St. Clair and after another couple of blocks he can hear the tires whirring as people try to drive up Bathurst Street hill.

When he talked to the boys down at the paper, they said Red tried every trick in the book to stay in the States, said he was going to take his case all the way to the Supreme Court. Tried to claim he wasn't born in Canada. But somehow, once Washington said they weren't going to grant bail, he found himself on the train out of town that night, even though "reliable sources" told the *Star* reporter Red had an appointment with his Minneapolis lawyer at ten thirty the next morning.

Hemingway's ears are freezing and he takes his scarf from around his neck, does up the top button of his overcoat, and ties the scarf around his head. His legs ache from tramping through the uncleared sidewalks. The roads are no better. At last he reaches the bottom of Bathurst Street. The streetcars on Front Street are running.

Duncan and company certainly took a circuitous route from Minneapolis. But to go through Detroit, they'd have run the risk of some other jurisdiction claiming him or some other person, like Red's brother, springing him. Apparently, the brother's fingerprints are all over this little caper of Red's from the get-go.

The station is full of people. The word seems to have gotten out. Red's train missed its connection at Sault Ste. Marie because of the weather and they had to catch up with the Toronto train at Blind River. One of the cops tells him there was a huge crowd in Blind River even though it was twenty-eight below.

Hemingway pushes his way to the platform gate. Standing there waiting for the train to hiss to a stop, he feels a hand on his shoulder. It's the doorman from the King Eddy. "Wasn't going to miss a show like this," he says.

When Red appears at the train's doorway, handcuffed of hands and shackled of ankles, the crowd roars.

"Do you recognize him?

"Red Ryan? Of course I do. I was the first one to cover this until Hindmarsh pulled me off the story."

"I'm not talking about Red Ryan, I'm talking about the guy who's got him by the arm. Did you do your homework like I told you?"

The man that Hemingway now knows is Inspector Walter Duncan clutches Red's right arm. The Deputy Warden of Kingston Pen, Rob Tucker, has the other one. Two other policemen who look smug and rough jump out of the train and stand on the platform. Duncan and Tucker lift Red down off the train into the arms of the other two cops.

The crowd starts to move as they escort the prisoner up through the grand hall. The press yell questions at him as he goes. Halfway to the station's front door, the tightly knit group pauses for a moment and a man walks up and speaks to Red Ryan.

"That's one of his brothers," the doorman from the King Eddy says.

"How do you know?"

"I told you, finger on the pulse, finger on the pulse of this whole damn city."

"Is that Frank, the rum-runner I keep hearing about?"

"Nope. I think this guy's from the straight and narrow branch of the family."

The conversation with the brother doesn't last long. From the look on Red's face, he didn't like whatever his brother had to say. Out on Front Street, the cops push Red into a police department limousine.

"No Black Maria for that guy, I guess," the doorman says.

"Coming up to city hall?" Hemingway asks.

"No, I saw what I wanted to see. I'm back to my little domain: opening doors, summoning the bellhop, getting big tips. Not one larcenous bone in my body."

Hemingway waves him goodbye and follows the crowd along Front to Bay and on to city hall. The clock in the bell tower chimes the half-hour. They must have dragged some hapless magistrate out of bed or out of church to deal with this.

When he reaches the front doors of city hall, someone tells him they've already taken Red to the Don Jail. "Come back tomorrow. He's supposed to be in court at two o'clock. He says he's going to fight it."

This story isn't over yet.

Hemingway climbs over the snowbank and looks down Bay Street to see if the Bay streetcar is running to take him back home. The city really is a mess. The snow must be three feet deep.

"Why did they take him to the Don?" he says to the man standing next to him. "What's the matter with the holding cells at city hall?"

The man laughs. "You're kidding, aren't you? It's Red Ryan. Don't you know? He escaped from Kingston Pen."

50

"THANKS, BOYS," RED SAYS WHEN THEY HAND HIM OVER TO the governor of the Don Jail, always looking for a friend. "See you tomorrow."

"Put him in solitary," the governor says. "We aren't taking any chances. He'll eat in his cell and no visitors."

"Not even my family?"

"Particularly not your family."

The front door of the Don looked like the mouth of the devil. The thing about being in custody is you never know what is coming at you. Cops, in his experience, often have a grudging admiration for you although they'd never admit it. You were all playing a game and they won and they are gracious and good sports in their winning unless, of course, you hurt one of them in the process. Now they're in control, they've got you. Except for denying him his right to talk to his lawyer, and the destination, and the handcuffs and shackles, and the goddamn cold, it was almost a pleasant trip, sitting and talking. Billy Meehan gave him a pair of gloves, his own gloves, to wear on the train ride back. And hell must have frozen over on the weekend because they gave him back his cashmere coat, after they checked it over.

So far at the Don, they've been all right. They brought him dinner on a tray. The jail is quiet at night but he cannot sleep. He cannot help but think of his comfortable bed in their apartment in Minneapolis or the dinner that Irene Adams made for them when life seemed good. The warm yellow glow that came from the houses on her street. Sully talking about his future. Red gulps to muffle a sob. Whenever he closes his eyes, he sees Sully lying on a slab but he'll be goddamned if he's going to let this bunch see him cry.

Sully's wife travelled all the way to Minneapolis to take his body home. She came with his brother, Daniel, the one in Detroit whose wife told them to get lost. The guards let him speak with her, although one of the detectives was always there. Red suspected she'd read the stories about Irene but she didn't mention anything. Just didn't want to talk to Billy Meehan, that was all. He had a haircut from the prison barber especially for her visit. Sign of respect. She was gracious to him, too, perhaps showing him more kindness than he deserved. At the end of her visit, he gave her his diamond watch and signed over the REO to her and said that he was very sorry.

The Toronto cops want to nail him for the robbery. Unlike the feds, they haven't won yet so they still have blood in their eyes. He may plead not guilty just to watch the look on their faces. Frank is supposed to be getting him a lawyer so who knows how tomorrow will go.

Every time he drifted off to sleep last night, he was awakened by the voices of the guards making their rounds. When he's awake all that he can think about is Sully and Babe and the REO and whether he'll get another chance to escape. But he's tired and that's not good. In a couple of hours, he is supposed to appear in court. Who knows what opportunities may present themselves while moving from place to place. He needs to keep his wits about him.

The Crown will no doubt be there with every witness they can get their hands on. He doesn't care. He's not going to plead guilty, to hell with that. To hell with the Toronto cops.

51

On Monday, at the City Hall courthouse, Hemingway stands at the back of the room and watches the lawyers confer. Red Ryan sits there as if he is a spectator, too, as if this is all about somebody else. The lawyers break apart and approach the judge's bench. The judge nods and then the lawyers sit back down.

Red turns and smiles at his lawyers when the judge says, "Bound over for trial in February." Hemingway cannot believe his ears. He'll be gone when Red's trial is on. Maybe he is missing out on the story of his life.

This crazy bastard is keeping it going, although, too bad for him, they are taking him back to Kingston. Is this like the letters? Something he didn't think through? They won't keep him in Toronto. Pleading not guilty will mean he's sent back.

The mumblings in the seats surrounding him rouse him from his thoughts. They grow louder and louder until the judge bangs his gavel and demands silence. The police hustle Red out and the crowd in the courtroom starts running toward the door. The onlookers race down the hallway, heading to the side entrance and around to the north end of the building, hoping to catch a glimpse of Red leaving in the police van.

But Hemingway doesn't follow them. He knows, because the weather is so bad and the streets still so full of snow, that with a bit of a head start he can probably make it down to the station before they get there.

The sun is still low in the winter sky as he trudges across Queen Street. When he reaches York Street, he looks back toward city hall. He can see the police van followed by the screaming crowd just turning the corner. If he hustles, he can still make it down to Front Street before they do.

When he reaches the station, there are eight or nine policemen standing on the sidewalk. No back door for Red Ryan or the police. Not like Sullivan's sad return home. He's not sure who is trying hardest to put on a show, Red or the police. He watches the van turn the corner, followed by the police limousine. Before they bring Red Ryan out of the van, Duncan, Tucker, and the two Minneapolis cops step out of the fancy car, followed by Dickson.

Duncan is quite a character with his fancy clothes and his handlebar moustache twirled into a curl at the end. He must spend a lot of time on that moustache, or maybe he has somebody doing the twirling for him.

They take Ryan out of the van.

"Red," Hemingway calls out. Red stops, turns, and looks him dead in the eye. He holds his handcuffed wrists up. A last defiant salute. Like a boxer, like in his dream. But a cop bats Red's hands down and Red shrugs his shoulders as if he is saying whatcha going to do? "Red," Hemingway says under his breath, "we are the bullfighters."

Red lowers his eyes. This is an act. Hemingway knows underneath that now-battered fedora the Red Ryan brain is working overtime. Just waiting for someone to make a false step or let their guard down for a minute. One of the Minneapolis cops pulls on

Red's arm and he shuffles his way into the station through the great hall and down onto the platform.

Two policemen stand beside the train. As Red hobbles toward them, a man runs up and grabs him by the arm.

Hemingway feels in his pocket for his notebook. Is he about to witness a Red Ryan escape first-hand? But to his amazement, the quartet of law enforcement officers surrounding Red step back and let the man who has approached be. The crowd stops talking and a silence falls over the cavernous open barn where the trains come and go. Red calls out to Inspector Duncan, and Duncan, looking like a shy girl who can't believe she has been asked to dance, walks over to where the two men stand. What the hell is going on?

Red's hands move up and around and Duncan nods his head and then looks back to where the police and Rob Tucker are waiting.

They step forward and take Red by the arms. But instead of heading toward the waiting train, they turn and head back along the platform, back into the station.

When this strange parade bursts through the station doors back out onto Front Street, the gentlemen of the press have caught up with them and are demanding to know what's going on.

"Who was that man?" Hemingway shouts.

His question is answered not by the police but by a pretty red-headed woman with a handkerchief in her hand. "Red's brother," she says.

"Frank?"

"I don't know."

The press clamour around the police car, screaming for an explanation.

Walter Duncan emerges from the back seat and holds his hands up in the air until he is surrounded by silence. He begins, a slight smirk tugging at his lips under his moustache. "Mr. Ryan," he says, "has decided to plead guilty."

The red-headed girl next to Hemingway starts crying.

"Why?" Hemingway hears himself shout.

Again, it is the girl who answers him. "The family's shamed him into it."

At that moment Hemingway feels the kinship he felt for Red move from a simmer to a full-out boil. How can this guy who has had the balls to escape from Kingston Pen, to rob a bank under the noses of the Toronto cops, how can he let his family shame him into giving up without a fight?

Hemingway turns to ask the girl another question but she has drifted off into the hundreds of people who are now travelling along the street next to the police van. They are taking Red back to city hall.

The tramping feet have finished the job the snow crews couldn't. The streets are beaten down.

Hemingway looks at his watch as he climbs the city hall's front steps. It's still early, ten thirty in the morning. He pushes through the crowd that surrounds him to make sure he gets a seat in the courtroom. The policeman standing at the door recognizes him and lets him pass. He slides into the last row of blond oak benches.

The crown is going through Red's record, crime by crime, starting in 1907. The red-headed girl he saw at the station sits several rows ahead of him. Almost directly behind Red. Red turns around once and smiles. The courtroom is warm. She has removed her coat. *It's odd*, he thinks. In her trim navy suit and her snow-white blouse, she looks like a young Rosedale matron.

The judge sentences Red to life in prison and thirty stokes of the lash: ten, the first month; ten, the second; and ten, the third. With each pronouncement, Red's shoulders flinch as if he has been hit already. The Crown says there's a train leaving for Kingston at ten minutes past noon.

The parade leaves again for the station. The cops and the convicted, the press and a healthy representation of the good citizens of Toronto. They follow the same path down York Street, they enter the station, they try to crowd onto the platform but the police keep them at bay.

Hemingway is waiting for something to happen. But nothing does.

And then Red is gone.

The same red-headed girl sits on a bench, wiping her eyes. He wonders if that is Red's friend, the one Red came to see. When he tries to approach her, she gets up and walks away.

Hemingway walks through the doors that lead into the station's great hall. The noon sun glimmers through the tall windows. The policemen and the reporters stroll across the marble floor. He cannot believe Red is captured — on his way back to Kingston Pen where the whole story began. Back along the same train route he himself took, so very unhappy, so late at night, the tenth of September, just four months ago.

52

The train rocks back and forth as it crosses the spiderweb of tracks that lead out of Toronto. They have been kind enough to take the shackles off and Red reaches down to rub his sore ankles. Sully always said their primary purpose is to humiliate rather than prevent escape. "Make a grown man waddle like a duck, what cop doesn't get a secret kick out of that?"

At every level crossing and suburban station, crowds gather to watch the train go by. They shout and wave. It's almost as if they are there to see him, not his captors. He tries to raise his handcuffed hands to acknowledge them, but Rob Tucker holds his arms down.

When they are out of the city, looking out over the lake where wind has blown shards of ice into the shoreline, Tucker agrees to take the handcuffs off. The sun is floating like an island of mercury across the rippling water. Small pieces of ice bob at the shore, glistening like handfuls of diamonds.

"We'll be arriving back at the prison around five o'clock," Tucker says. "Just in time for dinner. You'll be in solitary, no doubt about that."

"The judge didn't say anything about solitary," Red says.

"The judge isn't running Kingston Pen."

After that no one talks for a while until the conductor comes down the aisle holding a deck of cards. They pass an hour or so playing but then the talk returns to what Red's got waiting for him back at the prison.

"They'll search you within an inch of your life, my boy, after the stunt you pulled," one of the cops says. "If you have anything hidden anywhere, they'll find it. They'll search every nook and cranny. They'll be down your throat and up your ass."

Red stares out the window as the train travels through another small Ontario town. A tall man holds his tiny daughter by the hand and they wave as the train passes through.

Out in the open, the landscape stands stark white and black against the sky. The sun sets early in January so it will be dark by the time they get to the Pen.

"Any word on Bryans or Simpson?" Red asks Tucker.

"Now, Norman, you know I can't say anything about that."

"Call me Red, everyone else does."

"I think I'll just stick with Norman. That's how you're recorded on the ledger."

The train tilts as it goes around a long, slow curve like the one where they jumped the freight. The lake stretches out before them again, shades of faded blue with circles of dark black water.

When the train pulls into the station, there is another large crowd, pushing and craning their necks, trying to see him. The Kingston police hold everyone back while Tucker and Duncan hustle him into the waiting van. For a second, and even though it doesn't make much sense, he finds himself looking to see if that reporter fellow is in the crowd but he's not there.

The drive is much slower than his last trip through the streets of Kingston. There's the Martello tower. There's city hall. There's the corner where the guard's bullet caught Ed McMullen's hand.

And there's the wall they went over four months ago almost exactly to the day.

The prison seems quiet. "You're not a hero anymore," one of the guards whispers as Red passes by. Warden Ponsford stands in the doorway as they strip him of his clothes. They are rougher than he remembers ever having been handled before but Ponsford says nothing. They look in his mouth, his hair, they grab his legs and look at the soles of his feet. Then they make him bend over and touch the floor and he feels their fingers push inside him.

They put him in the cells in the basement of the keeper's cottage. The cold comes seeping in through the limestone walls. He wonders when he will see the sun again. The cell is so narrow that he can touch the clammy stone on both sides.

Ponsford is playing cat and mouse with him about the lash. Part of him keeps one ear cocked for the sound of multiple footsteps coming down the stairs. That's how he'll know. They come in fours or fives, like in his dream, so you won't know who strikes you.

He may be back in the joint, but he'd do it all over again if the opportunity arose. But this time, Red Ryan, you'll be smart about it.

"You talking to yourself again, Ryan?" the guard yells.

"Just thinking to myself."

"If I was you, I'd lay off the thinking. Look where it's got you."

⁂

How can it be that he is here, Sully is dead, and Gord and Tommy are still free? Gord, he doesn't mind so much but the dumb-ass kid, that really bugs him. Even the girls on Carlton Street couldn't stand him: always drunk, making stupid jokes. No class.

The thought of Carlton Street makes him sigh. Babe with her red hair spilled out across the pillow, her soft hands touching him, the sound of the sirens passing by.

"Ryan!"

He turns and squints through the cell door.

"The boss wants to see you."

⁂

"Let me formally welcome you back, Mr. Ryan," Warden Ponsford says as the guards lead Red into his office. They have him in handcuffs but at least his legs are free. "I hope everything is to your liking. I hear you had some complaints about the food."

"Do I have to be in solitary?"

"Afraid that can't be helped, my boy. After what you did, I'm not taking any chances. Don't want Ottawa breathing down my neck."

"I wouldn't put a dog in solitary."

"I want you where people I trust can keep a close eye on you. I do have some good news for you, though. I've decided not to lay a charge for the escape."

"Wouldn't make much difference, I already have a life sentence."

"Precisely."

The guards move forward and take Red by the arms.

"Haven't you forgotten something, Mr. Ryan? I told you I'm not charging you."

Red looks into the eyes of the man who just might be his keeper for the rest of his days. What does he see? Victory? Contempt? Respect? Fear? He can't tell.

Ponsford takes his fingers and pushes back a lock of hair that has fallen across his forehead. The guard who has hold of Red's right arm squeezes it and whispers, "Say thank you."

Red resists for a moment, then he remembers what the chaplain used to tell him. "You have to learn to pick your battles, son." After everything, he's not in the mood for fighting — at least, not today.

He straightens up and faces Ponsford square on.

"Thank you, sir."

"That's better. You try it again and we'll find you again. Take him back."

53

"You know what makes me angry?" Hemingway says as he throws the *Toronto Daily Star* down on the bed, one of the two pieces of furniture left in the apartment. Most of their belongings are gone.

"Don't worry, Tiny. We're leaving in a week."

"Look at this," he says jabbing at yesterday's paper. After watching Red Ryan's return in person, he is checking the *Star*'s account.

"They certainly are giving Mr. Ryan a lot of space," Hadley says.

"He deserves a lot of space. But that's not what I mean. Look. The reporter has a byline and copyright. How come?"

"I think you got off on the wrong foot with Mr. Hindmarsh."

"You think it's my fault, what happened?"

"I didn't say that."

"Are you forgetting all the crazy hours and the out-of-town trips? Are you forgetting about me not being there when my own son was born? Are you forgetting he embarrassed me in front of Count what's his name?"

Hadley laughs. "Count what's his name? Oh Tiny, you should listen to yourself. We're leaving. Is there any point in getting angry about something else now?"

"Well, I am angry. I don't like it. I'm going down to the paper."

"I don't think that's wise."

"I'm sure you don't," Hemingway calls back over his shoulder as he heads out the door. On the landing he hears the baby start to cry.

The air on Bathurst Street hits his face like a pitcher of cold water. For the second time in less than a week, he decides to walk downtown instead of ride. His feet take him past the Connables's house but when he rings the doorbell, the maid tells him no one is home. He continues walking and stops at the crest of Davenport Hill. From there he can see all across the city. He raises his hand in a farewell salute.

He passes by Casa Loma. The snow is piled high on the roof of the portico. The grand house is empty now. Henry Pellatt, the millionaire who built it, had a reversal of fortune. He drowned in debt. The Home Bank that lent him all that money is out of business too. The same Home Bank he was supposed to cover his first week of work.

Mr. Pellatt's money troubles remind him that neither he nor Hadley has heard any explanation from George Breaker about her money. In five more days, they will be getting on a train heading to New York to board the ship to France.

The cool air and the long walk calm him down. Hadley is right. What is the point of having it out with Hindmarsh? From now on his name goes on everything he writes. He'll make sure of it. No more assuming it will be so.

Although he has decided to forgo a showdown with Hindmarsh, he still finds himself on King Street looking up at the home of the *Toronto Daily Star.*

It's almost noon and the typesetters are singing while they get ready for the five o'clock edition. He heads down the stairs to the library and finds himself humming along.

The librarian is surrounded by books. The paper has been full of Red Ryan for days: his childhood, his record. His remorse? His Royal Hindmarsh must be happy, nothing like the capture of an escaped prisoner to sell a few papers.

"Can I help you?" the librarian says. She looks to be in her fifties; maybe she'll remember the events the doorman told him about. "I thought you resigned."

"I did resign but I'm looking for something to do with Red Ryan."

"You and everybody else in the building."

"About a cop that ... it was before the war. A cop that got fired for talking to the press. The doorman down at the King Eddy told me I should look into him."

"Oh," she says with a laugh. "An order from the doorman at the King Eddy. That's different." She goes back into the dusty shelves of the library and comes out with a huge file filled with clippings and drops it on her desk.

Hemingway looks down at the label on the file. DUNCAN, Walter, it says. "It is him. He's the cop that got fired?"

"Yes, sir. Doesn't seem to have done him a whole lot of harm. He's a big hero now."

Hemingway picks up the file and puts it under his arm.

"Just where do you think you're going with that? You don't work here anymore. I could get in trouble just letting you look at it. Go hide in the back."

He takes the file and moves off to a corner, his favourite refuge. When he opens it, the file is full of clippings about the fall from grace of one Walter Duncan. The clippings are from the fall of 1912. Another damn bank failure. It's a tangled web of investigation after investigation. Something comes out in the investigation of the Farmers' Bank that leads to the investigation of Inspector Walter Duncan.

In one clipping Duncan says he's going to write a book. Blow the roof off.

There's an idea. He could write a book about Hindmarsh. He pulls out his notebook and scribbles a few words about his nemesis, his editor, the son-in-law of the publisher so he can do no wrong. But he'd rather write about Red.

While he sits and smiles at the prospect of writing about whatever he wants to write about, Greg Clark walks by with an armload of books.

"What the hell or you doing here, Hem? I thought you quit." Greg sits down at the table opposite him, reaches out and touches the sleeve of his coat. "I wish you weren't going."

"Gotta go. O'Brien wants to publish my story. I'm going to be twenty-five this summer. I gotta get going."

"Twenty-five." Greg gives him a shove. "You're a baby."

"I need to be around other writers."

"You're surrounded by writers here."

"Some. You. Maybe that kid, Callaghan." Hemingway stands up and puts all the Walter Duncan information back in its folder.

"What about Cowan?" Greg says. "He founded a literary magazine for chrissake. That's pretty writerly."

"I know but I have to get out of here before it's too late."

Greg gets up and catches him off guard with a strong embrace. "We're going to miss you. I'd bet a lot of money we'll hear from you, pal."

It's hard to leave people you like but the *Star* has almost silenced him.

The librarian smiles up at him when he puts the folder down on her desk. "Interesting story, isn't it."

"Makes you wonder."

"About what?"

"About carrying on. You might lose a battle but win the war. Everybody gets a second chance, I guess."

"I hear you're going back to France, Mr. Hemingway," she says.

"That's the plan."

"Trying to be a writer."

"Yep."

"Well, son, you know I wish you all the luck in the world."

54

THE NEXT MORNING, HEMINGWAY LOCKS THE DOOR TO Number 19 while Hadley holds the baby close to her chest. They don't want him to cry and draw attention to the fact they're sneaking out, leaving the apartment — for good. Hadley has tears in her eyes but he cannot leave this city fast enough.

When they get down to the front door, he waves and Harriet drives from down the street to the front of the Cedarvale Mansions. She gets out and opens the passenger door for Hadley and the baby to get in.

"It's sad to say goodbye," Hadley says. "I've told Ernest's mother how kind you've been to us."

"It was our pleasure," Harriet says. "Ralph's going to walk down from the office to wave you off."

The car gathers speed as they travel down Bathurst Street hill. Hadley sits in the front seat next to Harriet, with the baby on her lap. The two women exchange frequent looks. Hadley wipes tears from her eyes with the baby's blanket.

Last night the Connables held a farewell party. The Connables don't drink but they have no objection if their guests do.

"You either got in line with Hindmarsh or you didn't," Jimmy Cowan said to Harriet after he'd had a few. "And Hem never did."

"That's our boy," Ralph said. "Rules are made to be broken."

"Or bullshit is not to be tolerated," Hemingway said.

"Do you know Hindmarsh wrote to Warden Ponsford at Kingston Pen, pointing out the inhumanity of solitary confinement for your pal Red Ryan?" Greg said.

"Really? I thought he believed in cruel and unusual punishment."

"But wait until you hear this," Jimmy said. "That muckety-muck St. Pierre Hughes wrote back, gave him the brush off, and addressed him as Mr. Hindman."

⁂

The train station is busy and Hemingway leaves everyone in the waiting room while he checks to see from which platform they are leaving. Somebody spelled Hindmarsh's name wrong. He's still chuckling about it when he gets back to where Hadley and Harriet are waiting.

"We're over this way," he says, picking up their suitcases.

He has dropped his ass in a train seat more times than he cares to count, graced this cave-like hall with his presence more times than he cares to count. But the last time was because of Red Ryan. Red's brother convinced him to go back and plead guilty. Abandon hope, all ye who enter here. That was true for him, too, when he arrived in September. Somebody should chisel that over an archway.

But for the living, there is always hope. Red believes that too. He's still never told a living soul about seeing Red that night.

Ralph Connable comes rushing through the station door and runs over to where they stand. Just in time, too, because when you start quoting Ecclesiastes in your head, it's time to go.

"You made it," Hadley says.

"One last hug," Harriet says. The two women embrace while Hemingway takes the baby. Tears stream down both their cheeks. Harriet holds Hadley at arm's length and Hemingway hears her say, "You'll be fine."

Ralph Connable slaps him on the back and says, "Make us proud."

"Oh Ralph," Harriet says. "We already are."

55

"Good job, gentlemen," St. Pierre Hughes says when his secretary shows Walter Duncan and Rob Tucker into his office. "Sit down, sit down. Let's have a wee dram to celebrate."

"We could use it," Duncan says. "There's nothing like Ottawa in January. She was a cold walk over here. Let's celebrate. Red's back in Kingston Pen and all's right with your world."

On his friend's polished oak desk, next to the bottle of Scotch and three glasses, sit two revolvers. Duncan knows them well. They belong to Red Ryan.

"I thought you two might like a souvenir. You pick first, Walter."

"Where's the blue steel automatic Sullivan had in his pocket when he knocked on his girlfriend's door?" Tucker says.

"We're going to sell it," St. Pierre Hughes says, "and send the proceeds to his wife. Least we could do for the poor woman."

Duncan approaches the desk, picks up one revolver, then the other. "You choose first, Robbie. You were a big help to me."

Life is very strange. You feel like you've been thrown down the outhouse hole and then the next thing you know everything's changed and you've set the world on fire.

"Kind of a sad ending to a sad story," Tucker says.

St. Pierre Hughes gives one of Red's guns a little push in Tucker's direction. "You deserve it, lad. You two are heroes."

56

STANDING ON THE DECK OF THE *ANTONIA*, HEMINGWAY watches the baby burrow into Hadley's coat, searching for her breast. The island of Manhattan ascends, then descends, then ascends again as the ship cuts through the incoming tide.

The January weather's turned warm, breaking records they say, hovering just below the freezing point. It's ten degrees warmer than it's supposed to be but still cold enough out on the water, cold enough to let the rain turn into snow.

Hadley opens her coat and tucks the baby inside to shelter him from the salty air. She wants Hemingway to come below deck but he says no. When he escorts her to the door, he sees his face reflected in a porthole. He looks older, he thinks. Four goddamn months and he looks older. What would a year have done? He walks back to the railing and a woman in a blue velvet coat nods at him as she passes by.

The waves roll into New York harbour from across the Atlantic. Hemingway shudders in spite of himself. At last they are leaving North America behind. He is going to start over with what they have from Hadley's small inheritance and the money they've saved and the stories inside his head. All they ever got from George Breaker was a telegram saying he'll talk to them in Paris.

He thinks often of George Breaker living the high life and Red back inside a cell. What's the difference? He doesn't see one except someday he may write about Red, but he will never write about George.

They say Red is accepting of his fate, but Hemingway doubts that's true. Red's sitting there in Kingston Pen, smiling at the guards, and figuring out how he is going to improve his situation.

As the bow of the *Antonia* swings toward the ocean, the woman in the blue coat passes by again. This time she smiles. He should probably go inside with Hadley but he wants to stay out until they pass the Statue of Liberty and the tiny *Antonia* works its way through the Narrows and out into the ocean. He wants to stand at the rail until he's safe: until North America is nothing but a dotted line of lights just above the water.

57

FROM HIS CELL IN THE MORNINGS, RED, HIS FANCY CLOTHES taken away, his itchy prison greys back on, sees a tiny sliver of light shining down from the top of the stairs.

One day a week he gets to walk in the open air of the tiny exercise yard. When he walks he always thinks about Babe back in Toronto.

He closes his eyes and reaches out to the limestone cell that surrounds him. He still has the ragged page he ripped out of the Bible at the Athletic Club in Minneapolis. What was it the Almighty had to say? "Be strong and courageous. Do not be afraid or terrified."

Babe is just down the lake that's hidden by the prison wall. You can't see the water from your cell or from the yard, but you can tell that it's there. In the yard just throw your head back and look past that twenty-foot wall up at the sky.

There's a different kind of light over a large body of water, even in the winter. Brighter, higher, it's extraordinary. Reminds you: Never forget the world is always full of possibilities.

Acknowledgements

AS WITH MOST BOOKS, MANY PEOPLE HAD A HAND IN BRINGing this novel to life. First, thank you to all my teachers in the creative writing program at the University of Toronto School of Continuing Studies: Lee Gowan, Kim Echlin, Michael Winter, Marina Endicott, and the late Peter Robinson. I learned a lot from them and still hear their sage advice in my ear.

Thank you to all the members of Bloor West Writers: Alison Gadsby, Pamela Ferguson, Ken Leland, Carolyn Charron, Gillian Kerr, Peter Timmerman, Jim Moore, Doris Muise, and the late Sten Eirik who were there from the beginning. With their encouragement, a short non-fiction piece about Hemingway turned into a novel. Thanks to Maaja Wentz, Bryan Dawes, Alexandre Leger, Rebecca Simkin, and Cai Guise-Richardson who also read many chapters. I always appreciated their input. Thank you to the members of 11th Story, Chris Briggs, Ann Y. K. Choi, Andrew Fruman, Melanie Hall, Saad Khan, Maureen Lynch, Njoroge Mungai, and Dianah Smith, for their invaluable feedback. A special shout-out to Andrew for sharing his knowledge of boxing with me. And thanks to Rosemary Aubert and the gang who attended her weeklong summer Novel Writing Workshops in Belleville: Duncan

Armstrong, Madelaine H. Calway, Rosemary McCracken, Roz Place, and Jo Anne Wilson. Helen Humphreys read an early draft and then a final one. Jeanette Lynes and Brenda Carr read early drafts as well. Thank you to Doris and John who said, "Let's try poetry," and started it all.

Although this is a work of fiction, I am indebted to the many fine biographers, editors, and institutional collectors and guardians of Hemingway and Red Ryan material. A salute to the Hemingway Society for all their work and clear-headed vision about their namesake. Thank you to Hilary Kovar Justice and the archivists of the Hemingway Collection at the JFK Library in Boston for their assistance. I thank Ernest for his great sense of humour. He often made me laugh out loud.

Thank you to everyone at Dundurn. Meghan Macdonald for her warm welcome. Laura Boyle for the great cover design. Karen Alexiou for her interior design. Thanks to my editor, Robyn So; my proofreader, Jennifer Rawlinson; my publicist, Rajdeep Singh. And to Erin Pinksen, my very helpful, kind, and patient project editor.

A special thanks to Jason Martin for listening, for helping, and for advocating on my behalf.

Special appreciation goes to all my family and friends for their on-going interest, support, and enthusiasm. Thank you to my friend Mary for her generous personal and literary support.

Last but not least, I would like to thank my late husband, Bill. He read many drafts with an engineer's eye and always had something helpful to say and some encouragement to give.

About the Author

Marianne Miller, like many of her contemporaries, was inspired to visit Spain after reading Hemingway's *The Sun Also Rises* in university. She didn't think any more about him until many years later when, challenged to write poetry, to her surprise, she wrote a poem (a very short poem) about Hemingway. Looking into his history, she discovered that the young, hungry, dying-to-get-published, twenty-four-year-old Hemingway lived in Toronto in 1923 and was very unhappy working for the *Toronto Daily Star*. It would be a turning point in his career. It piqued her interest.

Miller is a graduate of the creative writing program, School of Continuing Studies, University of Toronto. She enjoys reading, writing, theatre, and travel. She has crossed the Atlantic by ship many times. Crazy about Paris, she would love to live there, at least for a little while. She volunteers as a reader for a literary magazine and was recently asked to be a juror for the Penguin Random House Canada Student Award for Fiction given by the University of Toronto School of Continuing Studies creative writing program.

Miller presented a paper, "Hemingway in Toronto," at the 18th International Hemingway Society Conference in Paris, France, and is looking forward to the next conference in Bilbao, Spain, in 2024. She currently lives in Toronto — not Paris.